RETURN TO ROSELAND

RETURN TO ROSELAND

a novel

JOHN SHEFFIELD

Published by Deeds Publishing in Athens, GA
www.deedspublishing.com

Printed in The United States of America

Library of Congress Cataloging-in-Publications Data is available upon request.

ISBN 978-1-944193-58-4
E-ISBN 978-1-944193-59-1

Books are available in quantity for promotional or premium use. For information, email info@deedspublishing.com.

Cover by Mark Babcock and Matt King

First Edition, 2016

10 9 8 7 6 5 4 3 2 1

ACKNOWLEDGEMENTS

I dedicate *Return to Roseland* to my wife, Sharon, who has brought joy to my life following a difficult year. As always, I am grateful for the advice of Vicki Kestranek and Carolyn Robbins, my long-time writing colleagues. I appreciate the advice of Diane Douglas, Jeremy Logan, Lisa Youngblood, and Mary Wivell who have helped me to refine this novel. I am fortunate to be a member of the Atlanta Writers Club, and appreciate the advice of the Roswell Library, North Point, Barnes & Noble, and George Weinstein literary critique groups. Thanks also to Deeds publishing, Ashley Clarke and to Mark Babcock for another imaginative cover.

GENEALOGY
OF
ROSELAND

according to

ANDREW FERGUSON

ANTHONY:

George +   Ernest

John

BILLING: Florence (1882, grandmother)

Cap'n Hartley (1930)   Albert +

Young Hartley (1957)

COCKING: Jane (1905, née Pasco)

Anne   Edgar (1932) +   Primrose

Esther (1959)

GAY: Charlie + Petunia (née Quick)

Rodney   Jennifer

JAGO: Emily

Jacob +   Miriam   Mabel

Patsy (1958)   Paul (1960)

NANCARROW: George + Prudence (née Gay)

Isaac + Elizabeth   Arthur + Martha

Sandy   Samuel + Jennifer (née Gay)

NICHOLS: Agnes

John (dec)   Jane (1927) +   Susan

PASCOE

David (dec) + Mary (1935, née Billing)   Albert
|
Rose (1956)

QUICK

Peter (dec) + Clara (née Trevenna)   Petunia
|
Frankie (1948)

THOMAS: Albert + Emily

Morley + Hilda   James + Miriam (née Jago)

Nicholas   Susan

TREVENNA: John + Martha (née Cocking)

Charles (dec) + Jane (née Nichols)   Clara (1928)
|
John (1956)

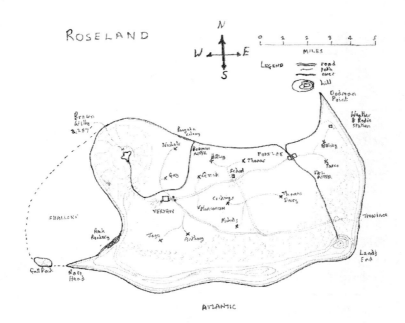

A MAP OF THE ISLAND, HAND-DRAWN BY PROFESSOR JONES

I.

We'd been six days traveling west out of Cape Town, and I stood on the bow of the *St. Just*, an ocean-going fishing boat, scanning the horizon, eager to catch sight of Roseland. The island had been settled in the 1800s by families from Cornwall in the west of England. Protectorates such as Roseland, the Falklands, and a number of other southern Atlantic outposts of the long-gone British Empire came under the jurisdiction of the Governor on Saint Helena. In Roseland's case, the island pretty much ran itself. More than two years had passed since 1978, when I'd left that isolated piece of land. I wondered how much things had changed.

My name is Andrew Ferguson. I grew up on a farm in North Carolina, my father Scottish in background and my mother Italian. My mother's dark hair and complexion and my father's blue eyes had combined well in me. Using my inherited good looks, I had played the field with women, more or less successfully. That was until I met Rose Pascoe, who was destined to become Roseland's doctor and its future leader.

I hadn't gone to the island the first time expecting to find the love of my life. I hadn't even considered the possibility of any relationship, particularly after my professor, Gareth Llewellyn Jones, had given me a strong warning that the Roseland women were off limits. No, I had accepted the opportunity to study the Roseland Auk for my PhD in ornithology to get over being dumped by my previous girlfriend, Annie. She'd caught me having casual sex with a pick-up at a party. Told me I needed to grow up. Lesson learned at that time…until the eccentric Clara Quick tricked me into an unwise relationship.

Initially, as a result of this islander's game, Rose had viewed me as a brash womanizer. That opinion changed gradually as she saw a different side of me: my genuine affection for the birds I was studying for my PhD in ornithology. While the birds had been important to my gaining Rose's love, she had made it clear that bird watching was not a justification for staying on Roseland.

To my farmer father's great disappointment, I'd initially rejected following in his footsteps for the two years while I completed my PhD. Then Rose made it clear that after having qualified as a doctor in England, she would return to the island for good. She said that despite the fact that she loved me, I would not be welcome to settle on the island unless I could contribute to its welfare. My qualifications in ornithology weren't useful in that regard, which was why I had finally acceded to my father's wishes and studied environmentally sound, modern farming.

During the two years that I pursued a master's in agriculture, I'd wrestled with whether I really could leave the States for good and settle on a remote island. Every time I'd felt uneasy, I would read one of Rose's letters telling me to not give up. Images of her would flash in my head and remind me that I didn't want a life without her. In fact, in my time on the island, I had grown to love the place and its people. I thought about all those things as I waited to catch sight of the island.

Captain Hartley Billing, pronounced Artley, had just left me, called away by one of the crew to receive a message on the ship's radio. It didn't take long for him to return, grim faced. "Best get below for time being, Andy," he said. "I just heard that the Maskers will be waiting for you at the dock. Seems like Johnny Trevenna doesn't want you on the island."

The news wasn't much of a surprise because, three weeks earlier, I'd visited the Prof. His housekeeper Mabel, who came from Roseland and kept in touch with family there, had taken me aside....

"Andy, you be careful," she said. "There's people on the island that don't want you back."

"You mean John Tre—"

"Not just him. I've heard Head of Maskers thinks Rose having you would be bad for island."

"I'll be careful." I'd often wondered who the Head Masker might be. Would Mabel know? "Can you tell me who it is?"

Mabel played with a curl. "Election of head is very secret. The oldest maskers choose. They're the only ones who know for sure. I don't want to give you a guess."

I'd come across the Maskers, a secret society whose members had beaten me up on my previous stay as a warning to keep away from the island's women. Before I went there, the Prof had warned me that the islanders still practiced pagan rituals. The Maskers, mainly or entirely men I suspected, were involved in them.

"Does Martha Nancarrow know about the reception planned for me?" I asked the Captain, understanding full well why not only the Maskers but also John Trevenna had it in for me. I'd taken

Rose away from him. But Martha Nancarrow led the island's government, the Seythan—Cornish for the seven, the number of representatives of the island's families. This current Penseythan, head of the seven, had been friendly to me on my previous visit. Surely she would help. "I thought the Penseythan outranked the Maskers."

"My informant thinks that Martha doesn't know what they plan yet, and I'm concerned that by the time she finds out, it'll be too late." He looked into the distance as if trying to understand what was going to happen. "This Penseythan and Head of Maskers are too close, maybe."

Not clear what he meant, but that could wait. I didn't want anything to get in the way of my seeing Rose again. My heart raced, and I had to hold on to the side of the wheelhouse to calm down. "What are you going to do?"

He shook his head. "Not sure 'xactly. Stay out to sea and think about it."

He went into the wheelhouse. After half an hour, during which he talked to his nephew, Young Artley, the boat headed south. I wondered what the captain was up to. It looked like he planned to drop me off secretly somewhere along the coast. But steep cliffs marked the eastern and southern shores, and the waves were far higher than on the western shore where a shoal broke them up. Probably, he would circle around from the south because very few people ventured above the high cliffs, and it wasn't likely anyone would be looking, unlike on the northern shore, which sloped gently down to the sea. That left the western coast: lower cliffs there, but harboring dangerous shoals in the waters below them. I knew the area well, having spent two years studying the Roseland Auks, relatives of the Atlantic Puffin that nested at the top of these cliffs.

The Captain circled the island at a distance, and only as the sun began to set did he head in from the west. I was soon able to make out the massive cone of the dormant volcano, Brown Willy. When we got close to the shore, he slowed down and put out a sea anchor to stop the trawler from drifting. While Young Artley and another crewmember lowered the lifeboat, I went to my bunk and put on my money belt, which contained Rose's engagement ring. Feeling insecure, I took out the ring for a brief moment. With my eyes closed, I held it while visualizing Rose: a comforting moment that gave me temporary relief. I'd not seen her in two years and I didn't want anything to screw up getting on the island.

The first time I had boarded the *St. Just* in Cape Town, I had been apprehensive about its small size—a mere hundred and twenty feet in length and sitting low to the water in my estimation. Now, as I scrambled down the rope ladder out to sea, I was happy it was a short drop and the *St. Just* felt like a cruise liner in comparison to the lifeboat.

"We'll deal with your luggage later," Artley said as I joined him. The engine coughed to a start and we headed into the shallow region flanked by the promontory of the Nare Head to the south and the vertical side of Brown Willy's base to the north. I knew the area was dangerous because the islanders left the fish to the birds that nested there.

"How did Captain Artley explain the delay in getting to Portloe?" I asked.

"Said something about engine trouble," Young Artley replied. "Told 'em he'd be a day late."

I didn't want to distract him anymore and kept quiet. Flecks of white in the massive swell showed where the rocks were close to the surface. Artley maneuvered the boat skillfully between them. After twenty tense minutes, we approached the base of the hundred-foot cliff below the auk rookery. The sight brought back my fear of heights and memories of the last time I had been there, when I'd nearly lost my life. I gave an involuntary shiver.

"Looking for bones?" Artley asked, his bright blue eyes searching my face for a clue.

"Hard to forget the Penseythan and Winston falling," I replied.

"Jane Trevenna got what she deserved," Artley said. "Though I felt sorry for the dog."

I nodded. It wasn't the bloodhound's fault that the previous Penseythan had wanted me dead: my death being her solution to preventing me from taking Rose away from her precious son, Johnny.

I glanced up and saw the ropes hanging from the cliff that were used by my onetime assistant, Frankie Quick, when he went to collect gulls' eggs. The greenish rock face was dotted with nests and bird droppings. *Slippery going.* My insides tensed. In the sky, the gulls and a few great skuas were circling, eyeing us in the hope we had gutted fish scraps to discard. At that point, a figure appeared at the cliff top and started a cautious descent.

"The Cap'n got word to Frankie," Artley said. "He's coming to help you."

"I'll need it," I replied, remembering the nausea I'd felt on the two occasions I'd been on the cliff face.

"Don't know if I can get close enough for you to jump on a rock," Artley said. "You may have to swim for it." He held out a lifejacket. "Put this on and wait till Frankie throws out a line."

Jump in the water? A frightening thought but, in fact, I was a strong swimmer and was more scared of the climb I faced. It took a long ten minutes for Frankie to reach the bottom. During that time, I tried to avoid watching the sea pounding against the rocks at the base of the cliff. My chest felt tight even before I put on the life jacket and inflated it.

"Get up on starboard side," Artley instructed as he swung the boat in an arc toward the rocks.

I clambered up and sat on the bulwark, watching the dark green water and waving seaweed fronds that I had to join.

When Frankie threw out a rope, I jumped. The shock of the icy water gave way to panic as the seaweed grabbed at my legs. I stopped trying to kick and used my arms to pull myself toward the lifeline but was unable to reach it.

Fortunately, the swell carried me in the right direction. Frankie quickly pulled the rope in and cast it again. The rope lashed my back, but again I failed to hold on. Gulls and one great skua swooped close in the hope food might be involved. I wondered if the skua was the one I'd named Dracula.

The initial surge of adrenaline when I jumped had worn off, and I felt the cold seeping into my body. I stopped moving and thought about Rose. No way was I going to leave her to Johnny Trevenna. The weeds fell away when I remained still. Frankie tossed the rope again and I was able to catch hold.

"Tie under your arms," Frankie shouted.

I rolled in the water, wrapping the rope around me until I could make a knot forming a loop, allowing Frankie to pull me in. He waited for the water to rise before landing me on the side of one of the rounder boulders. Relieved, I lay down for a minute, my body numb and my heart racing, before scrambling up to him. Out of the corner of my eye, I saw Artley heading back out to sea. I would never forget that date, Wednesday, September 17, 1980.

"Hi, Frankie," I said, peering up at his still youthful face. "Thanks."

"Glad you're back," he said. "Not studying auks this time, I hear." His look showed disappointment as he bent down and fastened the rope more securely around my chest, and checked to see that he and I were properly connected by it.

"You like the birds, don't you?" I said. "But sorry. It's going to be farming." I started to shiver.

"Need to get you out of these wet clothes," Frankie said. "Better hurry."

I glanced up at the crumbly and wet cliffs. I tried not to show the fear I felt. "Right behind you," I replied through gritted teeth.

Frankie started up the cliff. When the rope went taut, I followed. He seemed to have no trouble finding footholds and handholds but then, he didn't mind looking down. I was okay with the hands, but my feet kept slipping on the rock ledges, greasy with droppings, and my muscles were tight. *Thank God we are tied together.* To take my mind off the faint, fishy smell percolating down from the gulls' nests and my precarious footholds, I decided to find out about what would happen to me. "How's Rose?" I shouted.

"Fine. Said she was sorry she couldn't meet you." Frankie continued up. The rope jerked on me and I followed. "Didn't want to tip off that bugger, Johnny Trevenna, you were coming ashore here."

Of course. "Where'll I be staying?"

"George Anthony's tonight." Frankie peered down at me. "You know Ernie died?"

Mabel Thomas, the Prof's housekeeper had let me know. "Yes. I'm sorry."

"You bring your trumpet?"

Frankie had reminded me how I had replaced Ernie Anthony on the trumpet in the island's band when he had been sick with terminal cancer. "It's on the boat."

By now Frankie had reached the top of the cliff and I was right under the auk rookery. I put my hand over the edge, hoping to find a tussock of grass to grab but found only an old burrow. It was empty and, unlike the last time, there were no fish left for a chick. On the previous occasion, I'd hurled the offering at Jane Trevenna's head in a desperate effort to prevent her from shooting me. Dracula had saved me when he swooped to catch the fish, and the Penseythan had lost her balance and fallen to her death.

I pulled myself onto the edge of the empty rookery and studied the darkening sky.

"Auks'll be back soon," Frankie said. "Late September or early October, likely."

"I'll be visiting then." I had a name for each one I'd studied. "Got to catch up with Nellie."

"Your favorite *good time girl*, eh?" Frankie grinned.

I had a vision of Nellie scuttling around with her main man Fred, who'd been killed by Dracula. "She still around?"

"Was last year…but not so strong." Frankie held out his hand and pulled me to my feet. "Come on, we'd better get to George's before sun sets." He took my arm. "No talking now. Remember, sound carries a long way on the downslope."

No chance to ask him what he'd meant about Nellie. I started after him along the cliff-top, mindful of the thorny gorse that bordered the path. When we crossed a small rise, I could see the island spread out before me. It was early enough that lights still glimmered in nearby Veryan and scattered farmhouses. In the distance, I could just make out Portloe, where I should have landed. A flood of memories returned and I thought back over what had happened since I'd left the island.

Even though I'd survived Jane Trevenna's attempt to kill me, she had succeeded in shooting me in the leg. Because I needed time to recover, when the *St. Just* departed a few days later, I missed the opportunity to return to Cape Town with Rose. She headed on to England to attend medical school while I returned to the States two months later.

From my time on the island, I knew it would be lights out later that evening, and every evening, when the generators were shut down. I understood how difficult it was to provide the energy needed by such an isolated community. While the British government provided fuel to support the islanders' basic needs, they could use more electric power. I'd learned how crops and animals could provide not only food but also help meet that need.

With my parents' support, I spent two years at North Carolina State learning about agriculture and closed-cycle farming. A year earlier on a visit home, I'd seen my dad's new addition of a covered lagoon to contain manure from the hogs he was now raising. He proudly showed me the system he'd had a company put in to collect the methane, make electricity, and process heat.

This was an additional area in which I could prove my value to the islanders.

My grandparents had left me a tidy sum of money for when I'd turned twenty-four. It had covered some of my agricultural college costs and allowed me to purchase equipment for utilizing the methane from digested animal wastes. Communicating by long-distance radio with Morley Thomas, who ran the island's dairy, I talked him into building a pit to collect manure from his cows. Three months before I left home, having learned the pit's dimensions, I shipped him a thick plastic cover for the pit.

I confess that communicating with Rose at long distance had been frustrating, particularly in the first year, knowing Johnny Trevenna was also in England completing his engineering degree. His designated role on the island was to be the expert on generators and other electrical systems. I hung in there for two years supported by Rose's letters, which encouraged me to complete my studies. She pointed out that she was in the same position as me in needing to finish qualifying as a doctor. I wanted desperately to go to England to see her, but I couldn't afford it in addition to my other expenses. My reality was that, at that time, I needed to work all the time when I wasn't at college to repay my parents and also have enough money left from the inheritance to buy equipment to send or take to Roseland.

In my spare time, I helped out on our farm and learned some of the intricacies of converting manure to energy. Remembering how some maskers had beaten me up, I'd also taken karate classes to protect me in future attacks. Armed with my new knowledge, I'd left for the island.

2.

I STAYED IN STEP BEHIND FRANKIE AS HE TOOK THE PATH THAT skirted the cliff top so we couldn't be seen against the rapidly setting sun, and then descended through woods to George Anthony's farm. He had left all his lights on—a welcoming gesture—and met us at his front door.

"Andy, welcome, m'dear," he said, white teeth flashing in his weather-beaten face. "Come in the kitchen. It's warm and I'll make some tea. First some dry clothes." He bustled out.

M'dear, the traditional Cornish salutation, made me feel accepted, and I already felt warmer.

Frankie edged away. "Best get home," he said. "Mum and Esther'll want to hear everything."

"Say hi to them," I said, having an instant vision of his mother, Clara, who had a habit of playing games on people, including me.

Frankie looked puzzled and I heard him muttering, "Say hi. Say hi. Low," as he wandered off, taking an occasional skip. "Rum ti tum, tum," followed, the words used to match the lilt of the Floral Dance, a part of the rituals on Midsummer's Day. Acting the fool to mislead people as to how bright he was. Frankie hadn't changed.

I followed George and sat by the old-fashioned coal-burning stove—the coal provided by the UK government every year along with a supply of gasoline and diesel fuel for generators. A kettle hissed gently on the stovetop. I warmed my hands on the heat wafting from its warm black belly.

While George searched for clothes, I brooded about Captain Artley's mention of the Maskers. The Prof had explained that they were an ancient society derived from the islanders' Cornish background. And, to him, they appeared to have been established by the menfolk as a reaction to the matriarchal system, in which the Penseythan was always a woman. The Captain's hint that the present Penseythan, Martha Nancarrow, was too close to the Head Masker suggested that it might be her personable husband, Arthur. He had helped me the last time by providing materials for my blind by the auk rookery. Then again, I'd been present at a weird event, set up by Clara, when Arthur had acted the lead in a mask. I wasn't sure. Nevertheless, to me, more likely the leader was Arthur's intimidating brother, Isaac. My thoughts were interrupted when George returned. He was accompanied by a taller, thinner version of himself, with a sharp nose that might have been inherited from his mother and a pale face suggesting he didn't work on the farm. The man wore a suit that might have been from the thirties, a white shirt, and tie. The trousers stopped a couple of inches short of his black, lace-up shoes, and the jacket was a tad too big for his shoulders.

"Andy, this is my son, Harold," he said. "Come back to help me around the house."

"I've heard a lot about you," Harold said.

I'd heard mention of Harold, who'd been away in England on my previous stay. "All good, I hope."

"Not 'xactly," he replied with a tentative smile. "I heard—"

"Harold speaks in a very straightforward manner," George said, interrupting my opportunity to find out what I'd done wrong.

"But he asked?..." Harold left the kitchen shaking his head.

"Don't mind Harold. Takes everything very literal-like. Now, try these on," George said, holding out a pair of faded denim pants and a heavy woolen, brown sweater. "Ernie's. I hope you don't mind. We'll get the saltwater out of your clothes and dry them by the stove."

"Not at all. I was sorry to hear he...passed on."

George shrugged. "Had to happen. Better for him than all that suffering. Martha did the best she could." While I changed, he turned to the stove and put tea and hot water into a large blue teapot.

I put my money belt on the table. "Where do I wash my clothes?" I asked.

"Leave it to me. I've trough out back with rainwater." He took the clothes and went out.

The dollars and South African rand I'd purchased in Cape Town were sodden. I carefully extracted them from the money belt, reassuring myself that the engagement ring was secure, and laid them out on the table.

When George returned, he draped the wet clothes over a cord that stretched above the stove.

I hung my paper money in the gaps.

"That won't last you long," he said, eyeing my funds.

"It's pocket money. I made an arrangement with my bank in the States and Nancarrow's.

"Good." George made me a cup of tea, milk first. He added heaping teaspoons of sugar. "To warm up your insides."

I sipped the tea and silently debated whether I should ask about the Maskers. Curiosity won. "Captain Artley told me John Trevenna and Maskers were going to meet me at the dock. Is Johnny their head?"

George turned away. Before he did, I could see he appeared troubled. "Doubt it. Too young." He busied himself rearranging my clothes.

"Then how would he get others to join in?"

"Best ask him that."

Time to change the subject. "How's the band getting on? Charley Gay still leading it?"

"Course. They miss you." George chuckled. "Young Artley stepped in. He weren't very good. They'll be glad you're back.... Which reminds me." He scuttled out of the room and returned carrying a trumpet. "Ernie wanted you to have this." He held it out.

"Are you sure?" I asked, taking hold of the gleaming instrument.

"Ain't no use to me," George snorted. "T'was Ernie had the ear. Like you."

"Does it have a case?"

George scratched his head. "Ain't seen it in a long while. I'll have a search when I have time tomorrow."

"Thanks." I had played the instrument before, when I'd visited Ernie. It had a beautiful timbre. This time I inspected the worn brass for a maker's mark. The imprint of the stamping was very faint, Boosey and Hawkes, London, 1932. "Thank you. It's a real treasure. I raised it to my lips and played a few bars of "The Floral Dance."

"Rum tum ti tum, tum, tum." George warbled the rhythm of the song in accompaniment.

His words brought back memories of two Midsummer's Days when the band played the song and twice led a dancing procession to the village green in Veryan. On the second occasion, the Penseythan ushered the chosen Queen and seven men to the large Round House in the square. In this revived pagan ritual, which the Prof reckoned had been created as a response to a lack of women on the island, the Queen serviced the men—a hand job for the first six and the real thing for the seventh man, the King. As far as I could tell, the Queen usually married the King.

How much longer would this ritual continue now that it could no longer be attributed to what Jane Trevenna had described as, "a dearth of women"? My gut feeling was that the islanders enjoyed their bit of rum tum ti tum tum too much to give it up. I recalled what had happened to me on the Midsummer's just before I'd left the island when George interrupted my thoughts again.

"Next Midsummer's might be Rose and you," he said.

"You think so?"

"Could be."

I didn't like the idea of Rose being the Queen, but if it was going to be, I prayed that I would be the King. I suppressed the awful possibility that I might not be chosen and wondered when I was going to get to see her.

3.

Exhausted, I spent the night sleeping fitfully, fighting nightmares about maskers dancing around the bonfire on the night of Guy Fawkes Day and Johnny Trevenna usurping my role as the King. When I heard movement downstairs, I got up, dressed, and joined George and Harold in the kitchen.

George reached for the teapot. "Nothing like a hot cuppa to get you going."

"Dad's right," Harold said. He cleared his throat and tilted his head. "Do you know the origin of the word cuppa?" he asked, eyeing me sideways.

"I think it's a contraction for cup of, as in cup of tea," I replied.

"Indeed, but there's another definition." Harold looked up at the ceiling. His mouth distorted in what I took to be a conspiratorial smile. "It also refers to farting in to your hand while it is cupped so the smell doesn't get out, then holding it over someone's nose." He handed me my cuppa.

I took it, put in milk and sugar and sat at the kitchen table. "Fascinating," I said. "Now, where will I be going from here?"

George dropped a piece of butter into a warm saucepan on the stove, broke in some eggs, added pepper, salt and milk, and whisked it with a fork. "Clara's going to come and get you. Harold'll go with you…just in case…. You'll be staying with her."

"I guess it makes sense," I said. My hope had been to lodge at Mary Pascoe's, like before, so I could be with her daughter, Rose. The women had probably decided it would be inappropriate. Either way, it wasn't a big deal; Clara lived next door. "What about Frankie?"

"Since he got married, he's been living at Esther's place," George replied. "Clara's glad to have the company."

His comment brought me back to my memories of Clara Quick, a strange woman, who was too clever to be contained in the narrow confines of Roseland and exercised her imagination by playing games on visitors. I'd been the butt of her practical jokes. On my previous visit, she'd conned me into believing Rose would be Queen on Midsummer's Day. I'd spent that time agonizing in the stocks, while the band played "The Floral Dance" and the Queen—hidden from my view by the crowd—the King, Frankie, and six other 'lucky' men went about their business, only to find out the Queen had not been Rose but Frankie's future wife, Esther.

"I'll have to watch out, won't I?"

George grinned. "You'll be fine. Clara likes you." He finished scrambling eggs and ladled them onto two plates, handing me one. "Help yourself to toast and butter." He indicated the toast rack on the table.

"Do you know how much Clara's going to charge for full board?"

George scratched his ear. "Not really. I'd assume same as Mary did last time you were here."

After breakfast, I changed back into my now dry clothes. An hour later, Clara arrived.

"Hello," she said, looking at me with her head tilted. "We're glad to have you back, m'dear."

"I've missed you all," I replied.

"All?" she asked, a smile flickered.

"Not the Maskers," I said. "So tell me, what's up with John-ny Trevenna?"

"My nephew needs a spanking," she said. "No business stirring up Maskers like that."

"Anything I can do about it?"

"Best leave it to me and...." Again, a smile came and went. "Frankie's outside. He'll come with us, in case Johnny finds out you're here." Clara patted me on the arm. "We'll look after you."

George nodded agreement, but his face showed concern.

"Well, I guess we'd better be going," I said. "Thanks for letting me stay."

"'weren't no problem," George said. "I'm glad Arthur suggest-ed it."

We trooped out with me carrying my new possession, Ernie's trumpet. We came across Frankie by the gate. He headed off in his usual ambling style, punctuated by little jigs. Harold went with him, attempting to copy the actions. Clara and I followed them down the track to the Trewince-to-Veryan road.

Clara laughed. "That Harold."

"Is it a game?" I asked.

"No m'dear. That's Harold."

As we approached Veryan, a faint smell from Jacob Jago's pig farm wafted over the hedge on the breeze. Soon, we arrived at two small, round houses, one on each side of the Veryan-to-Port-loe road. The houses were copies of the originals in Cornwall, complete with a cross on top. They, so I had been told, were ef-fective in keeping the devil out; the devil likes to hide in corners. We turned left toward Veryan.

A short distance further on, Isaac Nancarrow's small slaughterhouse, abattoir to the islanders, sat behind his store on Veryan's main square. Another unpleasant odor emanated from the tank in which they dumped the wastes. A movement by the building caught my eye as a man appeared through a doorway. Wearing a bloodstained white coat and Wellington boots, he stared hard at us, then turned and shouted something through the door.

Frankie stopped and waited for me to catch up, then walked in step to my left. "Sandy Nancarrow," he said. "You're not a favorite of him or his brother. News you're back'll be all over the island."

"Let's really make it clear," I said and held out my trumpet. With Clara trailing behind, we picked up our pace keeping to the right side of the road, and soon entered the main part of Veryan with me playing the Imperial March from Star Wars.

Nothing had changed in two years. Nancarrow's store and pub still graced the east side of the village green. The Seythan House was on the south side. To the west, stood the large Round House with its white walls and a conical thatched roof with a cross on top. Two tiny windows were set high in the wall. On the green's north side, a track leading to the auk rookery ran past the entrance to the chapel where Isaac Nancarrow delivered hell and damnation sermons. The simple building had a corrugated iron roof running down its length to a tiny wooden steeple and a cross identical to the one on the Round House. "Veryan Baptist Chapel" was printed on a sign by the road. The village hall was beside and set back from the chapel. The two thousand foot peak of Brown Willy provided a backdrop. Carrying on around the green were the four two-story row-houses. Those closest to the hall belonged, respectively, to Clara Quick and Mary Pascoe. Fond memories of staying with Mary and Rose flooded my mind.

"What the hell are the stocks doing there?" Frankie exclaimed, pointing at the low wooden frame. The Medieval punishment structure sat on the grass in the center of the square, in front of the Seythan House—a place for meetings of the governing body, a library, the island's records, and the jail in which I'd spent time.

The sight of the stocks reminded me of my last Midsummer's Day on the island. I'd been trapped in those stocks in the square for trying to see Rose—a punishment meted out by Jane Trevenna and her allies.

"Warning for poor Andy, likely," Clara said. "Frankie, can you get it put away in the shed behind Seythan?"

Frankie scratched his head. "No point in asking the Nancarrow boys to help. Probably put it there. Maybe Harold and me could…?"

"I'll help," Harold replied. "We'll need to take it apart." He glanced at me. "Do you know the origin of stocks?"

No, but you're going to tell me, I thought. "Do you know?"

Harold smiled. "Yes. Stocks have been used for more than one thousand years, most likely starting in Asia. The Statute of Laborers in England became law in 1351 as a way to discourage any laborer from demanding higher pay following the labor shortage caused by the Black Death." He paused to see if I was listening.

"Most interesting," I said.

"There's more," Harold stated. "The Vagabonds and Beggars Act was enacted in1494. It provided that "Vagabonds, idle and suspected persons shall be set in the stocks for three days and three nights and have none other sustenance but bread and water and then shall be put out of Town."

By now, we had reached the four row-houses that faced the Seythan House across the village green. We came abreast of Mary Pascoe's house and I had the sudden thought we would stop in to see Rose.

"The Poor Law Act of 1531—"

Clara anticipated my intent and interrupted Harold. "Nobody in," she said, putting her hand on my shoulder and squeezing. "Mary's teaching. Rose has clinic in Portloe. I'll make tea and show you my new puzzle."

Damn. I wondered how often Rose would be away, recollecting that while she had a surgery in the Seythan house, her main office was in Portloe, where she could also do dental work. "Thanks, Clara," I said, not doing a good job of hiding my disappointment.

Frankie took Harold's arm, preventing him for bending my ear anymore. They veered off to work on the stocks.

"Call me if you need a hand," I shouted after them. Frankie waved me away.

Clara and I continued to her house and went in. The well-worn sofa and easy chair were turn of the century and reminded me of my grandparents' furniture. The layout was the mirror image of Mary's house where I'd stayed before; the front door on the right led into the living room, stairs led to the upper floor. Clara went past the stairs and down a short corridor to the kitchen in the back. I followed. The faint scent of bacon, cooked for breakfast, lingered in the air. The loo, visible from the kitchen window, was a one-holer with a kind of septic tank at the end of the garden.

Water came from the Bodmin River, a stream really, that started on Brown Willy and meandered down to the northern shore. A rainwater barrel outside the kitchen provided a backup supply. As at George's house, an old coal-burning stove delivered hot water and warmth for cold winter days. A small table and four chairs were squeezed in so you could sit near the stove on cold days.

"You're in the spare bedroom," Clara said and then looked sideways at me. "Think about what meals you'll need. We can discuss how much for board and lodgings over tea." She pointed at the coffee table. "You can start on the puzzle."

"What about my things on the boat?"

"I'm sure Cap'n Artley will arrange it," Clara said over her shoulder. "Best you not go to dock."

I knelt down and put my trumpet under the table. I'd been roped into doing Clara's puzzles before. They always consisted of one of her paintings stuck to cardboard; in this case, not a watercolor. She used a curious Victorian device to stamp out the pieces. Scattered among the sepia photographs of island folk on the walls were Clara's watercolor seascapes: a reminder of what a brilliant woman she could be.

Previously, her puzzles had seemed to relate to something that was going to happen to me; like being put in the stocks on Midsummer's Day. I never worked out how she knew or whether she was a party to engineering my fate. What was this one going to be?

Intrigued, I glanced at four photos resting by the pieces on the table. The photos appeared to show scenes in the puzzle. In one, a young man knelt by a Maypole, looking up as if pleading. In a second, a slim, dark-haired woman stood in front of the large

Round House. The other two photos showed groups of people, one looking happy, and one wearing devil's masks. I suspected Clara was depicting Rose and me, our friends, and the masked characters. I turned the photo over. On the back was scrawled, "Romeo and Juliet." I remembered another of Clara's talents: putting on plays.

Clara returned with a teapot, milk, sugar, cups, and plates on a tray, which she placed in front on the hearth.

"Are you doing another play?" I asked.

Clara fussed with pouring tea, turning half away, her face blank except for yet another faint smile. "Could be."

I held up the photo. "I can tell you're going to put on Romeo and Juliet." Her last play had been The Tempest, with Prospero replaced by Prospera, the Penseythan of Tristan da Cunha.

"You've caught me out, Master Andy." She grinned. "Milk and sugar?"

"Please."

"Want to be in it? You could play Romeo."

"It didn't end well for him and Juliet," I said. "And who's going to be Juliet?"

She stood and posed dramatically. "Aye, there's the rub." She handed me my teacup.

"So, who's going to play Juliet?"

"Might be Rose. I'm sure she'd do it if you were Romeo." She paused before continuing, a mischievous look on her face. "Of course, if you're not interested, I'm sure Johnny—"

That hit a nerve. "Clara!" I'd reacted too quickly. Embarrassed, I put down my cup and busied myself sorting out edge pieces of the puzzle.

"There, there, Master Andy, don't fret yourself, we'll deal with Young Johnny." She patted my hand. "Now—"

A knock on the front door interrupted her. "I wonder who…?"

Clara went to the door and opened it. Martha Nancarrow, the Penseythan, came in. The smile normally on her chubby face was missing. She was followed by her husband, Arthur, who nodded at me. I joined Clara in looking at Martha uncertainly.

Martha smiled. "Andy…Dr. Ferguson, I hear, on behalf of us all." She glanced at Arthur, who nodded. "Well, anyway, most of us, welcome back. Captain Artley called the store and explained what happened. I'm sorry you had to come in the way you did."

"Without Frankie I couldn't have done it." Clara squeezed my arm. "Anyway, it was nice to see the auk rookery again."

"I've called a meeting of the Seythan to discuss your situation. I'm sure that it was just youthful high spirits, Johnny…." Martha seemed uncertain what to add. "Arthur, do you want to say something?"

Arthur, a pinch-faced man with thinning hair and deep-set, dark eyes, shifted on his feet and rubbed his head with his right hand. A nervous habit I'd noticed my previous time on the island. A glint of red light flashed off the carved stone in the ring he wore on his pinkie. "Nice to see you," he said. "No auks this time, they tell me. But I've still got bits of the blind if you need 'em." He waved in the direction of his store.

The red glint was the clue that had identified him as the principal actor in the mock trial of me Clara had staged in the Round House. "Thanks…. But, I'm sure I'll need help finding things in your store for the digestion system I'm going to build for Morley Thomas's dairy. I couldn't bring everything."

"Everybody's been talking about it." Arthur chuckled. "The island's largest septic tank." He scratched his head. "That cover you sent came on the last boat. Morley told me it fits a treat."

"Great." Thank God for that. I'd worried the cover wouldn't fit: one hurdle overcome. "I brought some piping, a generator, and other electrical equipment with me."

Silence. Arthur studied the floor.

Martha cleared her throat. "Andy, there was a problem at the dock…. When everything was unloaded, some maskers took packages and threw them in sea."

Just like the Boston Tea Party. "Can we recover them?"

Arthur seemed to be struggling to hide a smile. "Not where they threw them."

"Even things addressed to Morley Thomas?"

Martha smiled. "Those didn't have your name on 'em?"

"No."

"Maybe the equipment for Morley is all right. But I'm afraid anything with your name on it…."

"I hope so, but my clothes, my books on agriculture, sheet music for the band…my trumpet?"

"Likely gone," Arthur muttered. "Charlie Gay'll have to find you another horn."

"I've got that covered." I went and retrieved my new trumpet from under the table. "George gave me Ernie's. It's a beautiful instrument." I played a few bars of the old Cornish song, Starry Gazy Pie.

Clara giggled. "I'll have to make that pie again so Frankie can see your expression."

Three years earlier, they'd caught me out with Frankie pretending to eat one of the little fish heads that stuck out of the piecrust. "Not—"

A knock and the door opening interrupted me again, and Young Artley appeared. "Penseythan." He ducked his head. "Andy, I've got bad news."

"I heard."

"We tried to stop 'em but they took us by surprise…I managed to salvage this." He pointed to a sodden suitcase sitting on the front step: a small case I'd added at the last minute for extra clothes. "It floated."

"Thanks Artley." I picked it up and shook off beads of water. "At least I'll have some clothes."

"I shouldn't mention it," Artley said with a grin. "But you should have seen Elizabeth Gay's face when maskers were about to chuck her precious ornamental plants off the boat. She laid into them and they backed off. Right funny scene."

I had not interacted with her on my previous stay, but recollected that she lived in the farm across the Bodmin River to the north of Clara's house. I smiled weakly. "Artley headed off before I could comment."

"Bring it in the kitchen and put it on the sink," Clara said.

"Come on Arthur, we'd best be getting to Seythan House," Martha said as they passed me on my way to the kitchen. "Hope you have enough clothes and things. I'll talk to Seythan about this. Maybe we can help out with what's missing."

I turned to see Frankie holding the door open for them. "I'd appreciate that," I said.

"Stocks are stored again. Harold has gone home. I've got to get to work. Um, I'll drop by lunchtime." Frankie closed the door.

In the kitchen, I opened my suitcase and emptied it onto what the islanders called a draining board. "I guess, I'll be growing this beard," I said, realizing that my razor, along with my books, had been in my backpack that had been disappeared by the Maskers. Fortunately, I had packed my notes and instructions on assembling the methane collector, piping, and electrical equipment in the boxes for Morley.

Clara and I rinsed the salt water out of the clothes and hung them on a line in the backyard to dry, then returned to the living room.

By midday, we had completed half the puzzle and I was busy finding pieces of the Maypole, when I heard the front door open. I had my back to the door and didn't look up. Frankie, I thought. But shortly after, a soft pair of hands gently stoked across my face. I dropped the puzzle pieces and my heart raced.

"Welcome back," Rose said. "Andy, you might look good in a beard. What do you think, Clara?"

Clara sniffed.

I stood and faced Rose. My heart rate sped up again and, like the first time I'd met her, I couldn't breathe. Her curly black hair was tied up, Grecian style, with a blue ribbon. Her cheeks were as rosy as I remembered, and her black eyes sparkled.

"What are you waiting for? Kiss her," Clara giggled.

My feet wouldn't move and my chest was still tight, so I reached out. Rose's arms went around my neck, her mouth came up to mine and she kissed me long and, it seemed, thoughtfully. God, I hope she hasn't decided I'm the wrong person. She trembled and clung tight. At last, I relaxed and pulled back to look at her. "Boy, I've missed you."

"And me you." She stroked my face. "But I think I prefer you without a beard." Her eyes twinkled.

"Rose, you staying for lunch?" Clara asked.

"Can't. Jacob Jago's lacerated his left arm. He needs me now." She kissed me quickly. "Sorry, Andy, I'll see you later." Rose turned and went to the door.

Too stunned by seeing her again after two years only to have her leave, I followed and opened the door without thinking. The old Lagonda that Jane Trevenna had used was parked outside Nancarrow's Store. James Thomas, the car's driver, stood by the passenger door.

"I've got my own wheels," Rose said.

"I thought the Trevennas owned it. What does…?" I didn't want to mention Johnny's name.

"John does…sort of. But I need it to get around quickly with my first aid kit when there's an emergency like Jacob's arm." She started off across the green.

The slight delay brought me back to my senses. What was I waiting for? In our interchange of letters over two years, after I had committed to agriculture as my passport to live on Roseland, we had discussed getting married and where we might live. But I had never actually proposed. I ran after her and tapped her on the shoulder.

She turned looking puzzled.

I dropped to my knee and felt in my money belt. "Rose, will you marry me?" I said, holding out the ring. "It was my grandmother's." I remembered what my mother had said when she gave it to me. "The diamonds are rose-cut."

She glanced toward Nancarrow's Store. One of the Nancarrow boys stood on the veranda eyeing us. Concern showed briefly. "Yes, Andy, I want nothing more." She pulled back, her face showing concern. "I know this isn't a good time to tell you, but it's possible I'm going to be Queen." The words came out in a rush. "You know what that means."

George had been right. Another obstacle. Rose would have to service six men in the Round House—with hand jobs—and then have sex with the King. I wasn't happy about the first part but had assumed the Seythan would choose me for the latter role. The way she had spoken seemed to put that in doubt. "Yes. Do you have to do it?"

Rose bent down and stroked my cheek. "I know this custom seems weird to foreigners. Remember, it's our tradition. All us girls were brought up to accept it. I should have been Queen before.... You understand. And Johnny Trevenna would have been King. The Seythan thought it was more important we both finish our education. I can't put this off any longer. I'm sorry, but as a future Penseythan, I'm not going to buck the island's customs."

I recalled my mother's horrified reaction when I'd told her about the island's strange ways. I'd tried to compare Roseland to countries and religions that accepted polygamy. She wasn't impressed and asked me to consider seriously whether I wanted to return to Roseland, finally accepting that I was determined to follow through with my plans. Damn their primitive rituals.

I studied her face. Rose seemed to be on the point of tears. "I can be King. Surely, now we're engaged, they'd have to...."

She brushed a hand across her eyes. "That's up to the Seythan. I don't decide."

All this way to fail? My head started to sink at the thought. No. Whatever happened, I wasn't going to lose her. "I love you, Rose." I looked into her eyes. "More than anything…anywhere. But if I'm not King, I don't know if I could stand it."

Her face softened. "I love you, too. We will work it out."

She held out her left hand and I placed the ring on her finger. When I got to my feet, she put her arms around me and we kissed again.

After a minute, she pulled back. "I have to get to Jacob," she said.

I watched her, a slim figure in khaki pants and blue sweater, until she got in the car. The Nancarrow boy was gone.

I returned to the house to be greeted by Clara. "Relieved?" she asked, arching an eyebrow.

"You could say that." I returned to the puzzle, spotting a part of Juliette. Still savoring the relief that Rose had not cooled on our relationship, I said, "I'll do it." For emphasis, I added, "I'll be Romeo."

"Thought you might." Clara's pale green eyes twinkled. "I'll get your lines." She rushed upstairs.

4.

THURSDAY NIGHT, ROSE DROPPED BY AFTER DEALING WITH JA-
cob and holding a clinic in Veryan. We talked for hours, catching
up on some of what had happened since I'd left Roseland. When
she left, I went to bed and dreamed happily about her. The next
morning, Clara headed to her job in the library and I decided to
go for a walk. I had planned to visit the auk rookery, but seeing
the dark clouds moving in from the west, I studied my lines and
worked on Clara's jigsaw puzzle.

Early on the Friday afternoon, Clara returned, and a knock
on the door came just as I completed eighty percent of the puzzle. I opened the door to find Arthur Nancarrow looking pleased
with himself.

"Seythan agreed to replace whatever you lost, long as we carry it in our store." Arthur gave a wry smile. "Isaac wasn't happy
about it until he realized we'd get paid."

"Thanks. It's mainly some clothes, shaving stuff, notepads and
pens. There's nothing you can do about my books. Pity. Fortunately, I packed instructions for using Morley's manure in with
his equipment."

Arthur chuckled. "Morley's manure you call it…I'll have to
tell him." He glanced at the puzzle and the "Romeo and Juliet"
script. "You going to be Romeo?"

"I guess so."

"Good luck…. You can come by the store now if you like. Get a razor. I hear Rose doesn't like your beard."

My God, news travels fast.

"Off you go," Clara said from the hallway. "Before Isaac changes his mind."

We turned left out of Clara's house and crossed the village green, walking past the place where the Lagonda had been parked, to reach the verandah that fronted Nancarrow's Store. The upper floor of the two-story, two-house-wide building housed two flats: one for Isaac Nancarrow and his family and the other for Martha and Arthur. The smell of cheese and dried fish greeting us at the door reminded me of the first time I'd been there. Today, Isaac was behind the counter serving Petunia Gay, wife of Charlie the bandleader.

She turned, giving me a radiant smile that illuminated her flower-like face; a face no longer marred by the broken nose given to her years earlier by the Russian, Pavlov. An unpleasant visitor, he'd been the victim of one of Clara's games that had gotten out of hand and led to the injury. I guessed that Rose must have performed the corrective surgery. Petunia rushed over and threw her arms around me. "Andy, I'm so glad to see you're all right. All the way from Cape Town and having to climb that cliff. I can't imagine it."

"It wasn't so bad," I lied. "Frankie helped me."

She pulled back. "You ready for the band? Charlie's keen to get you back. I can tell him."

"Absolutely…." I stopped on seeing Isaac looking with irritation at the packaged food resting on the counter, waiting for her to pay. "Looks like you need to finish your order," I said.

"Right, m'dear. Can't afford to offend his lordship," Petunia whispered, gave me a squeeze, and returned to the counter. "I think we're all done, Isaac. How much do I owe you?"

I heard the till go ker-ching as Arthur and I reached the room where men's and women's clothes were arranged on racks. Chests of drawers lined the back wall on both sides of a door, the right marked men's, the left marked women's. A few pairs of shoes were displayed by a window. "I lost pants, a jacket, two shirts, underwear and my dress shoes," I said.

Arthur eyed me. "Assuming pants is trousers, I think I have what you need." He pointed at one of the chests. "Men's underwear's in there. Help yourself."

I went to the chest and found what I needed, then checked the shoeboxes, finding a pair of black Oxfords that fit well.

In the meantime, Arthur had rummaged around on the racks, returning with a pair of corduroy pants, a blue blazer, and two shirts, one white and one plaid. He held out the white shirt. "For best." He came around behind me and held it against my back. "It'll do. Now try these." He handed me the pants. "Go through that door over by underwear. I'll sort out some shaving equipment and other stuff. Then, I need to tell Isaac what you're getting."

The door led into a small, windowless room that looked as if it had been tacked onto the back of the building. It contained a bench on one side of a second door—leading outside I guessed—and a mirror and hooks to hang clothes on the other side. I took off my pants and bent down to put on the new ones. The corduroy was stiff, but I managed to shove my left foot in. I hopped as I tried to repeat the process with my right leg, but it stuck and I ended up standing on the pants cuff.

Distracted by my predicament, I barely registered a door opening. "Arthur, can you steady me?" I asked. The response was a savage blow to my side that made me double over and caused my eyes to water. Through my tears, I saw blurry, masked figures reflected in the mirror.

Remembering my karate training, I stayed crouched over and tried to lash backwards with my right foot, forgetting I was standing on the cuff. My action caused me to rotate wildly. As I spun to the floor, I could now clearly see the three men who had been behind me. One of them raised his foot and kicked at my side. I managed to grab his ankle and twisted it before his boot hit me.

"What the…?" he shouted as he fell into a second man.

The third man came at me. My left leg was free to move and I kicked him in the crotch as he bent over to throw a punch. He staggered back against the bench, knocking my shoeboxes off.

By now, the other two were hitting and kicking at me, and I was soon overpowered. Blows rained down from all sides. "Get off the island," a gruff voice said. "This is the last warning."

Something hit the back of my head and the world went black.

I regained consciousness to find Arthur bending over me.

"What happened to you?" Arthur asked, his face showing consternation. "I was with Isaac out back. Then he sent me to deliver a package to the Seythan. When I came into the store, I heard a crashing sound. Did you fall over?"

"Maskers," I said groggily. "Three of them attacked me."

Arthur now looked puzzled. "I don't see any damage."

I hugged my aching sides. "They kicked me," I said, and lifted my shirt gingerly.

"Oh dear, I see. Not good. I'll get liniment and bandages. You all right to putting trousers on?"

Not really. My head ached and it hurt to move. But not wanting to appear like I was a wimp, I nodded.

Arthur hurried out.

I managed to get to my feet and finished putting on the corduroys. A moment later, I heard the sounds of an argument. Arthur and Isaac. Was Arthur blaming Isaac for what had happened to me? It would figure, if Isaac had sent him on an errand to give those maskers time to beat me up. The thought drove me to consider who the three men had been. Frankie had said that Sandy and Sam Nancarrow, Isaac's boys, didn't like me. And Sandy had seen me earlier proposing to Rose on the village green, and there'd been time for them to get Johnny Trevenna to join them. It all added up. So, what to do? No way was I going to leave the island, I decided. I'd have to tough it out. Maybe Clara could help me deal with the Maskers. Better still, I thought, as a stab of pain went through my side, get back at the men who had beaten me up.

5.

Arthur insisted on accompanying me back to Clara's. He carried a bag with the shaving equipment, pen and notepad, and most of my new clothes. I walked stiffly, holding my shoes away from my tightly bandaged chest and sides. I must have looked like Frankenstein's monster. Arthur opened Clara's front door for me and I preceded him in.

Clara was sitting in a chair, writing on a notepad. She looked up and, seeming to sense a problem, stood and came over.

She sniffed. "Liniment…what happened?"

"Maskers gave Andy some trouble while I was at Seythan," Arthur said over my shoulder. "Don't think anything's broken. I fixed him up. He'll be fine."

Clara hesitated before speaking. "Put those clothes on the sofa. I'll make Andy some tea." Clara emphasized the 'Andy' in a way that implied Arthur wasn't invited. Odd, I thought and then forgot about it as she took the shoes, and led me to the chair.

Tea, the solution to all problems, I thought as I settled gingerly onto the seat.

Arthur laid the clothes down. "Best get back before Isaac finds I'm gone," he said as he left.

I closed my eyes and tried to will the aches away as if I were a yogi.

"What happened?" Clara asked, waking me from my vain attempts at meditative pain killing.

"Three maskers beat me up when I was in the dressing room."

"Where were Arthur and Isaac?" Clara asked sharply.

"Back in store. Then Isaac sent Arthur to Seythan House." I tried a smile when I realized I'd dropped the—just like an islander—a habit I'd picked up on my previous stay. "I was trying on these pants." I pointed at the corduroys.

"Does Rose need to take a look?"

I was about to say yes, but decided I didn't want to worry her. "Think not. Nothing's broken. I'm sore, that's all." I stood, holding onto the chair back. "Actually, that's not all."

Clara looked at me quizzically.

After what had been done to me, I was pissed off and decided to be blunt. "Rose is going to be Queen. I need to be King. I'd like to put an end to this crap. Can you help?"

Clara turned and glanced sideways at me. "Could be…. But King's up to Penseythan."

"I know."

She reached out and patted my cheek. "Understand, whatever I decide to do will be done my way…and I won't necessarily tell you everything."

What did she mean by that? "Can you explain?"

"You may not like what I do." Her face became serious. "And you mustn't tell anyone, not even Rose."

"Do I have a choice?"

Clara tilted her head. "Not really."

"Rose won't be happy when…if she finds out." Clara's expression didn't change. "Okay, I'll trust you," I said.

"I'll see what I can do." Clara's fleeting smile was one of delight. "You still going to play Romeo?"

I hoped acting wouldn't be that difficult. "Yes, I guess." That wasn't my main priority. "Tomorrow, I need to get over to Morley Thomas," I said. "Do you have a bike I can borrow?"

"Frankie's got his, but you can use mine, if you don't mind ladies'." She tugged at her ear. "Watch out for highwaymen."

***

Early the next morning, I headed for the Morley farm, which was on the road from the schoolhouse to Trewince, where Johnny Trevenna lived. On the way, I daydreamed about Rose. I'd hoped to see her the previous evening and had gone next door. After Mary had raved about the engagement ring and how happy she was for Rose and me, she told me Rose had gone to stay with the Billings on the other side of Portloe, because Artley's mother was ill. It was then I realized I would have to get used to Rose being absent a lot of the time. I decided I'd use the time to concentrate on consolidating my role on the island.

Riding the bike was more difficult than I'd expected; 'ladies version' was not a problem. In fact, it made it easier to get on and off. By the time I reached the turn-off by the school, I had aggravated the sore areas on my sides. I got down and walked with the bike for the remaining couple of miles to the farm.

Nothing had changed from my visit two years earlier. A hand-painted sign that read "THOMAS" pointed down a rutted, fenced-in track to my left. Jerseys munched grass in one of the fields.

I proceeded toward the two-story farmhouse, and soon saw the blue cover I'd shipped covering the pit that Morley had dug by the side of his barn. Next to it was a second open pit to collect the run-off. This pit would retain most of the nutrients after the methane had been removed. The residue would hardly smell at all, and it would have a much lower concentration of noxious bacteria than the manure. The liquid in it would be put back on the fields to fertilize them.

A new open-sided shed next to the pits housed a large white tank and a pump. I assumed it was to collect the methane gas given off by the manure. The crates I'd shipped sat unopened to the side.

Morley, wearing blue overalls, was on his knees in front of the tank fiddling with some pipes. He looked up when he heard me coming, and stood. "Master Andy, I wondered when you'd get here." He pointed at the pipes. "I put in a small pump, temporary-like. No point in wasting gas."

"Great," I said. "So you kept the cows in the barn over winter?"

"Yes. I collected everything I could and shoveled it into pit." Morley sniffed. "Barn don't smell so bad anymore. Thanks to you." He wiped his hands on his trousers, extended one and shook mine firmly. Morley pointed at an open pipe that protruded from the edge of the cover. "That's for hot water to warm up slurry on cold days in winter."

"Good. You'll need it."

I glanced around. "I see my crates arrived. There's a lot more piping and cable, and two each of a larger pump, water scrubber for the carbon dioxide and hydrogen sulfide, generator and controls, and spares."

"Must have set you back a bit? Before I forget, we need to discuss how much I owe."

"Thanks, but that can wait until we know it all works properly," I replied. "Other than the piping, it was all surplus stuff my dad helped me find. So less than seven thousand dollars…about five thou in South African Rand plus shipping. " I gestured at the shed. "Where'd you get the tank?"

Morley beamed, his angular face with its faint scar on the right cheek lighting up in a way that dispelled the first impression that he was an overly serious man. "World War II, Navy used island to store fuel and the like. They left a number of tanks and the small pump I found…covered in grease it was. Took me a while to clean it off. Oh, and I followed your instructions and made a simple scrubber. The waste water goes into a little pond away from the house." He paused. "The smell, you know." He gestured at what I'd sent. "Good thing you labeled these items to be delivered to me," Morley said, gesturing at the crates. "I heard what happened to your luggage. Not right. Gives island a bad name."

I bent down to check the generator crate, forgetting the tight bandages. "Oof." I rose up slowly and, grimacing, held my side.

"You all right, Andy?" Morley's tone of voice showed his concern.

"Slight problem with some maskers," I replied. "I'll be fine."

Morley glanced in the direction of Trewince. "Hilda heard something about it. That Johnny Trevenna needs to grow up," he muttered. "Want me to open this?" He gestured at the crate.

"If you don't mind…that and the other crates. I'd like to check everything's okay."

We finished unpacking and as far as I could tell, everything was in good shape, unlike me. I was now hot and sweaty under the bandages in addition to feeling sore.

"Fancy a cuppa?" Morley asked.

Tea, also the British solution to being too hot. "Absolutely."

I followed Morley into the farmhouse, where his wife, Hilda, was in the kitchen peeling potatoes. She wore a plain blue dress, no makeup, and her hair was pulled up into a bun. She smiled, flashing white teeth in a tanned face.

Hilda put down the knife when we came in. "Andy, I heard what happened. We Roselanders aren't like that.... You sit down." She turned away, brushing at her face with the hem of her apron.

Sensing that this might be a good opportunity to get answers to questions I'd had for a long time, I said, "Morley, I don't like to ask, but what can you tell me about the Maskers?"

Morley shifted nervously on his chair, studied the far wall and didn't respond.

Hilda brought over two mugs of tea. She'd already added milk and sugar. "You tell him. It's only fair," she said.

"Don't rightly know all the history. Let me think." He played with his cup. "My granddad told me about geese dancers back in Cornwall. They used to perform between Christmas and Twelfth Night, play games on people hoping to get food or money."

"Like trick or treat on Halloween? I used to get dressed up as a kid."

"Suppose so." Morley scratched his head. "Anyway, back in the last century, some of the men revived it."

"Getting back at the Penseythan, we women reckon," Hilda said. She added, as if she was remembering something she'd learned, "Didn't like our matriarchal society. Your Professor explained that to me."

"Could be. Anyway, it's what I think started out as a lark."

Morley glanced at me. "When you were here you saw what happens at Guy Fawkes. We all dress up."

"Yes, and cavort around the bonfire.... Last time, some maskers attacked me." I took a sip of tea. Too sweet, but I'd grown used to that on my previous stay.

Morley sighed. "I didn't know that. I did hear that the young lads didn't appreciate your turning the women's heads."

Hilda grinned. "Patsy Jago and the like." She returned to peeling potatoes.

A wry smile crept onto my face. "Clara set Patsy up to make a fool of me."

"So I heard," Hilda chuckled.

"Anyway, Maskers got more serious around nineteen thirties when Agnes Nichols was Penseythan," Morley said. "They weren't just young lads having fun. Whoever was their head was older and wanted to take over. Agnes Nichols tried to put a stop to it...but problem hasn't gone away."

"Were you ever a masker?"

"When I was young. Not after I got married and had to make a go of farming."

"I made sure of that," Hilda said, cutting a potato in half. "Maskers weren't happy, but...." Her swift quartering of the potato emphasized a disdain for those men.

I thought back to what had happened at the culmination of Clara's games with me. I was positive that Arthur Nancarrow had played a role. "Getting back to Clara," I said. "She got Patsy to make a pass at me, as part of a game. I ended up in the Round House in some kind of mock trial. The players wore masks. Were they part of the Maskers?"

Morley glanced at Hilda. She shrugged. "Didn't hear about that either. Doubt it. Clara does some weird things, but as far as I know she never let Frankie join them. That should tell you something."

Now to the critical question. "Do you know who is Head of the Maskers?"

Hilda stared at Morley and shook her head vigorously. Morley raised his mug, hiding his expression. After taking a long time sipping his tea, he said, "Can't rightly say. Best not for me to guess and best you don't know, anyway. Your first problem's with Johnny Trevenna. Worry about that."

So, Johnny wasn't the leader. I guessed he was too young. I wondered if Morley knew who was and wouldn't tell me or didn't want to hazard a guess. I bet Clara knew. I'd ask her. Time to change the subject. "I really appreciate what you've done, Morley. When I was here before, I mentioned the possibilities of digesters to Jacob Jago and Edgar Cocking. Do you know if they would be interested in a methane project?"

Morley scratched his head. "I don't reckon Edgar's got enough litter from his chickens. Then there's Fred Nichols across the road. He has a few sheep for wool and mutton when they get old." He scratched again. "Not much there. As to Jacob, I'm not sure about the hogs. He lets 'em roam. You need to talk to him." His voice gurgled with suppressed laughter when he said, "Folks downwind in Veryan wouldn't mind losing the stink."

I decided to forget about the chickens and concentrate on trying to persuade Jacob that it would pay to enclose the hogs and collect the manure. I also needed to help Morley put his system together. My aching chest told me that might have to wait. I finished my tea. "Can putting everything together wait a couple days?" I asked. "I'm a bit sore."

"Certainly, m'dear." Morley's voice showed his concern. "No great rush. I'll just get things ready. Tidy up a bit." He ushered me out into the yard.

As I was about to leave, I had a thought. "You mentioned the Navy had left a lot of stuff…like that tank you got. Where is this place?"

"Outside Portloe, off track to radio station," he replied. "There's quarry dug out to get stone for building houses. That's where they're stored."

"I need to go there sometime. Could be more useful stuff for digesters." I started to leave then had a thought. "Can I get in to see what's there?"

"Yes, m'dear. There's no fence."

Having put on a foolish show of male pride in riding the bicycle back to the road, I got off the minute I was out of sight and walked slowly most of the five miles back to Veryan.

6.

I woke up on Sunday morning still very sore. At breakfast with Clara, hoping to see Rose, I accepted the invitation to attend chapel: a hope soon dashed when Mary told me Rose was still in Portloe. I'd been celibate now for more than two years, unless you count an occasional personal relief. Being so close to her now was, in a strange way, more frustrating than being thousands of miles apart when nothing but memories had been possible.

Clara wore a floral-patterned dress with a lacy collar—frock to her—to the service, her going-to-church outfit. The dominant color matched the pale green of her eyes. I did the best I could to look respectable with a mixture of the clothes I'd obtained at Nancarrow's Store and those salvaged from the sea.

The walls of the chapel were constructed from whitewashed, volcanic rock. White wood-framed windows with plain glass ran down each of the long walls. The sloping roof was constructed from corrugated iron, painted green. A short, wooden steeple with a cross on top of it was mounted on the north end, which faced approximately toward Jerusalem. A porch and wooden double-door looked out on the village square. Inside the chapel, twelve rows of wooden pews sat on each side of a stone aisle that led to where an altar and a lectern graced the area under the steeple. The interior walls were white, and the only splashes of color came from a small, stained glass window on the wall beyond the altar and the gold and white altar cloth.

As on previous occasions, Isaac Nancarrow conducted the service. Like the other men, he wore his Sunday best blue suit, a white shirt with stiff collar, and a blue tie. The style would have fit well in the British movies from the forties that I'd seen. The theme of his sermon was the parable of the Good Samaritan. As far as I could tell, he was sending a message to those who'd beaten me up, which was odd given the likelihood of his kinfolks' involvement.

"Take it as an apology," Clara whispered halfway through his rambling speech.

"I will."

Isaac clasped his hands and ended the sermon with, "Therefore, we should offer aid to those in need, regardless of where they come from."

The remainder of the day, I spent resting, eating, and practicing my lines with Clara.

***

On Monday, after hearing that Rose had stayed in Portloe, yet again, to run a clinic, I decided to visit the auk rookery. Clara was about to leave for her job at the library across the village green. If I were asked to explain what she did, I might describe it as a *sometime* job. Sadly, owing to a tragedy early in her life, on occasion she would seem to lose her focus. I had observed her wandering the aisles of the library, dithering about where a returned-book should go. At other times, she was sharp and decisive. I wondered which version would turn up today. As she opened the front door, I called out, "I'm going to see the auks."

Clara paused in midstride. "There's bread and cheese. You could make a sandwich." She pointed at the larder. "There's paper bag in cupboard. And best go out back way," she said, her pinched eyebrows showing concern. "You don't want those Nancarrow boys to see you." She closed the front door firmly to emphasize the point.

I made a sandwich, placed it in the bag, then finished the washing up, muttering to myself that I could handle Isaac's boys, while being conscious of the fact that I didn't relish an encounter. A sharp twinge as I put the plates away reminded me I couldn't. Holding my side, I went upstairs to get a sweater and picked up my binoculars, which by good fortune had been left on the boat and not put out with the rest of my luggage. The late September weather on Roseland was inclined to suffer from sudden rainy squalls and I grabbed my parka, too.

It was a challenge to scramble over the low wall at the end of the tiny back yard while trying not to aggravate my bruised sides. Task completed, I rested for a few minutes before circling the chapel to reach the track to the rookery: all out of sight of Nancarrow's store. I trudged up the rock-strewn path, eager to reach the site of the blind from which I'd studied the auks. Fluffy clouds scudded across an azure blue sky, driven by a breeze from the west. Memories of the auks provided the wind that blew my thoughts toward my father, the bird watcher. He'd been disappointed when I ignored his advice to study farming, and pursued a PhD in ornithology; even though he was the one who had gotten me hooked on bird watching.

"I love birding," Dad had said, pausing to add, "As a hobby. But it's not a profession."

He'd been right in the long term. But, if I'd followed his advice at the beginning I wouldn't have met Rose. *One up for me.* The fleeting exultation was quickly replaced by the realization I hadn't yet closed the deal.

My father, a stern, upright Scotsman, or at least descended from Scots, wore a kilt to the Highland Games at Grandfather Mountain in North Carolina to remind us of his heritage. My ex-girlfriend, Annie, was the one who'd pointed out that he was jealous of me. Jealous of the time my mother spent fussing over me: time that should have been his. Seeing them together, their love for each other, had amplified the pain and the loneliness I'd felt when Annie dumped me. I like to believe that learning from this experience had improved my attitude and the more mature image I now presented to women. Rose, who had been wary of me when we first met, finally had seen this more mature version. I supposed that's what people meant when they talked about growing up.

I reached the top of the hill and started the shallow descent to the rookery. Since I'd been gone, the gorse bushes, originally imported to stop soil erosion, had grown back onto the un-trodden path. I picked my way cautiously, not wanting to tear up my calves on the prickly sprigs, and reached the once-bare spot where Frankie and I had built my blind.

George had informed me that the onset of spring had been colder than normal. The auks had not yet returned, and the fishy smell that normally pervaded the area was subdued. However, the constant sound of the waves sloshing against the base of the cliff and the whispering noises of the wind were still present and had a therapeutic effect taking my mind off my precarious situation.

Lost in memories of my time studying the birds, I remained for well over an hour. The topic of my PhD had been to explain why there were more male than female auks. Each female, my good-time-girls, had a mate and three gentleman friends. My favorite was Nellie and her main man, Fred. The reason for the abundance of males was a tragic one—the females killed the weaker female chicks. The reason for this horrific act was a relative scarcity of the kind of fish they ate. They needed the helping male hands to catch fish and feed the next batch of youngsters.

Sadly, the islanders, led by a nineteenth-century Penseythan, had adopted a similar practice to control the island's population. Traditionally, the Penseythan had been the midwife and was responsible for the infanticide, allowing only one female child per family to survive. This barbaric practice stopped with the death of Jane Trevenna. Unfortunately, the auks were not capable of making such a change.

My thoughts turned briefly to my situation. On the plus side, Rose and I were engaged and I had a number of good friends made during my previous stay. On the negative side, some islanders weren't convinced I'd be a useful addition to their community, and others wanted me gone. Hopefully, when I demonstrated the value of the digester system on the Morley Thomas farm, some of the doubters would change their minds. I wasn't sure I would be viewed as indispensable, but with my knowledge of agriculture, I knew I could be a positive addition to the island's well-being.

The digester had better work, because failure might tip the balance against me. Further studies of the island's birds would be interesting, but not a solution for my future. I wondered if the auks had started collecting out to sea beyond the Nare Head and Gull Rock, and whether Nellie would be among them.

I headed off across the rookery and took the path to the end of the Nare Head. The sea birds circling the Gull Rock and cormorants fishing in the bay provided an hour or so of entertainment before I decided to get a better view. Retracing my steps through the gorse, I started my ascent up Brown Willy, the dormant volcano that towered over this northwest corner of Roseland. The path followed the stream that drained the lake at the top of the mountain: a stream that provided water and a small amount of hydropower to Veryan and the neighboring farms.

Unlike other parts of Roseland, where the islanders had planted a variety of non-native trees and shrubs, the mountain was covered with native vegetation. Spread around the base were tussocks of grass and what Jane Trevenna had told me was a variety of buckthorn. Higher up, I worked my way through a band of three-foot tall dwarf tree ferns with their cluster of feathery fronds on a short trunk. Three quarters of the way up the two-thousand, two-hundred-foot mountain, the foliage was close to the ground with mats of crowberry and moss. The black fruit of the crowberries was used by the islanders to make a jam; just like my mother made blueberries.

I reached the dam by the lake, turned to the west and scanned the sea. Sure enough, patches of black spotted the water a few miles off the coast, showing that the auks were congregating and would be back on the island soon. I then turned my attention to the colony of rock hopper penguins on the shore to the north of Veryan. The males were stationed across the shoreline, waiting for the females to return. They were guaranteed female company and relief. The sight made me depressed. Until we were married, and I prayed Clara would be successful in helping us, my lot was to wait and pray. I decided to revisit in a week's time and check if the rock hoppers' dreams had been realized.

Satisfied that for some the world was normal, I turned my powerful, bird-watching binoculars to look east. Morley's farm came into view and, in the woods beyond it, so did Trewince House, the home of Johnny Trevenna, about ten miles away. Seeing no activity there, I looked down at the base of the mountain to the Jago farm. A figure was working in the small field that housed the pig shelters. *Probably Frankie.* Jacob Jago might be resting his injured arm. I decided I might as well go down there and find out if Jacob would be interested in collecting the manure.

The hike up the mountain had given me an appetite and I sat on a mossy patch and ate my sandwich. I knew from working at the rookery for months that the stream water was fit to drink, and I scooped up a couple of refreshing handfuls before starting back. Halfway down the mountain, I paused to view the area around Nancarrow's store. A flicker of movement around the abattoir out the back suggested the Nancarrow brothers were working. If they were busy, it would be safe to visit Jago's farm, I decided.

By now, the wind had picked up and a bank of darker clouds had moved in from the west. Rain would follow. I increased my pace. The path wove down the hill, past banks of blackberry bushes to reach a stile and the field next to the one with the pigs. The wind was at my back and I hadn't smelled them yet.

Frankie, who had been moving the pig shelters to new positions, saw me and ambled over to meet me at a gate. He tilted his head and, in his typical fashion, eyed me sideways. "You looking for Jacob?"

"Yes. I want talk to him about ways of collecting the manure. He might be interested in the electricity and heat it would generate."

Frankie's upper lip wrinkled. "I'd wait. He's grumping at everybody. Rose told him not to do anythin' active-like until his arm healed."

"That why you're out here?"

"Tossed a coin with Paul for who got to work in the yard." Frankie gave a sly grin. "I won." He glanced at my paper bag with its half-eaten sandwich, and pulled an old coin from his pocket. "You want to toss for what's in there? I go first."

Paul? Oh, yes, Jacob's son. A nice kid. His sister Patsy was the one who'd first got me into trouble with Jane Trevenna, but it had all been a part of Clara's game with me. As always intended, Patsy had married Young Artley. "What are you offering?"

He scratched his head. "Either way, I'll walk home with you."

"Why?"

He gestured to the west. "It's going to rain." Without turning, he pointed to the east. "*Probly* don't want to talk to Sandy Nancarrow."

I looked where he was pointing. The Nancarrow boy was standing on the track from the farm to Veryan smoking a cigarette. "Okay."

Frankie flipped the coin. "Heads," he said, catching the worn silver piece before it hit the ground and held his hand out flat. Queen Victoria's head in profile eyed a grimy fingertip.

I reached out and turned the coin over. Her majesty was now

looking at his tanned forearm. "Very clever." I handed over my sandwich. "Does Paul know?"

A smile flickered. "No, and don't you tell him." In two gulps, he stuffed the half-eaten sandwich into his mouth. "Come on," he said, spluttering breadcrumbs.

From past experience, I knew this was all a part of his act to appear the simpleton. Why he was still trying it out on me was a mystery. I followed him. We were now downwind and the acrid smell of the pigs was overpowering. Stepping carefully, I avoided the splotches of manure.

Sandy Nancarrow stood with his back against the gate, watching us. A muscular man, he wore a blood-stained apron, showing he'd come straight from the abattoir. I assumed that his wearing the apron was an added attempt to intimidate me.

Frankie stopped in front of Sandy, bowed, and said, "Prithee, kind sir, open yon gate for us."

Nancarrow looked bewildered for a moment. "Bugger off," he said. A smile crossed his face as he unlatched the gate, pulled it forward, and stood behind it. He watched us under lowered brow, while dropping his cigarette and grinding it out with his heel.

Frankie ushered me forward. As we walked steadily through, I heard a scratching sound. Out of the corner of my eye, I saw Frankie catch the gate as it swung violently at us, and hurl it back. The gate hit Nancarrow's outstretched arms.

"Damn you," Nancarrow shouted, rubbing his fingers.

Frankie bounded forward and pushed again, knocking Nancarrow to the ground onto an offering from one of the pigs. "Learn manners, kind sir." Frankie grabbed my arm. "Run. Sandy's got no sense of humor."

I started to break into a jog, stopping when stabbing pains hit my left side. Slowing down, I gasped, "Sorry. This is too much for me. I've got to rest a minute."

We stopped for me to catch my breath, in silence, before strolling the mile over fields to the village green. The Lagonda was parked outside Nancarrow's store. Rose and Clara were engaged in what appeared to be an animated discussion as they headed to their respective homes. At that moment, the rain started. I trailed Frankie to Clara's house.

Mary Pascoe opened her front door and Rose waved at me as she ducked inside.

Clara met us at her front door. "Andy, Mary invited you for supper," she said. "Any time after five-thirty, Mary said. You two can rehearse. Take your lines. Rose has hers."

An opportunity to be with Rose. Thank God.

7.

Mary answered my knock on the door. "Come on in. Rose'll be down in a minute."

In the living room, the fireplace with a hearth at floor level and brick seats on each side took up most of the wall that was shared with Clara's house. Over the fireplace, a photograph of Rose graduating from medical school had replaced a painting of a seaside village that had reminded me of Portloe. The other pictures all looked familiar—an old, hand-drawn map of Roseland, with annotations in spidery writing, and sepia photographs of groups of islanders.

For once, the coffee table lacked one of Clara's jigsaw puzzles. I assumed that the pile of paper I recognized as being in Clara's elegant writing was the script for a role in the play. "You got a part in Romeo and Juliet?" I said.

"Not yet. That's lines for Rose."

"How are you feeling, Andy?" Rose's voice drifted down from the stairs as she joined us: a trim figure in neatly pressed jeans and a pale blue sweater.

I glanced up. "I'm sore, but I'll get over it."

Mary stood. "I'll finish getting supper ready. Leave you two to talk."

"You've been working hard, I hear," I said to Rose after she had given me a tender kiss.

Rose had pulled her hair into a ponytail; the tips were damp. Her face—no makeup and beautiful as ever—showed signs of tiredness that washing with cold water hadn't hidden.

"For some reason everything happened at once: Jacob Jago's accident followed by Artley's mum's illness." She smiled. "But we all got through it. Two weeks ago, it was Patsy Billing deciding to have her second child late at night."

I had the idle thought that in the past, when the Penseythan practiced female infanticide, the sex of the two children would have mattered—no two females allowed. But I was more curious about the play. "How do you feel about us playing Romeo and Juliet?"

"Fine, really." She frowned. "Except, Clara says she's going to ask Sam Nancarrow to play Tybalt."

I recalled, earlier, seeing Rose and Clara arguing. "Is that what you and Clara were discussing when the rain started?"

Rose's lips compressed. "Partly." She leaned over and picked up her lines.

Apparently, there had been more to their argument. "So, you're unhappy with her choosing Sam because he was probably one of the maskers who attacked me?"

"Do you remember the details of the Romeo and Juliet plot?"

"Not really. Except, it's real gloomy and they both die." Hold on. "Do you think Clara's trying to make a point?"

Rose raised an eyebrow. "You're not a scholar of Shakespeare, are you?" Rose put on her doctor's, explaining face. "Tybalt is Juliet's cousin. He's aggressive and hates the Montagues...which means Romeo. After he kills Romeo's friend Mercutio in a duel, Romeo kills Tybalt."

"So?"

The face grew more serious. "If Sam Nancarrow's going to be Tybalt. You're going to have to do the sword fight scene with him. Do you understand now?"

"I guess so. But surely he wouldn't try anything in front of everybody...would he?"

"Probably not, but you two are going to have to practice and he could always make a mistake."

"But we're not going to use real sharp swords...are we?"

"I suppose not for practice, but he could always jab you in the eye. Ask Clara what you'll use."

Fair point. I'd have to be careful. "I can handle it," I said, recalling that, for fun, I had tried my hand at Japanese sword fighting, kendo, when I was learning karate. "Was there anything else?"

"Clara tried to get my goat." Rose grinned. "Said she'd offered Johnny the part of Romeo."

"Did you believe her?"

Rose made a face. "Wasn't sure and now I'll never know."

"Supper's ready," Mary shouted from the kitchen.

A fishy smell met me in the short corridor before I reached the kitchen, where a tiny table had been set up with three places and glasses of water. Mary motioned for me to take the chair furthest from the stove. "Fish pie," she said with a grin. "But not Starry Gazy."

I had a mental image of a Starry Gazy, piecrust holding up little fish heads and vacant eyes staring at the ceiling. "Phew," I said

Mary spooned a layer of fish, breadcrumbs and parsley onto a plate. I could see it had been baked in milk. She added boiled potatoes and cabbage, and handed it to me. "Fish is what we call five-finger," she said. "Watch out for bones. I never get 'em all out."

"Thank you." I took a sip of water.

The stew was delicious and the few bones easy to find. By the time we finished, a new aroma, apple pie, pervaded the room. Rose picked up the plates and took them to the sink.

Mary pulled the pie from the oven, cut three portions, and delivered the plates to the table. She returned with cream.

"That looks wonderful," I said.

"Not my best," she said, always the perfectionist. "Had to use apples stored over the winter."

"My mom also stores apples over winter…on newspapers in the attic." I took a bite. "Just like Mom's, I can't tell the difference."

Mary smiled.

"Have you had a chance to look at your lines, Rose?" I asked.

"Two weeks ago, while I was waiting for Patsy to produce." Her forehead wrinkled. "They're not quite what I remember of the play."

"In what way…? Wait a second. She had you lined up for Juliet before I got here?"

Rose chuckled. "Yes, and I think she planned to have you be Romeo. Now where was I?" Rose took a spoonful of pie. "Oh, yes. Clara's changes. For one thing, Juliet's mother, Lady Capulet, has become Penseythan Capulet," Rose replied. "She seems to have the role that had been her husband's, and he has hers."

I recalled Clara's version of The Tempest had also managed to bring in a Penseythan and Tristan da Cunha. "Does the play still take place in Verona?"

"Not exactly. More like the island of Verona…somewhere near Tristan."

"I wonder who Clara plans for the role of that Penseythan," Mary mused. "She hasn't asked me."

Rose finished a mouthful of pie and waved a finger. "Has to be Martha Nancarrow."

"I've glanced at my lines," I said. "But I don't remember much about the play other than a lot of people die. Has she changed that?"

"Not as far as I can see." Rose spooned up the remainder of the pie, and used a finger to pop a recalcitrant piece stuck on her upper lip into her mouth. "Not yet, anyway." Rose glanced at me. "There are quite a lot of crossed out and rewritten lines, but it shouldn't be difficult to ignore them. Anything you want to add?"

We seemed to have beaten that topic to death, and I didn't want the conversation to turn to whether I'd asked Clara to help me. I stood. "Not really. Let me do the washing." I picked up plates and moved toward the sink.

Mary pushed me back. "You and Rose need to practice your parts," she said. "Off you go."

Rose took my arm. "Don't argue. Mum knows best." She led me back into the living room, where she picked up her lines. "We meet first in act one, scene five. It's quite brief. We can do it another time. Let's start with the famous balcony scene in act two, scene two."

"Okay. We're going to stand?"

"Yes, I'm on a balcony."

"Right." I grabbed my pages. "Let's see." I struck a pose and declaimed Romeo's first line. "It's easy to joke about an injury if you've never been hurt."

Rose raised an eyebrow.

Be serious, I thought. "What is that light in yonder window to the east? It is Juliet. Rise up, oh sun, and kill the jealous moon. The moon is pale with grief because Juliet is more beautiful than she. If I could but say how much I love her. The brightness of her cheeks outshines the stars." I wasn't acting anymore, and tried to convey that was how I felt about Rose.

"Oh, my." Rose looked up from her script.

Is she suppressing a giggle? Whatever. "You are as glorious as a bright angel, who makes us men look up at the sky to see you."

"Oh, Romeo, why can't you change your name? It's not you that's the problem. It is the Montague name." Rose looked away. "A rose by any other name would smell as sweet. Tell me you love me and I'll risk the wrath of Penseythan Capulet and forsake my family and my name."

I had only had time to do a cursory scan of my lines. Now I focused on the reply Clara had conjured up. "I believe you. Just call me your love and I will call you Rose. For indeed no other could be as sweet."

Rose did not respond immediately, but studied the script. "Andy, what game is Clara playing? She's changed the plot so I am Juliet and you are Romeo. Listen to this. 'Tell me how you got to this island. I heard my father's men had barred your passage at the port. Surely you did not scale the cliffs. I'd give all to prevent my relatives from finding you or it will be the end.'"

"Don't worry, fairest Rose. The darkness will hide me. I'd rather die than lose you."

Rose dropped her script and came into my arms. She was trembling. "I hope Clara knows what she's doing."

"Have you any idea how she plans to get us married?"

"Not yet. It's typical of Clara. We'll just have to be patient."
Her face came up to mine and she kissed me passionately.

When I responded, she pulled back.

"Not here, Andy. And not now. I've been saving myself for you.
I don't want to spoil things." Her face showed determination. Dr.
Rose Pascoe had returned.

Damn. I'd been waiting, too. Don't screw up. "Sorry. It's not
been easy, but I can wait."

She rubbed her forehead.

"You're tired," I said. "We can pick it up later."

Rose kissed me again, tenderly. "I do have to get up early to
check on Patsy and the baby. I'll send word when I'm going to be
free." She clung to me briefly. "Look after yourself."

On the short walk back to Clara's, I brooded about the fact
that Clara had probably chosen to stage Romeo and Juliet with
Rose and me in the key roles before I had arrived back on the
island. Why? I decided to go over my lines thoroughly to see if I
could work out what other adjustments Clara had made.

8.

I HAD STUDIED ONLY A SMALL FRACTION OF MY LINES BY THE time the electricity switched off promptly at nine. While I'd seen "Romeo and Juliet" in high school, I'd been with a hot date and really didn't remember much about the plot. The only way to discover what Clara had changed would be to get the original script. The thought that there should be a copy in the library came as I fell asleep.

***

"Is there a copy of Romeo and Juliet at the library I could borrow?" I asked Clara at breakfast.

Clara toyed with a slice of bacon, cutting it into smaller and smaller pieces, but didn't reply.

She doesn't want to answer.

"Surely you must have used one yourself for the lines you gave Rose and me."

She forked a small piece and chewed on it. "That was some time ago," she said vaguely, long after I had seen her swallow.

"Do you know where it is now?"

Clara finished the bacon, a piece at a time before replying. "I'd have to look." She glanced sideways at me, and spoke, her voice no longer hesitant. "Why do you want it?"

Can't tell her the truth.

"I realized I didn't know the plot. It would help me understand my lines."

"I see." Clara stood. "I need to go. Please wash up and put dishes away." She walked out before I could respond.

I decided to wait before going to the library, and read my lines more carefully. "It's no use," I muttered to myself following a fruitless two hours. "Without the original, I can't tell what she's changed." I stuck my head out the door. The sun was shining on this late spring day, but a cold breeze ruffled the grass and the yellow heads of daffodils on the edges of the uncut village green. Wearing my zipped-up parka, I crossed the green to the library. Some idiots had replaced the stocks—likely the Nancarrow boys.

The library was eerily silent and at first I thought Clara wasn't there. I tracked down the S-section and found a number of Shakespeare plays, but not the one I needed. A faint scuffling sound coming from a far corner drew me on a circuitous route through the bookshelves to see her crouched down with a book in her hand.

"Now, where do you go?" she said, trying ineffectively to insert the book into an unyielding slot.

I glanced around the shelves and noted a large gap in the shelf behind her. "I think it's in back of you."

"Oh." Clara put her free hand over her heart. "Mister Andrew, you gave me a shock."

64

I had seen her act before and ignored her reaction. "I'm looking for Romeo and Juliet."

She stared silently at me.

"You know, Shakespeare's play?"

"I know it's a play by Shakespeare, m'dear. I'm putting it on." She smiled triumphantly. "And you and Johnny Trevenna are going to be in it."

What the hell. Was she trying to sidetrack me?

"What role will Johnny have?"

"Paris, of course. The man, the Penseythan wants to marry her daughter, Juliet."

I scratched my head to gain time in preparing my next question. "Fine, and where can I find the play?"

"Should be filed under "S" for Shakespeare," Clara replied, her voice showing both hope and doubt.

"Already looked there."

"Maybe Johnny has it."

"Well, see if you can get him or whoever"—I looked hard at her—"has the play to return it."

"I will, m'dear. Do you want to look at it?"

"Yes."

"Do you have a library card?"

What was she up to now? "No."

Clara smiled sweetly. "I could arrange to get one issued by the Seythan at their next meeting."

Game set and match to Clara.

"I would appreciate that."

"I'll have to find the form. You could come back this afternoon."

And she'd tell me it's out of print. I could ask Rose to get a copy. "Let's forget about it. This afternoon I have to help Morley with the digester system."

"I think that would be better," she said, her tone of voice no longer hesitant. "Just mind you don't hurt yourself." She turned away and held the book out. "Now, where do you go?"

"Behind you."

Clara ignored me and went back to trying to fit the book into the narrow slot. As on previous occasions, I was unable to tell whether this was an act put on for my benefit or, as the Australian aborigines might describe it, she'd gone on walkabout.

***

I cycled to Morley's, managing to stay on the bike the whole way, though it still hurt. Morley had laid out the parts of the methane extraction and energy production system. Good. It would save me the pain of doing it.

As my wheels scrunched on a patch of gravel, Morley looked up from the assembly instructions. "You're just in time," he said, smiling. "I think we're ready to put everything together, but I'm having trouble with this." He waved the sheets of paper. "You Yanks use different words. I think I've got them right." He pointed at the instructions and recited, "A wrench is a spanner, a generator is a dynamo, an oil-pan is a sump.... But what's a spigot?"

"Tap," I said with a grin.

"That makes sense. Where do you want to start?"

I glanced around the yard and spotted the generator and a hot

water heater that I'd shipped from the States. They were still bolt-
ed to their shipping pallets, and sat underneath a small, wooden
roof that projected from the side of the barn nearest to the covered
collection pond. Morley had already connected the new pump,
scrubber, and dryer to the tank, which would hold the methane.

"We need to tie those pallets down to the slab," I said. "I assume you'll be using the hot water in the barn."

"Yes, and in house later. Hilda wants it."

"Then, we'll put the heater closest to where you can run a pipe
on to the house. The electric cable's easier to fit…. Oh, and we'll
leave a space between the two units for the junction box that
allows you to switch the methane from one unit to the other or
operate both. Was there anything else? No. I think that's it for
the moment."

"I'll get my tools and watering can." Morley went into the
barn. He returned carrying a toolbox, an ancient hand drill, and
the can.

Without thinking, and forgetting that electricity was rationed,
I'd assumed we'd use power tools. Just what I needed with my
sore body, I thought ruefully. I decided to check the instructions
before starting. "Let me refresh my memory," I said. "I think we
need to lay out the piping before anchoring the generators."

It took us all morning to cut and temporarily fit the pipes
and junction box. We then marked where the holes were needed
in the concrete. After lunch, we removed everything and started
the long process of drilling. At that point the weather, which had
been cloudy and warm, turned colder.

Morley looked at the sky. "It's going to rain." He smiled.
"Keep concrete dust down."

He was right, but by the time we finished making the holes, the constant drizzle had soaked my pants, and water had managed to get under my parka. Though Morley had done most of the drilling, my contribution had aggravated my bruised sides and I started to shiver.

"We can finish tomorrow," Morley said. "You best come in and dry off. Can't have you getting ill. A cuppa's what you need. You go on in, I'll cover the generators."

"You look a right mess," Hilda said when I reached the kitchen. She was not alone. A girl with curly brown hair, bright blue eyes, and sunny smile that compensated for a prominent nose sat at the table. I recognized her as the grown up version of one of the gawky, giggling teens who on my previous stay had once asked me to dance at a Saturday night social in Portloe.

"Andy, this is my daughter, Susan," Hilda said.

Susan stood and held out her hand. "Pleased to meet you, Andy, I've heard all about you."

"Andy, you get those clothes off. I can hang them over the stove. You can wear Morley's overcoat. Come on Susan." She bustled out of the room, Susan following slowly and pausing at the door to wink at me.

Flirting? What is it with these island women?

I heard some sharp words from Hilda. By the time Hilda returned, alone, I had stripped to my underpants.

"Oh my," Hilda exclaimed. "I heard you took a beating. I had no idea. Those boys should be jailed." She handed me the coat and took my clothes. She hung them on a cord that stretched above, what I knew from my previous time on the island to be a coal-burning, Aga cooker and space-heater. A cup of tea and slice of a fantastic sponge cake followed shortly afterward.

Morley soon appeared, and he and Hilda peppered me with questions about my father's farm and life in the States in general. I sensed they might be avoiding some issue connected to my presence on the island.

By the time my clothes were dry enough to put on, our conversation had become forced with long periods of silence. I noticed that Hilda was staring at Morley with raised eyebrows.

Morley shifted uncomfortably in his chair. "Andy, there's something we think you should know."

Hilda nodded her agreement.

I'd guessed right. What now? My heart rate increased.

"It's time for the Seythan to meet with its new members."

I knew that no family could have two members of the Seythan during the same term. "I think I understand the system. What's the problem?"

Morley shrugged. "Word is that some of the new members aren't favorable to your being here."

"Who, in particular?"

"Not for me to say."

"I know Martha Nancarrow's the Penseythan. Who are the other six members?"

Hilda held out her hands and ticked off the names on her fingers as she recited them, "Elizabeth Gay, Jacob Jago, Arthur Nancarrow, Daisy Quick, James Thomas, and…Johnny Trevenna." She looked at me expectantly.

I could see the problem with Johnny. I didn't know the two women. Oh. James Thomas and his wife had worked for Jane

Trevenna. He had chauffeured her, a job he now did for Rose. Hard to tell how he felt about me. I believed that Jacob had gotten over my brief fling with his daughter, Patsy. That left Arthur. Wait up. "How come Arthur's on it with Martha?"

"Her maiden name was Nichols. There was some argument about it. Pressure was brought to bear from certain quarters." Hilda didn't choose to elaborate on the comment. "Finally, they agreed that Arthur could replace Isaac."

"How do you think Arthur might vote?'

Hilda looked puzzled. "On you or Rose?'

"Me."

"Don't know. Rose though might be…."

"Why?" She glanced at Morley, who shrugged.

"Arthur weren't happy when Mary chose David Pascoe. Most he got was hand assistance if you know what I mean."

"That was a long time ago."

"Arthur's not the kind of man to…."

Hilda's lips pursed and it was clear that was the end of that discussion. "Can you tell me something about Elizabeth and Daisy?"

Morley glanced at Hilda, who gave a slight shake of her head.

"Best ask Petunia Gay and Clara," he said.

"I will." I walked to the door. "I hate to do this but I'm still very sore. It may be another few days before I can help put the system together."

Morley came over and opened the door for me. "You take all the time you need. I think I've got the hang of things now. If I get stuck, I'll get a message to you."

The rain had abated and I cycled slowly back to Veryan, lost in thought about what I'd heard. Obviously, Morley and Hilda believed the Seythan would be stacked against me. On what particular issue, I wasn't sure. On the anti-side would be Trevenna and maybe Thomas, who'd worked for his mother. Martha and Arthur had always seemed friendly, but I had seen Arthur in a mask. Jacob had been hard on me when I'd faced the Seythan two years earlier, and I'd have to find out about the two women. I shivered, a reaction to being worried and to the cold as the rainwater remaining in my damp clothes evaporated.

Clara took one look at me as I hobbled into the living room. "You're shaking," she said. "Come in kitchen. It's warmer. I'll get you some tea, bread and jam…and a blanket."

After she had me seated and bundled up and I'd eaten, she asked, "How did it go with Morley?"

"Fine. We got a lot of the equipment installed before the rain came."

Clara eyed me with her head tilted. "I bet you had a lot to talk about."

She knew. "You mean about the new Seythan?"

"Maybe."

Knowing how everything traveled fast around the island, I decided not to tell her about Hilda and Morley's concerns. "I know all the members except Elizabeth Gay and Daisy Quick. What can you tell me about them?"

"Elizabeth's married to Charlie's brother. She lives in farm just by Veryan on other side of Bodmin River."

I knew where she lived but hadn't remembered she was married to Charlie's brother. It could be useful since I played the trumpet in Charlie Gay's band and got on well with him.

A sly smile flickered. "Elizabeth was Jane Trevenna's best

friend. She and Fred don't have any children. She's Johnny Trevenna's godmother. Dotes on him"

Not so good. I suppressed the comment, 'and you're his aunt.' "What's Fred like?"

"Nice man but under her thumb. Not outgoing like Charlie."

"How about Daisy?"

"Couldn't say."

What did that mean? "Surely you're related?"

"Sister-in-law. She doesn't like my plays, says I shouldn't mess with tradition." Clara stared at me, implying, I guessed, that there was a message in what she'd said.

Tradition. That could mean foreigners like me are a problem. Doesn't sound good. So, what did I have? Martha, Arthur, and Jacob might be on my side; but Johnny, James, Elizabeth, and Daisy might be against me. Which left the question—what would they be debating? "Do you know what's on the Seythan's agenda?"

Clara gathered up my cup and plate and went to the sink. She hummed "The Floral Dance" as she washed up.

Oh, my God! I'd played that song on Midsummer's Day as the band marched to the Round House by the green. We'd led a procession including the chosen woman, the Queen, the King and six other men she'd service there. The Seythan was going to pick them. It seemed they would choose Rose to be the Queen. "Do you know who they're going to pick for Midsummer's?"

"They'll decide," Clara replied vaguely. She kept her head down and busied herself with washing up.

"When do they do that?"

"Some weeks after Guy Fawkes."

I remembered that Guy Fawkes Day, which commemorated

the Catholic rebel's attempt to blow up the Houses of Parliament in the Gunpowder Plot of 1605, was held on November fifth. So it would be more than a month before I'd find out.

9.

AFTER A FITFUL NIGHT TRYING NOT TO THINK ABOUT ROSE AS Queen and Johnny Trevenna as King, I fell asleep exhausted and woke up late. Clara had already left for work. A note on the kitchen table read, 'Make yourself breakfast.' Bread with jam, and tea were all I could stomach before washing in cold water and shaving with hot water from the kettle.

I then went to the library to see about the play. No sign of Clara. "Clara, are you here?"

"In back."

Her voice came from an open door on the far wall. I remembered that was the room where stacks of older books, Seythan reports, and island newsletters were housed.

Clara was seated at a desk. She held out a sheet of paper. "Library card application," she said.

"What?"

"You'll need it to take books from library." Clara placed what I now saw were two sheets onto the table next to an inkwell. With one hand holding the paper down, she pulled the lower sheet out to reveal a second signature section, and handed me a quill pen. "Sign here and here. Full name." She indicated the bottom of each sheet.

What was she up to now? I had an urge to pick up the both

sheets and study them. But I needed Clara's help and decided there was no need to aggravate her.

I glanced at the form. It listed my obligations and the penalties if I failed to return a book in a timely fashion. "Do I need to put the date?"

"It's on form." She indicated penciled-in crosses. "Sign here."

"Why do you need two forms?"

"Regulations. Other two lines are for sponsors."

I dipped the pen in the inkwell and wrote Andrew Ferguson next to the crosses.

"Don't have a middle name?"

"No. When will I get my card?"

Clara picked up the forms, being careful to keep them with the lower one displaced. "When I've finished filing and sent to Seythan. Should be tomorrow." She paused. "You had a message from Charlie Gay. Can you come to band practice at four in village hall?"

When did she find out? Never mind. "Sure." I'd considered visiting Jacob Jago to talk about his hogs, but wasn't sure whether it was a good idea. Having to go to band practice was a good rationale for putting it off. "That'll be fine. I can practice my lines."

Clara's smile showed pleasure. "What a good idea."

***

I left at ten of four, trumpet in hand and made the short walk to the hall, a tin-roofed, single-story building, which was set back from the green between Clara's house and the chapel.

75

Charlie greeted me at the door. "Right nice to have you back, Andy. We need a good trumpet." Inside the hall, ten chairs were arranged in an arc in front of a low stage. Charlie waved a hand at the three people who'd arrived earlier. "I think you know Jim Nichols, Jacob Jago and Paul."

I glanced at their faces quickly. Jim and Paul, Jacob's son, smiled. Jacob showed no expression. What did that mean? "Indeed," I said. "It's great to be back. I've missed playing the trumpet with y…you all." I walked over and shook hands with Jim and Paul. Jacob hesitated slightly before he held out his hand. His heavily-bandaged left arm rested on his drum.

I still had mixed emotions about whether to try and sell Jacob on installing a digester system. This might be an opportunity. However, further discussion was halted by the arrival of the other band members, including Arthur Nancarrow with his violin, and Roddy Gay, who played the clarinet.

When everyone was seated, Charlie walked to the front. "The first order of business is Guy Fawkes. We'll start with *Star Wars* march and the "The Oggy Man". As I expect you know, some idiots dumped Andy's belongings in the sea. Unfortunately, that included new music for us and the dance band."

"John Williams music for the Superman movie for us," I said. "Some big hits, "I Will Survive" and "The Rose" for the dance band…. I'm going to write home and get my mom to resend them."

"That's real kind of you," Jim Nichols said to murmurs of appreciation.

"Now to business," Charlie said. He handed out the *Star Wars* music. "You can all remain seated. It'll make it easier for Jacob with the drum." Charlie grabbed a chair and helped Jacob lift the heavy instrument onto it.

Jacob held on with his left hand and tried a couple of drumbeats. "Good enough to keep time."

We practiced hard for over two hours. I found it easier than expected to pick up where I'd left off. As we packed up, Charlie said, "I need a beer. You're all welcome to join me."

I had nothing else to do. "I'll be there in a bit."

I walked back to Clara's, took my trumpet up to my room, and pocketed a few South African rand, the most common currency on Roseland, from my money belt. Glancing out the window, I watched most of the band following Charlie across the green to the Roseland Arms, the pub that occupied the south end of Nancarrow's Store.

When I arrived, the band members, without Arthur, were clustered in the far corner. Mary was at the bar, wearing her usual low-cut blouse. I leaned over a bar stool and, trying to keep my eyes off the inviting cleavage, ordered a pint of St. Austell best bitter.

"You've got to hear this," I said as she drew the beer. "I wanted to look at *Romeo and Juliet* in the library. Clara said someone borrowed it and she'd put me on the list. Then she told me I couldn't, anyway, without a library card."

Mary giggled. "I know. She got Rose and me to sign as sponsors…with a quill pen, for heaven's sake. What was she thinking of?"

"I've no idea. I simply want to look at the original version." I said. "Compare it with the lines she gave us." I would have liked to get her opinion on Clara's plans, but Sam Nancarrow elbowed me aside and sat at the bar.

Mary's face showed brief irritation before she forced a smile. "What'll you have, Sam?"

"Pint."

I nodded at Mary and joined the band, finding a seat next to Jacob. He had a half-finished pint in front of him and appeared more relaxed than when I'd met him earlier. *What the hell. Go for it.* "I'd like to drop by sometime, Mr. Jago, when it's convenient for you to talk about digester systems."

Jacob tilted his head. "Heard you went to some fancy agricultural college," he said. "So those academics taught you about farming on Roseland?"

Keep your cool. "I grew up on a farm...chickens, corn, and soybeans...pigs added recently," I replied. "Most of what I know comes from my dad. He was the one who encouraged me to go to the Agricultural College at North Carolina State. Most of the farmers I've met went there. He wanted me to learn about new opportunities in farming."

Jacob stared at me. "Morley thinks you're onto something. Come round tomorrow morning and we'll see...." His smile was mirthless. "Try not to bring the Nancarrow boys."

Paul, who was sitting next to Jacob, raised his flute and grinned.

So everybody knows about that incident. "I'll certainly try." Out of the corner of my eye I noticed Petunia Gay, Charlie's wife, patting an empty place on her bench, a signal for me to join her. "Excuse me," I said to Jacob. His glass deflected slightly in acknowledgement.

Before I got to her, Petunia stood and held her arms out. She kissed me on the cheek. "Andy, I'll say it again, it's wonderful to have you back. Rose showed me the lovely ring you'd given her. When's the wedding?"

We sat down.

"Beginning of next year when I'm hoping my parents can visit."

Her smile disappeared. "Oh, such a long time."

Was Petunia trying to tell me something about the new Seythan? Such as they wouldn't be favorable to me. "Petunia, I have a question for you. I heard your sister-in-law's going to be on the Seythan. That must be exciting for her."

Petunia finished her drink. "Elizabeth ain't one to get excited about anything 'cept island's history," she said.

"Sounds interesting." I noticed that Petunia was toying with her empty glass. "What are you having?" I took the glass from her.

"Port and lemon, please."

I got Petunia's order filled and returned to sit by her. "If Elizabeth's written it down, I'd like to read it."

"Doubt she'd show it to you." Petunia downed half her drink and, wide-eyed, touched a finger to her nose. "You being a foreigner an all."

A clear message that Elizabeth wouldn't be on my side if my being King came up before the Seythan. "Are there many islanders feel like that?"

Petunia indicated the crowd in the pub. "You've got more friends than enemies," she said. "And we all love Rose and want her to be happy. It's just a few…and I expect you know who they are."

Our discussion ended when Charlie took me away so I could tell him and Jim Nicholls about the latest music fads in States. That led to another couple of beers and dart games, where I got soundly beaten. As I left around ten, Sam made a move as if to follow but stopped when Charlie stepped between him and the door. His action brought on an overwhelming feeling that, despite the actions of some maskers, I was accepted as a part of the strange Roseland community. A warm glow enveloped me from more than the beer as I returned to Clara's.

10.

On Wednesday morning, I waited until ten before going to meet Jacob Jago. While crossing the square, I glanced back to check for the Nancarrow brothers. *No sign of anyone.* I continued between the Seythan and Round House and took the path across the field to Jacob's farm, reaching the farmyard about fifteen minutes later. Two barns with sloping roofs stood across from the main house. Each had stone walls with windows and a main door on the side facing the homestead. The remaining sides and roofs were covered in red-painted, corrugated iron. Jacob was in his yard supervising Frankie, who was cleaning one of the barns. Through the doorway, I saw that this barn had a partial concrete floor, but the other barn appeared to have trodden-down earth. Both had partial flooring on their rafters. For storage, I guessed.

Jacob waved for me to come over. "I keep pigs here and in yard over winter," he said by way of a greeting. He gestured at two bales of hay, and we sat down.

"Tell me some more about those farms in America you've visited." His arm still seemed to bother him and he hugged the bandaged part to his side.

"I guess the most interesting one was a hog farm in North Carolina," I replied. "The farmer had sows and their farrow. He sells the farrow to other farms for fattening."

"How many?"

"A few thousand total, I think."

Jacob snorted. "What's that got to do with my situation?"

Don't react. "The principle's the same. He collects the manure in a covered lagoon and uses the methane for electricity and to provide process heat. The heat keeps the sows and their litters warm in the cold months. What's left can be used for fertilizer or in his case to grow duckweed in a second lagoon to feed tilapia."

"Tilapia?"

"It's a popular fish."

"Maybe you didn't notice." Jacob shook his head. "We're surrounded by sea. We don't need more fish."

Shouldn't have mentioned tilapia. "That's not all. He uses the liquid left over to fertilize *tom-ah-toes*"—I was careful to use the English pronunciation—"in greenhouses."

"Hmm. That could be interesting." Jacob scratched his head. "Let's say I did this. How much electricity would I get?"

I fished for the notes I'd had the foresight to put in my back pocket. "Dad gave me these numbers. For a thousand pounds of hogs it's maybe two kilowatt-hours a day."

Jacob tilted his head and did some counting on his fingers. "I think I use a few of those units," he said.

"Let's find out what you could produce then. How many pigs do you have?"

My question brought a frown. "You mean all sizes?"

"By size would be better."

Jacob scratched his head. "Eight sows for breeding, twenty young'uns, and another fifteen fattening up.

"Any idea of their typical weight?"

"Their what?"

"Weight. I can estimate the dry weight of the manure from that."

"Big'uns are heavier than you and me."

I'd looked up typical numbers before I left the U.S. Having seen his pigs, I guessed an average of 150 pounds for the small ones and 300 or more for the large ones. I took out my pencil and did a quick calculation on my note pad. "I'd say a total weight of about ten thousand pounds." I glanced at my notes. "So as much as twenty kilowatt-hours a day or less if you decide to use some process heat beyond what you get from the generator."

Jacob eyebrows scrunched and he turned away. I reckoned he was doing some more calculations. He took a couple of minutes before turning back to me. "Just in winter?"

"I think so. That's what Morley's doing…. Unless you can find a way to collect manure from the field the rest of the year."

"Hmmf. I'll think about that. Now, heat could be useful in smoke house where I cure hams…also in farmhouse. Miriam's always complaining about cold." He pointed a gnarled finger with a chipped nail at me. "What would it cost?"

I knew of Jacob's reputation for being a tightwad with his money and had thought about an answer. "I brought an extra generator, er…dynamo, furnace, piping, and controls. They're at Morley's. The deal I have with him is that he can start paying me back for his system when it works. I'd do the same for you."

Jacob lips quivered in a suppressed smile. "Then what does it cost me up front?"

"Have you seen what Morley's done?"

"Dug two big pits next to barn where he keeps cows o'er

winter." Any hint of being pleased disappeared. "His barn has concrete floor. Where I keep pigs mostly doesn't. We put down straw and scrape everything into large piles to put back on fields in spring."

No point in pretending. "My dad had the same problem. He put down a concrete floor and we wash the manure into the pit. When I—"

Jacob scowled. "You want me to concrete the big barn? That'll take time...and money. I'd have to find out how much cement is here on island."

"Let me know what you find out. Then, when I know your pit size, I could order a cover for you. In the meantime you could make a temporary cover."

"And who'd pay for that?"

As the islanders would say, "he had me by the short and curlies." *Here we go again.* To stay on the island, I had to establish myself as the agricultural guru. Having two systems operating would give me more credibility. "I would get the permanent cover and you'd pay me back when the system is up and running."

"All at once?"

"No. In installments."

I thought I detected a smile before he said, "I'll let you know."

I took my leave and headed home. In case one of the Nancarrow brothers was waiting for me, I took a circuitous route back to Clara's.

Clara came in around five just as I finished the latest puzzle. The photos I'd seen earlier had not depicted the actual layout. The full picture revealed a pleading young man, backed by a group of smiling people. A group of maskers stood between him and the dark haired woman to whom he was appealing. The maskers were pointing toward the Round House, clearly indicating the woman had been chosen. Clara had predicted the maskers would try and thwart my efforts to marry Rose. I prayed she had a plan to stop them.

"How did it go with Jacob?" she asked.

"All right, I think. He said he'd let me know. I think his delaying tactics were a way to ensure the best deal."

"That's Jacob. Did he offer to put up any money?"

"Not yet. I told him I'd provide the equipment and he could pay me back when the system works." Clara's raised eyebrows indicated she wanted to hear more. "He'll have to pay to dig a pit and concrete the floor of his bigger barn."

Clara chuckled. "Make sure you get it in writing." She started toward the kitchen then turned around. "By the way, Saturday morning I'm having the first general meeting on the play. Not everyone can come." She gave a furtive smile. "I expect Johnny'll be there. You need to come to Village Hall at eleven."

I'd seen Johnny only once, years earlier on the dock in Cape Town. Now I'd have to face him. I tried not to grimace. "I'll be there."

11.

Two hours after breakfast on Friday morning, I cycled to Morley's farm. As I approached the farmyard, I spotted him in a pasture.

Morley waved and ambled over to join me by the barn. "It's all together and working," he said. "Got confused with the circuit diagrams, and had some trouble with electrics. Johnny Trevenna helped straighten it out."

I'd forgotten that Johnny was an electrical engineer. "Of course. He just graduated, didn't he?"

"Top of his class, so they say."

That made me think about who Johnny was: one of Roseland's brightest, sent to England to get an education that met the island's needs. He and other islanders had expected that he and Rose would marry. For a second, I felt sorry for him. That feeling evaporated when a residual ache in my side reminded me of the beating he and the Nancarrow brothers had put me through. Morley had said the system was working but I couldn't hear anything. "Is the generator running?"

"Been waiting for you to turn it back on." Morley beamed. "A celebration like. Hang on." He went into the farmhouse, emerging with two mugs. "Best cider." He handed me a mug, and pointed at the master switch above the generator.

I switched it on and as the generator spun up, we toasted each other. The rough cider warmed my insides and I felt elated at my first success in proving I could be useful on the island.

"You'll be pleased to hear I succeeded in getting my drains reconnected," Morley said. "The waste that had gone to the septic tank now goes to the covered lagoon."

Another positive result. "Congratulations."

We chatted about maintenance and possible upgrades to the system until I remembered I had another appointment. I glanced at my watch. "I've got to go to the radio station," I said. "Some maskers dumped the music I'd brought for the band into the sea. I need to telegraph my mother to send replacements."

"Hilda's real eager to talk to you. It's a bit early for lunch, but surely you've got time for a bite?"

I was curious about what Hilda wanted to say, though torn by the need to get my telegram off, and I wanted to see the Navy surplus in the quarry. Morley looked so hopeful and I didn't see how to refuse. Maybe she'd tell me something useful. "Thank you."

"Andy's here," Morley shouted out as we entered the kitchen.

I heard the sound of her footsteps as Hilda came downstairs, wearing the same dress as the last time I'd visited. She turned to Morley and made a shooing motion with her hand.

Morley went back to the door. "I have things to do." He left.

Hilda sat me down and made me a cup of tea. "Bread, cheese and pickles all right?" she asked. Not waiting for an answer, she carved two slices from a farmhouse loaf, placed them on a dinner plate, added cheese and pickled onions, and brought them to the table.

When I'd eaten half my lunch, she came and sat with me. "I've been asking around," she said. "Rose'll be Queen. The odds are against you being King. That'll be Johnny Trevenna."

Despite the fact that I'd already reached the same conclusion, my face must have showed unhappiness, for she patted my hand. "He's not a bad lad, really. A bit spoiled by his mum, and led in wrong direction by maskers."

"I know Penseythan Trevenna had convinced Johnny that Rose would be his. It must have been a shock when I appeared and screwed things up...." I shrugged. "Not helped by what happened to the Penseythan."

"From what I heard, she had it coming to her." Hilda smiled sympathetically. "Now if you and Rose were married, they'd have to find another Queen."

What's she after? "Who might it be?"

"Could be Susan."

"Your daughter?" I started on the second piece of bread and cheese.

"Yes."

So that's what it was about. Hilda wanted Susan to marry eligible bachelor, Johnny Trevenna. "But, I've been told that nobody on this island would marry us."

Hilda looked at me closely. "Not on this island, maybe.... How about on Tristan?"

"I hadn't thought of that.... Wouldn't we have to be residents for some time?"

"Not sure." Hilda closed her eyes for a moment before her words came out in a rush. "Talk to Clara. She might know."

It began to sound like she was letting me know what Clara had planned. "Have you talked to Clara?"

"Not directly, but you hear things." Her mouth closed firmly.

Obviously, I wasn't going to find out any more. On the bad side, if Hilda knew or suspected, Johnny Trevenna might have worked it out, too. I finished my lunch. "Thanks for the food and for the information. I'd better be leaving. It looks like it might rain and it's quite a way to the radio station and back to Veryan."

Hilda showed me to the door. Morley had returned to the pasture, and waved as I cycled down the road.

By the time I reached Portloe, my side had started to ache again. From there, I walked with the bike out of the village. About half way to the radio station, I spotted a track to my right and a sign that read, "Navy Property." A decayed slab of wood with the remnants of "Keep Out" lay beside it. In fact, I'd noticed it on my previous time on the island and paid no attention. The full quarry came into view when I rounded a bend. A cliff, cut in steps, provided the backdrop to the quarry floor, which was covered in rows of equipment: various sized crates, dusty gray paint, rust-covered tanks and the like. Walking down the rows, I soon spotted two more tanks like Morley's and four huge open, rectangular structures next to piles of metal pipes. What was in most of the crates remained a mystery because the painted information was unreadable, though I did make out a couple of "Pumps" and what might be a reference to a generator.

Satisfied that I'd learned all I could, I went back to the main track and continued up the hill, soon spotting the radio tower. After cresting the rise, I walked a quarter mile to a single-story white building with an array of aerials, and various weather meters on a flat roof and around it.

Inside, I was greeted by Douglas Billing, the radio operator and weather recorder—a softer and gentler-looking version of his brother, the Captain. Douglas ushered me into his radio room and indicated one of two upholstered chairs. The room smelled smoky and I noticed a well-used ashtray on the coffee table.

"It's grand to see you again, Andy. Artley told me what happened on dock. Not right." He handed me a pad and a pencil. "Write down your message and the addressee. I'll get some tea and biscuits."

I really didn't need more food, but bowed to the custom. "Thank you." I wrote a note to my mom and dad, telling Mom that she could find my original order for sheet music in my room, filed under Roseland, and to please airmail new copies. I listed the books on agriculture I'd lost and asked Dad to mail me replacements. I told him about Morley's digester system working and my hope to repeat the process for Jacob Jago's farm. On the subject of Rose and me, I was upbeat. No reason to upset my mom.

Glancing around the room, I noticed watercolors of whalers interspersed among faded photos of the island. One particular photo drew my attention, a scene from Midsummer's Day. A young Douglas stood outside the Roundhouse with a smiling brunette. His wife, I guessed, who was now ill.

Douglas, a briar pipe clenched between his teeth, returned with tea and digestive biscuits.

"That you?" I asked.

He removed the pipe and grinned. "Yes. Jill and me, 1956. Rum tum ti tum ti, eh?" he said as he quickstepped out of the room before I could ask how she was doing.

While I munched, Douglas telegraphed my message. After

checking to see it had transmitted properly, he came and sat with me. "I hear new Seythan isn't likely on your side," he said, by way of introducing the topic of my problem.

I was resigned now to being the focus of attention. Maybe he would tell me something new, like Hilda had done. "So I've heard. Anything I can do about it?"

Douglas's mouth half opened, as if he were surprised by my suggesting the possibility of influencing that august body. He emptied the ashes from his pipe into the ashtray. "Don't rightly know. It's new Seythan. Generally they do whatever they think is in the island's interest."

Try another tack. "Will Martha Nancarrow be able to influence them?"

"Some, maybe." He pulled a wad of tobacco from a pocket and tamped some into the pipe, lit it, and took a puff before replying, "Don't reckon Elizabeth Gay will be easy."

"I guess I'll find out soon enough."

Douglas appeared to be about to say something, when he was interrupted by the sound of rain beating against the roof. He walked to a window and looked to the west. "I don't think it'll last long. Watch out though, I can see there'll be another band of showers coming through. If you ride fast, you should be able to get back to Veryan before it hits."

I joined him and we watched as clouds passed overhead and a flicker of blue sky showed. I thanked him for his help, said that I hoped his wife would get well soon, and headed down the hill. His estimates of my cycling speed were optimistic. Foolishly, I hadn't brought my slicker and I was drenched on the road between the schoolhouse and home.

Clara was at work. I stripped off in the kitchen and wrung out my wet clothes before hanging them over the stove. Upstairs, I dressed and picked up my lines for Romeo and Juliet, hoping that in them, I might find another clue to Clara's plans.

12.

I was apprehensive about the meeting Clara had set up. Johnny Trevenna would be there. How would he act? The minute Rose and I entered the village hall, a dark-haired man with a short beard, which hid what I suspected was a receding chin, came over. "We haven't met," he said. "I'm John Trevenna. Congratulations to you and Rose on your engagement."

I shook the proffered hand. Not what I'd expected. *What's he up to?* Out of the corner of my eye, I noticed Rose raise an eyebrow. "Thank you," I replied. "And thanks for helping Morley with the electrical work."

"Glad to be of assistance. When's the wedding?" he asked.

"Not set yet," Rose interjected. "We're hoping Andy's parents will be able to come."

"On the next boat, I suppose." Johnny seemed to be suppressing a smile. Did he believe that would be too late for me to have captured Rose? "After the…New Year?"

"Could be sooner." Clara's voice came from behind me.

The partially suppressed smile disappeared. Johnny appeared to be about to fire off a retort. Instead, he bit his lip and remained silent for a moment, before saying, "So, what other surprises do you have for us, Aunt Clara?"

I turned to see Clara, Frankie, and Harold Anthony, who nodded my way, solemnly. "You'll find out soon as everyone's here," she said.

An elderly woman with her hair pulled up in a tight bun came in with Charlie Gay. Johnny walked away to speak to them. I wondered who she was.

"That's Elizabeth Gay," Rose whispered as we sat down.

I had vague recollections of having seen her on my previous stay, but had never spoken to her. Other cast members appeared, including Cap'n Billing, Paul Jago, and Isaac Nancarrow.

After everyone was seated, Clara moved in front of the stage. "Frankie, please give them the handout saying who's playing each part. Each of you can take a moment to read it."

I glanced at the handout…

ROMEO AND JULIET CAST.

Juliet.. Rose Pascoe
Romeo .... Andrew Ferguson
Mercutio .... Frankie Quick
Tybalt... Sam Nancarrow
The Nurse... Clara Quick
Friar Lawrence.................................... Cap'n Hartley
Capulet .... Charlie Gay
Paris... Johnny Trevenna
Benvolio... Paul Jago
Lady Capulet .... Elizabeth Gay
Montague .... Isaac Nancarrow

An Apothecary....................................... Arthur Nancarrow
Lady Montague .... Martha Nancarrow
Governor .... Harold Anthony
Paris.. Harold Anthony
Stand in .... Harold Anthony

"No surprises, really," Rose whispered.

"I've met Harold. Why is *he* the stand in, too?"

"Harold is different," Rose replied. "He's good with numbers and does everybody's accounts. He also e He also has a photographic memory. He can remember everybody's lines in case there's a problem at the last minute."

"Won't people notice?"

"If it's a woman's role, yes. Though he loves to do different voices." Rose chuckled. "You may end up marrying him if I have to drop out. Anyway, from something Clara told me, I think we'll all be wearing masks. Anything else?"

"Yes. It confirms I'll be sword fighting Sam, and—"

"If there are no questions, I'll start by going over the plot, briefly," Clara interrupted me. "I've tried to simplify it and make it more relevant to us."

I heard Isaac mutter. "Huh. If it's like you usually do, I doubt it."

Clara glanced around before reading from a thick sheaf of paper. "Young Romeo and Juliet fall in love, but there are people who don't want them to marry. Andy will play Romeo and Rose will play Juliet. Juliet's nurse and a kindly friar try to help them. I will take the role of the Nurse. Cap'n Artley has graciously agreed to play Friar Lawrence." She paused.

"In Shakespeare's original play, the setting is Verona. I have moved it to the island of Verona, which I've placed midway between here and Tristan."

"Don't you think you should stay with the Bard's setting?" a female voice asked. "And replacing Shakespeare's Prince with the Governor doesn't seem right."

"Elizabeth is such a traditionalist," Rose whispered.

"It wouldn't work because of my role reversal between Capulet and Lady Capulet," Clara replied. "Now, Lady Capulet is not only Juliet's mother. She's also Penseythan Capulet."

"But—"

"Which will be a most important role for you, Elizabeth." Clara tilted her head.

Elizabeth stared hard. "I suppose so. And I see Charlie will play my husband?"

"I haven't had the opportunity to ask him, but I hope he will."

"Fine with me," Charlie Gay replied.

"Good." Clara continued to read. "The Penseythan organizes a feast for Juliet to meet Count Paris...Johnny will have that role. By mistake, Romeo and his friends Benvolio...Paul here, and Mercutio...played by Frankie...go in disguise. This is when Romeo falls for Juliet. Unfortunately, Juliet's cousin, Tybalt...er, Sam Nancarrow couldn't be here, recognizes them and they have to leave." Clara looked at her audience. "The famous balcony scene follows."

"Will we have to build a balcony?" Isaac asked. "Don't think there's enough height."

"A raised part of the stage will have to do," Clara replied. "Romeo can stand where I am.... No, no, that's not right. We won't be here."

"What!" Isaac's voice rose above the murmuring that followed Clara's announcement.

Clara fiddled with her papers. "I should have said. The play will be in Portloe. Village hall. It's bigger."

"Makes sense to me," Johnny said.

Clara smiled at him. "Continuing. Tybalt picks a quarrel and Mercutio is accidentally killed. Romeo kills Tybalt and is banished by the—"

"Clara, aren't you missing something?" Elizabeth snapped. "Don't Romeo and Juliet get married?"

"What, what?" Clara shuffled her notes. "Sorry. Isaac addled me with his question. Yes. Then the Penseythan, not knowing what has happened, is furious when Juliet doesn't want to marry Paris. Finally, Juliet agrees because she plans to fake her death and flee with Romeo. Briefly, she obtains a sleeping potion from the Apothecary.... Oh, where's Arthur...?"

"Running store," Isaac interjected.

Clara fiddles with a loose strand of hair. "I see. Well, he takes the potion to her. Romeo finds Juliet, apparently dead, and kills himself. Juliet wakes up, discovers Romeo's body and commits suicide."

"Clara you seem to have taken great liberties with the play," Elizabeth commented in a sharp tone of voice. "I mean, you haven't mentioned Romeo's parents, the Montagues?"

I turned so I could see them both. Elizabeth's face showed great irritation.

"Oh dear, I did miss some of the plot." Clara played with the papers again. "Thank you for reminding me. It's on your cast sheet. Isaac will be Montague, and Martha will be Lady Montague.... I think that's everybody."

"Is there anything else you've *forgotten* to tell us?" Elizabeth demanded.

Clara eyes opened wide. "I don't think so, dear. Unless it's that you'll all be in modern clothes…it's so much simpler…and wearing masks."

Elizabeth stood and glared. "What?"

"I think it will make the play more interesting. I got the idea from the Greeks and the Japanese." Clara smiled sweetly. "We won't need makeup and we do all have masks, you know."

"I think it's an interesting addition." Captain Billing's comment echoed around the room. "Makes a connection to our culture."

I didn't have a mask and made a mental note to talk to Clara about it.

"How about all the servants Shakespeare has?" Elizabeth seemed to be on the point of saying more. Instead, she sat with her lips pursed.

"And thank you for reminding me about the servants," Clara said sweetly. "Some of you can put on a different mask and also play one of them."

Clara removed the top three sheets of paper and laid them on the stage. She held out the remaining sheets. "Frankie, please distribute these."

While he did that she continued, "I've written out a rehearsal schedule for each of you. After you've had a chance to study it, please let me know if you won't be able to attend any of them and I'll reschedule." She glanced around. "If there aren't any questions, I think that's everything. Thank you all for coming. Oh, and bring your mask to the first rehearsal."

"I need to talk to you for a moment, Clara." Martha Nancarrow's voice came from behind me.

Clara frowned briefly, and she walked away from the stage.

"Clara's forgotten her notes," Rose said. "I'll get them."

When she came back, Rose had a strange look on her face. "I don't know what to make of it, Andy. The writing on those pieces of paper had nothing to do with the plot. They were just random scribblings."

Another part of the game? "She's an actress," I said. "She memorized the plot."

"I suppose so, but what about the hiccup with the wedding scene?"

"That was after Isaac interrupted her."

Rose looked thoughtful. "Yes, he did. That must explain it. How about the masks, then?"

"Maybe she's getting at the Maskers."

"Could be."

Angry voices emanated from the group of people clustered around Clara.

"Seems we're not the only people with questions," Rose said. "What a dance she leads us in…Which reminds me, dance tonight in Portloe. Johnny will be there. Do you want to go?"

He seemed to have got over his problem with me, I guessed. "Sure."

13.

WHEN I WENT TO PICK UP ROSE AT SIX, THE ISLAND'S BUS WAS parked outside Nancarrow's store. A few faces peered out at me as I reached her door. Cap'n Artley, Mary's beau, let me in. He wore the standard white shirt and tie expected of the men, with a blue blazer. Fortunately, with my replacement clothes from Nancarrows', I was able to follow that convention.

The Cap'n smiled and shook my hand. "Rose'll be down in a minute."

When I had first met him, I'd gotten the impression he didn't approve of me. Given he'd helped me get back on the island, and the warmth of this greeting, I felt that situation had changed. Pity he wasn't on the Seythan anymore.

"You look real smart, Andy," Mary said from near the stairs. She wore her curly black hair piled on her head and tied with a red ribbon—eye-catching. I was about to compliment her when Rose came down. My chest tightened and I swear my heart missed a beat at the realization that, for real, she wanted to be my wife. Rose also wore her hair up and she wore a simple white dress with a scalloped neckline. The dress was tied high above the waist with a blue ribbon, accentuating her bust. "You both look stunning," I said.

"Best get to bus," Mary said, hustling us out.

Clara was already on-board, sitting next to Sandy Nancarrow, whose brother, Sam, and wife, Jenny, were seated behind them. Jenny smiled at Rose and me. Sam acted as if he were going to trip me up, withdrawing his leg at the last moment. "Thank you," I said, pretending to step over it. He scowled.

"Idiot," Mary muttered.

As we stopped at the school to pick up more passengers, Rose leaned over and whispered, "You know I'll be expected to dance with—"

"Johnny Trevenna. I know. It's okay." I remembered how the lights dimmed at the end of the dance. "Just remember to save the last dance for me."

Rose pinched me. "And I thought you'd be fine with me choosing Johnny."

"Hmm."

"He's not as bad as you think," Rose said. "He must have been talked into beating you up. That's not like the Johnny I grew up with. I hope you get to know him better. Please try, we're all going to be here for a long time."

"I hope so and I'll give it a shot," I replied with a sigh.

Forty minutes later, having stopped to pick up passengers on the way, we reached Portloe. I hung my jacket on a peg in the entryway, remembering that as the evening progressed, the hall would get hot and humid. This hall was larger than the venue in Veryan, and it had a bigger raised area at the far end, more suitable for staging a play.

Conversation stopped momentarily as Rose and I entered. She and Mary immediately left to join the other women on one side of the dance floor. The Cap'n and I joined the men on the other side, sitting with Roddy Gay, Charlie and Petunia's son. Roddy's sister, Jennifer, waved to me from across the room. Shortly afterward, Paul Jago joined us.

Women's fashions hadn't changed much in the two years since I'd left. Most of the older women wore dresses with a floral print. The younger girls generally had on festive blouses and dark skirts, some quite short. As had been true before, the number of young women was fewer than the number of young men. Fortunately, Jane Trevenna's death had ended the practice of population control through female infanticide. The imbalance would gradually disappear.

"Band's grown since you were here, Andy." Roddy pointed at the quartet on the stage, consisting of a piano, clarinet, base, and drums.

"They still playing same music?" I asked, recalling the previous combination of thirties and forties songs with some Beatles and Elvis thrown in to show they were up to date.

Roddy chuckled. "More or less. I heard you'd brought some of the latest music from the States, but those silly buggers..." He nodded to where Johnny Trevenna sat with Sandy and Sam, "dumped it in the sea."

"I'm getting my mom to send more sheet music...enough for a bigger group."

"Is this a spare seat?" a voice said.

I turned to see Harold Anthony. He wore the same suit as at the play rehearsal and hadn't removed his jacket.

"Certainly," I replied, edging over. Having forgotten that Harold took everything literally, I added, "We were saving it for you."

"You were? Well, thank you very much." He sat.

Roddy nudged me. At that point, the band started up, and

Rose came toward me, stepping aside when Susan Thomas brushed past. Rose chose the Cap'n. Susan, dressed provocatively in a pink blouse and a short burgundy skirt, came directly to me. She leaned over and her blouse, left unbuttoned at the top, swung open as she grabbed my hand. "My dance, Andy," she said. "You can show me all the latest moves."

I hadn't been dancing since the last time I'd been on the island. "I'll do my best. Is this a foxtrot?" I followed her onto the dance floor.

Susan ignored my question and held me so close it wouldn't have mattered what tempo was being played as we shuffled to the beat. All the while, she pumped me with questions about teen fashions back home. From my previous time on the island, I knew this would happen and had read teen magazines at the dentist. Faced with answering the question, I could only remember one item. "Tube tops," I said.

"What's them?"

I wasn't sure how to respond and said, "Ask Rose."

As the song came to an end, Susan said, "I hear Rose is going to be Queen. Are you going to be King?"

Not what I wanted to discuss. "Up to Seythan," I replied curtly.

"Oh…. I'll be Queen sometime," she said.

"Who do you want to be the King?"

"I'd love it to be Johnny, but…."

The dance ended. I assumed that saved her from adding that she'd also heard Johnny was going to be picked this year. Shit.

I had barely sat down when Clara grabbed me for the next dance. At the same time, I saw Rose pick Johnny. Even though Rose had warned me, my gut ached. Get over it.

Clara had a great sense of rhythm and I had no trouble keeping up with her in a quickstep. When no one I knew was in earshot, I asked the obvious question. "Is it true that Rose and Johnny will be chosen as Queen and King?"

Clara's grip on me tightened and for a moment she stutter-stepped. "Don't you believe all the rumors put out by some people," she replied. A quick hug followed. "Leave it to me."

"What are you going to do?"

"Best you don't know."

"Oh. You said we'd all be wearing masks in the play. I don't have one."

Clara patted my back. "I'll make you one."

I sat the next dance out, and watched Clara masterfully maneuvering Harold around the floor. His body had all the stiff appearance of a marionette, and his face had a permanent look of bewilderment as they twirled slowly.

Jennifer Nancarrow, who was a pleasant person, unlike her husband Sandy, then grabbed me for an energetic Scottish reel. In between twirling, she said in gasps that she hoped things would work out for Rose and me.

"Thanks, Jenny," I said, giving her a quick hug.

No sooner had I sat down than, to my amazement, Elizabeth Gay, wearing an ankle-length blue dress, selected me for a waltz. As we rotated around at arms' length, she said, "You may have heard that I am a traditionalist. I hope that your efforts to improve farming practices will not lead to problems."

I hoped that was her only concern. "I pray so, too," I replied, trying to show sympathy for her position. "As I told Jacob Jago, I grew up on a farm. My father's parents came from Scotland. He is also a firm believer in tradition." Now for the clincher, I hoped. "He was the one who encouraged me to learn about conservation farming. That is how I hope to help Jacob and Morley."

We twirled a couple more times. "Is that the limit of your knowledge?"

"Oh, no. I also took courses on diseases that are threatening key crops and how to limit the damage they could cause. Through my father, I have access to advice put out by agricultural organizations."

"And you think what happens in the United States will be relevant here in the southern Atlantic?"

I glanced at her as we spun slowly at the end of the dance, remembering one of my dad's favorite comments. "In the words of that great Scot, Robbie Burns, 'A spud's a spud for a' that.'"

"Hm. Thank you for the dance, Mister Ferguson," she said, her face expressionless. She returned to the ladies' side of the hall.

One thing was clear from her tone of voice. She didn't approve of me. Not good.

The band took a break, and many of the men went outside to have a smoke. Paul Jago was about to leave and I took the opportunity to grab him. "How does your dad feel about the digester?" I asked.

"Doesn't say much, but I think he likes the idea. We've started digging a pit." A worried look crossed his face. "I didn't tell you that." He continued on his way out.

"Understand."

I remained behind. When Roddy and Jennifer returned, I asked him a trickier question. "Roddy, what do you hear about the Queen and King this year?"

Roddy shifted in his seat. "Don't rightly know." He looked across the hall at Jennifer, as if seeking guidance. "What do you hear?"

Back in my court. "That Rose will be Queen."

Roddy relaxed. "I've heard that, too." Then in a rush, "But the King's up to Seythan."

Obviously, he's heard or believes it won't be me. I glanced across the hall to see Rose staring at me with a worried expression. I stood and motioned for her to follow me outside.

She took my arm in the entrance way and we went around the other side of the hall from where a group of men were smoking.

Rose turned and faced me. She held both my hands. "You heard, didn't you?"

"You mean, you'll be Queen and, from what I'm hearing, I'm not going to be chosen as King?"

"Yes. I can't say exactly how the Seythan will vote, but the odds have been stacked against you."

I remembered how Johnny Trevenna had looked pleased when I'd told him that Rose and I likely wouldn't marry until January. "What if we got married before Midsummer's? Clara hinted at something. I hate to do this to my parents…"

Rose's grasp tightened. Her head tilted down and a tear trickled down her cheek. She let go of my hands and brushed it away. "There are only two people on the island licensed to perform marriages: the Penseythan and Isaac Nancarrow."

"So, what's the problem?"

"Mum hears they're not willing to preempt the Seythan."

Shit again. "So, this is all so Johnny Trevenna and you can…" I said bitterly. "Can't you say no?"

Rose came into my arms and buried her face on my shoulder. She was shaking. "I have to." After a moment, she said, "Would you still want to marry me if...?"

My kneejerk reaction was to say, I'm not sure. Then I thought about my former girlfriend Annie, who'd dumped me after catching me with another woman. "Yes. And I'd go beat the shit out of him."

Rose relaxed. "I love you." She kissed me affectionately.

While we were kissing, I had a thought. "Can't Cap'n Billing marry us at sea?"

Rose pulled away. "I asked Mum that. She said, she didn't think so. In his case, Captain is a courtesy title."

"Oh. So it looks like we're screwed."

"Unless Clara can come up with something." The band started a waltz. "Come on, we'd better get back," she said. We returned to our respective sides of the floor.

By the time I sat down with Harold, the next dance had started, a Gay Gordons.

Without thinking, I wondered aloud why the Gordons were gay.

"I expect they had much to be happy about," Harold volunteered.

A waste of time explaining that it might have been because of a lack of women, I thought. "I expect you're right. Life must have been good in their part of Scotland."

"I'm good at working things out," Harold said proudly. "In fact, it does come from Scotland and is a popular dance at social gatherings, made popular in the late nineteenth century. The name refers to the Gordon Highlanders, a Scottish regiment."

He appeared about to say more when the time for the last dance came. Rose and Mary started in my direction. I watched in dismay as Susan ran past them and grabbed my hand. I knew the custom—first come, first served— and signaled to Rose with my other hand in an appeal for help. She shook her head, and picked Cap'n Artley. Mary hesitated before opting for Johnny Trevenna.

The band started to play the Tennessee Waltz. Susan held me lightly, but I could sense she was waiting to pounce. As the lights dimmed, I turned my head in an effort to limit her assault. She let go with her right hand, grabbed my head and kissed me quickly.

I managed to detach myself as the music stopped and wiped my mouth. "Thank you," I gasped. "That was very nice. I can see you've been practicing."

Susan gaped at me.

"American sense of humor," I replied.

"Oh." She looked flustered.

Rose grasped my arm. "Come on, Andy. Fun time's over." She faced Susan. "Who put you up to that stunt?"

"Dunno, really. The boys, I guess." She gestured at Johnny, Sam, and Sandy, who were clustered across the hall.

"Typical," Rose muttered. As we continued on our way to the bus, she said, "Susan's not as flighty as she acts. She's one of the brightest young people on the island. Here, she'll be a teacher. The plan is to send her to Cape Town for training."

14.

"I NEED TO START ON YOUR MASK," CLARA SAID, WHEN I CAME down to breakfast on Sunday morning. "Normally, papier-mâché would do, but I think you need more protection." She pulled a tape measure from a pocket and took measurements of my head, noting them down on a piece of paper.

"What will you use?"

"Metal from petrol can."

Mind boggling. "How?"

"Beat it into half globe-like on wooden mandrel. Cut out around ears. I'll show you after breakfast. This is what I plan to make." Clara handed me the paper with her notes

Above the numbers she'd written down were a series of penciled sketches, starting with a metal skullcap, a blank mask, and finally, an exaggerated, smiling face under some kind of hat.

We cleaned up the dishes and I followed her into the yard. She went into her small garden shed, emerging with a rectangular gas can and a log with a rounded end, which she placed on a flagstone. A hammer, a metal saw, and shears followed. Clara then sawed off the top and bottom of the can, and cut what was left down one side, before flattening it to make a metal sheet, which she cut into quarters. Each quarter was placed on the log and hammered to form part of a bowl. Clara consulted her notes, took a pencil and marked the metal pieces before cutting them into triangles.

"How do you join them?" I asked.

"Solder. I'll do it later. Garage in Portloe," she replied. "For now, let me check parts on your head. In kitchen."

Inside, I sat down and Clara placed the metal petals on my head. She made further marks and trimmed them until she was satisfied. "That'll do for now," she said. "You'd best get ready for chapel. I'll wait for Frankie."

Beneath overcast skies, I accompanied Rose and Mary to chapel. The Captain was at sea on the St. Just, fishing to the south of Gough Island. He wouldn't return for twelve days. In his absence, we sat three rows back with Clara, Frankie and his wife, Esther. Afterwards Isaac Nancarrow welcomed his flock. A selection of psalms and hymns followed. Mrs. Nancarrow provided the accompaniment on a nineteenth century reed organ. The music was interspersed with the creaking sounds of the foot pumps.

When Isaac returned to the lectern to give the sermon, he rambled on for a few minutes before holding up his Bible and opening it at a page marked by a piece of paper. "Pay heed to what is written in 2 Thessalonians 2:15," he said. "So then, brothers, stand firm and hold to the traditions that you were taught by us, either by our spoken word or by our letter." His sermon was interrupted by the noise of a rain shower beating against the corrugated iron roof. Isaac put the Bible down on the lectern, clasped his hands in what I now recognized as a characteristic gesture, and waited patiently before adding, "The Lord has sought to emphasize my admonitions, and as the Bible says we should hold to traditions. I counsel all of you to remember that, when you observe people making decisions that affect our beloved island." He'd said all of you, but he appeared to be staring at me.

Mary nudged me gently. "That sounded like a warning," she whispered.

"Back in the States we call it a 'heads-up'," I replied. "The question to ask is, a warning about what?"

"Hmm." Mary looked away.

The remainder of the sermon dealt with the subject of tradition through Christ's meeting with the Pharisees. The final hymn was Onward Christian Soldiers. I joined in the vigorous singing.

Clara was going to Frankie and Esther's house, and Mary invited me for lunch. I waited until we were in her living room before asking my question. "If Isaac was giving me a warning, what do you think it was?"

Mary and Rose exchanged glances. Rose raised an eyebrow.

Mary shrugged. "I suppose he was referring to the tradition of the Seythan choosing the Queen and King. Everyone's talking about who's going to be King."

"What do they say?"

"Island's split. Some, like me and the Captain, think it should be you and believe you have a chance. Then there's Clara, Charlie and Petunia, George Anthony and lots of others, who support you but they're not convinced the Seythan will give you a fair chance. Then there's those don't think it should be you at all, seeing as you're a foreigner." She patted me on the shoulder. "They've nothing against you...most of them. However, we've never had something like this before."

"So Isaac was reinforcing the point that they should let the normal process run its course?"

"Yes."

I'd already heard that and, in some strange way, felt relief. The tightness in my chest relaxed. There was nothing to be done. "Guess I…we'll just have to live with it. Unless Clara…."

Rose snuggled close and kissed my cheek. "We'll get through it." We held onto each other.

"When you two have a moment, we can start lunch. It's ham and salad." Mary walked toward the kitchen.

The scattered showers of the morning had stopped by the time we finished lunch. I'd heard from Frankie that the auks had returned and suggested to Rose we take a look at them. I was curious, hopeful even, that my favorite, Nellie, would have survived. Rose changed into a sweater, jeans, and what she called an anorak—another Eskimo name used by the Brits for a parka. She followed me to Clara's where I changed out of my Sunday best. I grabbed my binoculars and we headed up the hill. As we neared the top of the rise, the fishy smell wafted toward us well before we saw the gulls and great skuas above the cliff. Mating had started in the rookery, but it would be around six weeks before the eggs were incubated. In the meantime, the auks would be busy housekeeping, cleaning out the burrows for the new clutch of chicks.

We cleared the rise. I led Rose down through the gorse to the site of my blind. On the way, I checked the area of Nellie's burrow to see if she'd returned. An auk came out of the burrow, kicking debris away. Even from a distance, I had the feeling it wasn't Nellie. I blinked back a tear, tripped on a loose stone, and fell toward the gorse. I twisted to ensure I'd fall backward into it. My parka and corduroy pants protected most of me from the thorns. The back of my neck was not so lucky.

"Don't move Andy," Rose shouted. "I'll help you out."

I tried to remain still, while she maneuvered into a position where she could reach down and clasp my outstretched hands. When she had a firm grasp, she pulled me up to a crouching position. From there, with Rose helping me keep my balance, I managed to get upright and return to the path.

"What happened?"

"Nellie's not there. I wasn't concentrating and lost my footing."

Rose put an arm around me. "I'm sorry. Do you want to go back?"

I nearly said yes, but curiosity about the rookery won out. "No. I'd like to see how the birds are doing." I leaned forward. "Can you check my neck? I feel like I'm being attacked by a multi-clawed insect."

Rose chuckled and picked pieces of dry gorse off the back of my head before we continued to the site of my blind.

We sat on the ground, my arm around Rose, and watched the auks. One of the new occupants of Nellie's burrow, my guess the female, was inside kicking out debris, which splattered all over the auk standing outside: again at a guess, her main man. This male took a brief turn at cleaning the burrow before they scuttled away to collect dry grass for the nest. Two other males helped occasionally. They stood around the rest of the time and, to me, mainly looked hopeful while watching the main man and the female engage in courtship, wagging their heads from side to side and knocking their beaks together.

The sight aroused me and I kissed Rose. She embraced me and we lay back. The sound of voices singing, "rum tum, ti, tum tum tum," to the tune of "the Floral Dance" put an end to the passionate interlude.

I sat up. "Damn."

Rose giggled. "Better luck next time."

I glanced around and saw the approaching figures of Young Artley and his wife, Patsy.

"Having a quick cuddle, were we?" Patsy called out. "We were visiting Dad and saw you come up here. How's Nellie?"

I noticed Patsy had put on weight. Of course, she'd just had her second child. "Gone, I'm afraid."

"Sorry. I know how you felt about her and, what was his name?"

"Fred." The memory of Nellie's main man, killed by Dracula and the skua who'd saved my life, brought another tear. Rose gave me a sympathetic hug. Change the subject. "How are the little ones doing?"

"Albert and Anna," Rose whispered.

"Anna. That's a pretty name," I said to cover my confusion.

"Got it from a book," Patsy said as she sat down beside Rose. "Albert and Anna are with Grandma. She can't get enough of them."

We sat in silence for a couple of minutes, occasionally commenting on the auks, I waited for the inevitable question.

Patsy came up with it. "We're so looking forward to the wedding," she said. "When is it?"

I nudged Rose.

She took a deep breath. "Andy's parents are planning to come here after the New Year. That's—"

"Isn't that a bit late?" Patsy blurted out.

Artley jumped in with, "Patsy, you shouldn't—"

Patsy ignored Artley and, apparently to cover her embarrassment, stammered out, "I mean, what with Midsummer's and all."

"No point in doing anything until Seythan meets," Rose said firmly.

"But…."

"Patsy. We need to go and check on Albert. He can be a bit of a terror." Artley stood and helped Patsy to her feet. "We'll leave you two lovebirds to…."

We watched them leave. "I don't feel like a lovebird anymore," I whispered.

"Me neither. Why can't people leave us alone?" Rose kissed me tenderly on the cheek, then turned my face so she could look into my eyes. "I'm glad Artley got over what happened with you and Patsy," she said.

"You mean when Clara set Patsy up to make a fool of me?"

"Yes."

"I asked Artley about that afterward. He said he argued with Clara, but she persuaded him to take part in her game, too…. Clara must be very persuasive."

Rose chuckled. "You can say that again." She didn't explain what that meant, and added, "Let's go home and practice our lines. There's this marriage scene Clara wants us to rehearse."

That was news to me. "I think Clara's in that scene. If she's back, we could see if she'd join us."

"Good idea." Thoughts of Clara turned quickly to her house and Mary's next door, reminding of a question I'd been meaning to ask Rose. "Have you made any progress on where we'd live…" Be positive. "When we're married."

"Yes. I talked to Mum, and she and the Captain are going to get married…. Promise you won't tell anyone. It's a secret."

"About time, "I said without thinking.

Rose punched me on the arm. "Don't be judgmental. Mum will move to his house in Portloe. Leaving us the house in Veryan." She stood and started away

One thing settled. Now to get married. I followed Rose up the gorsy path.

We reached the top of the rise as a shaft of sunlight illuminated the house at Trewince on the east end of the island. Light glinted off one of the lower windows. I closed my eyes and recalled an image of the living room and the powerful binoculars, mounted by the window that Jane Trevenna had used to spy on me. A second flash of light came. I took Rose's arm and pointed. "Someone's watching us."

"Could be Mr. Thomas, looking for me," she said.

"Or Johnny."

"You worry too much." Rose patted my cheek, stood, and patted my butt. "If you can handle it, I'll race you back."

She was gone before I could reply. I kept up with her until my sides began to ache.

15.

We strolled past the Round House and arrived home. Rose went ahead to see if Mary, in the absence of the Captain, would read the Friar's part. I went into Clara's house to find out if she would join our rehearsal.

Clara had just answered that she would love to do it, when Rose and Mary knocked and came in. Rose joined me on the sofa.

"I don't have the Friar's lines," Mary said as she closed the front door. "Are you sure this will work?"

"Don't you worry, m'dear," Clara said, winking at me. "Just take a seat." She gestured at the remaining seat by the coffee table. "I've got a copy you can use." She went upstairs, returning with scripts for herself and Mary. "We'll read act two, scene six. In Shakespeare's version, it takes place in the Friar's cell and finishes in the church for the wedding scene. I have placed it all in the cell to avoid a set change. The scene begins when the Friar and Romeo enter stage left. Right, Mary. You're the Friar."

Friar: "May the Penseythan bless this union."

Mary gave Clara a puzzled look. Clara nodded for her to continue.

Friar: "And prevent any actions that might make us regret it."

I wondered where Clara was going with this scene and read my first lines.

Romeo: "Amen to that. Whatever happens, it won't ruin my joy when you have joined our hands with holy word so I can call her mine."

Mary, as the Friar, wagged a finger at me in admonition.

Friar: "Be careful such a joy has a happy ending. The sweetness of honey is a delight, but too much sickens the stomach. Love in moderation is the key to a long-standing partnership."

"Rose this is where you rush in and embrace Romeo," Clara said. "I, as your nurse, follow."

Nurse: "One as light as she needs a spider's web for her feet. They will not survive the stony path of life. How transient their pleasure may be."

Juliet: "Good evening my ghostly confessor."

Friar: "Romeo will thank you for both of us."

Juliet: "Equal thanks from us, too."

Romeo: "Juliet, you have a better way with words. Tell me of the happiness you anticipate in our marriage."

Rose leant across and patted my cheek.

Juliet: "Words cannot express what I imagine. Your love had brought me riches that I can hardly count."

Friar: "Let us not delay your union. Come, we'll complete the job quickly. I now invite you two to join hands and make your vows in the presence of God and these people. Face each other and—"

"That's enough, m'dear," Clara said. "It's the standard wedding vows and so on…. I, Romeo, take you, Juliet, to be my wife, to have and to hold, et cetera. She repeats the same with I, Juliet. They exchange rings, and the Friar says, 'In the presence of God, and before this congregation, Romeo and Juliet have made their wedding vows to each other. They have declared their marriage by the joining of hands and by the giving and receiving of rings. I therefore proclaim that they are husband and wife. Those whom God has joined together let no one put asunder.'"

"Amen," Mary stated with conviction. "I hope the Seythan thinks on that when they pick the Queen and King."

"Do you have rings for us to use?" Rose asked.

Clara reached into a pocket and pulled out a gold ring. "This was my mother's. Mary, can you come up with another?"

"I'll see what I can do."

"We won't be using them until the dress rehearsal." Clara studied her script. "There'll be one other thing. Romeo and Juliet will sign the wedding certificate, witnessed by the Friar and her Nurse."

Rose wiped her eyes. "It's sad the Captain can't make it a real wedding."

I reached over and held her hand.

"By the way," Mary said. "Clara, you've used our standard wedding ceremony. Didn't Shakespeare use an Italian, Catholic version?"

Clara toyed with the script. "Not exactly, Catholics weren't popular in his time. And remember, this is on the island of Verona. Marriages have to satisfy our governor on St. Helena."

"I suppose so." Mary's brow wrinkled.

"I've got to get a copy of the play," I whispered to Rose.

Rose squeezed my hand. "Good luck with that."

"Let's run through it one more time," Clara said. "And, Andy, next Saturday I want to rehearse with you and Sam in the sword fight scene. So, learn your lines."

"Will do," I said. "That's going to be fun,"

Mary looked concerned. "You be careful."

In fact, we ran through the scene two more times before Mary announced she had to get supper ready and I was invited.

"I'll leave you two alone," Mary said when we finished her delicious apple pie. "I'm going to my room to read while electricity's still on. You can wash up."

After completing our chores, Rose and I went back to the living room. She snuggled up against me on the couch. When I tried to go beyond gentle petting, she drew back.

"I know it's frustrating for you, Andy, but I want to wait until after we're married."

"You mean after you and Johnny...?" The words spilled out before I could stop them.

"No," Rose snapped back. "Clara suggested something. There's a way we can get married before Seythan meets."

I recalled what Hilda had hinted at. "We could get married on Tristan da Cunha?"

Rose's face showed surprise. "Clara didn't say she'd spoken to you. You know how she likes to keep things secret."

"She didn't. Hilda Thomas said something."

Rose frowned. "I wonder who else has thought of it."

"But the Captain would have to take us. What reason would he give? It must take quite a lot of fuel. Does the Penseythan have to approve it?"

"Yes, and that's not a problem," Rose replied. "Once a year, the doctor on Tristan comes here and there's a joint clinic and he helps handle deferred, tricky operations at my surgery in Portloe.

Tuesday seventh I'll be going to Tristan to do the same thing for him. If you join me, we could get married."

Sounded great. Wait a second…. "Is there some kind of residency requirement?"

"Clara says that shouldn't be a problem. We'd be there for two weeks. Get back October twenty-fifth."

So that was what they'd been discussing when Rose wouldn't tell me what the argument was about. "You didn't agree when she suggested it, did you?"

"Look. I didn't anticipate a problem in doing what we planned." Rose put her arms around me. "After what happened to you and realizing the Seythan wouldn't be favorable, I changed my mind."

"You could have told me earlier."

"Clara made me swear I wouldn't."

"Is there anything else she's got in mind I should know about?"

"Not that I aware of but, knowing her, I bet there is." Rose kissed me. "I've got to check on Young Artley's Mum, Jill. She's not getting any better. Then I'll be doing house visits all week," she said. "Anyhow, I'll try to be there for your fight scene. Stay out of trouble until then."

"Will do. I think Clara planned the rehearsal here in the village hall."

16.

MONDAY MORNING, STILL CONCERNED ABOUT THE NANCAR-row brothers lying in wait for me, I took a circuitous route to Jacob's farm. I started out north, crossing a flimsy wooden bridge over the Bodmin River. I strolled past the Gays' out-buildings, noting the tomato plants and a fancy flowerbed on the north side of the farmhouse: the ornamentals Young Artley mentioned that Elizabeth Gay had saved from the Masker's Tea Party antics. I chuckled and continued on, following a path over the Gays' and Nichols' fields to the seashore where the Bodmin River met the Atlantic. The northern rock hopper pen-guins nested there. The Professor had suggested these birds as an additional PhD topic if the auks had turned out to provide insufficient material for a robust thesis.

On my previous stay, I'd visited their colony a few times but had not paid much attention to them other than to check wheth-er they had similar issues to the auks—a lack of fish to support the continually growing population. They didn't because they weren't as picky in their diet, and the seas had plenty of the fish, crustaceans, squid, and krill they consumed.

The rocky shore was dotted with male penguins waiting pa-tiently for females. The smallest of the penguin family stood at about twenty inches. These rock hoppers had orange-red beaks, similarly-colored eyes, and their webbed feet were pink. Incongruous tufts of yellow feathers sprouted from the sides of their head. Like the auks, they were gregarious, loyal to a mate, and pecked at any birds encroaching on their nest in the tussocks of grass. The return had started and I saw females popping out of the waves as they approached the shore, where they belly flopped onto the rocks. Each of the previously-attached females called out to her mate, found him, and they paired off. Unattached males waited expectantly for single females. The sight reminded me I was a partially-unattached male, too.

After amusing myself for an hour or so watching their antics, I skirted the base of Brown Willy. When I reached the field with the pigs, I was surprised to see Paul Jago with a shovel scooping pig manure into a large wheelbarrow.

He stopped when he saw me approaching and removed a blue rag from a pocket. "Dad wants to be ready when you set up the digester," he said, wiping his brow. "Bloody waste of time, if you ask me, but that's Dad for you."

Not wanting to get into a father-son argument, I said, "Where's Frankie?"

"Tricked me with his two-headed coin into doin' this." Paul mimicked flipping a coin and grinned. "Got him the wrong end of the stick. He's digging the pits. Come on. This barrer's full enough. I know Dad's eager to talk to you."

"How's his arm?"

"Better, but not good enough for digging yet, if you know what I mean."

Cagy old devil. I wondered what he had up his sleeve for me this time.

I stayed slightly ahead of the 'barrer' to avoid the stench as we made our way to the farmyard.

"Frankie's all excited about the sword fighting scene," Paul said. "Clara and him's going to teach you and Sam how to do it. It's quite an art."

"You think Sam will fight fair?"

Paul stopped and looked to me. "Can't say rightly." He pushed ahead. "Of course, could be an accident, like."

I hurried to catch up, deciding not to mention my training in Japanese sword fighting. Word had an unfortunate habit of getting around on the island, so I would keep my limited skill as a swordsman to myself. In kendo, the sword was held in two hands and I suspected that parrying an opponent's thrusts would use a similar technique to that with rapiers.

Jacob came out of the barn and waited for us to reach him. One pit was complete and Frankie's arms and shovel were just visible as he excavated a second one. Jacob and I had discussed whether to dig one hole and split it in two with a wall. He'd gone for the cheaper option of separating the two holes by five feet with a plastic curtain in the first one to limit seepage.

Paul went into the near barn, which had a completed concrete floor, and dumped the manure onto a pile where, later, it could be hosed into the collection pit.

"What do you think?" Jacob asked.

I paced out the sides of the first hole and estimated its depth at about six feet. A quick mental sum and I concluded it would be more than big enough to handle the manure from Jacob's pigs. "Looks good," I said. "If you've got a tape measure, I'll get the measurements for a permanent cover."

Jacob sniffed. "In house. I'll get it."

Frankie waited until Jacob was out of earshot before straightening up. "Sword fighting scene's Saturday," he said. "How about you and me get together before then and I'll teach you some tricks? Wednesday evening work for you?"

"Fine. I could use them if Sam gets too aggressive."

Frankie grinned. "That's the idea."

Jacob's footsteps interrupted further discussion. Frankie returned to digging.

Jacob handed me the measure. "Ordered cement and gravel," he said. "Barn'll be ready in about a month." He grunted. "Cost me a pretty penny."

I ignored his attempt to make me look like the villain in this. "Good. We're making progress."

I made my measurements and was about to leave when Jacob said, "About temporary cover. Anything I should know?"

Good question. "You're probably okay if it's only for a short time; however, manure gives off some pretty noxious fumes: ammonia, hydrogen sulfide, for example. It would corrode corrugated iron. Plastic would probably be best. Morley may have something." I remembered something else I'd read. "You can get explosive situations with the nitrates. But they'd take a long time to build up, and shouldn't be a problem if you follow the instructions in the booklet I brought."

Jacob frowned. "Explosion, you say. Better not happen. Wouldn't be good for your standing on island."

Concern for me or a threat? To hell with him. "Follow the instructions and it won't," I snapped.

***

The rest of the week went by in a blur. I studied my lines, checked on the auks, and cycled to Morley's to make sure the digester was working properly. It was. Best of all, I was able to meet Rose one evening and go for a walk to show her the rock hoppers.

Saturday morning, I dressed in my jeans, short sleeved shirt and sneakers and went down to breakfast.

Clara glanced at my shoes. "Leather soles better for fencing," she said. "Like dancing. Feet won't get caught up on floor." I was about to go upstairs to change when she added, "Not so important this time, since you'll be practicing with sticks. Leather soles next time."

After breakfast, I walked with Clara to the village hall. Chairs were assembled in groups with small tables. A set-up for Bingo night, Clara informed me. The room smelled musty. Roddy Gay and Sam Nancarrow were already there. Frankie Quick arrived shortly afterwards, wearing dusty work clothes that did nothing to improve the ambience. Roddy and Sam wore their Saturday-go-to-the-dance outfits of white shirt and gray trousers, sneakers, and no jacket and tie.

Clara went into a room backstage and returned with two long sticks and two short ones and laid them on the stage. "You'll use these in place of rapier and dagger while we're training," she said.

She beckoned for Frankie to join her and motioned for the rest of us to sit. "First, I'm going to explain the basics of stage sword fighting," Clara said. She pulled yellow and red ribbons from her bag. "I'll demonstrate on Frankie. We have to keep it simple. There are five cutting areas on the body and two point areas you thrust at."

She took two yellow ribbons and pinned them on Frankie's arms just below the shoulder. Two more went on his thighs midway between his waist and his knees. "You strike at these points coming in sideways," she said. "Frankie'll demonstrate how to parry in a minute."

The fifth yellow ribbon she pinned to the front of Frankie's cap so that it hung over his nose. "For this cut, you strike straight down. Now to the points you lunge at. One's in the middle of the chest." She pinned a red ribbon. "The other's lower part of belly." She paused. "Is that clear?"

"What if I wanted to go for Romeo's eyes?" Sam asked.

Clara glanced at the ceiling. "You'll have a hard enough time doing what I just said. Find out soon enough when you train with Frankie."

"You mean I won't train with Roddy…and er, Sam?" I said.

"Not until both of you have shown that you know what you're doing," Clara replied sweetly. "Now to parrying." She moved to face Frankie, with both of them sideways to us.

"Cut one," Clara said, sweeping the stick horizontally toward Frankie's right arm.

Frankie held his stick out pointing up, intercepted it and brushed Clara's weapon aside.

The same process was used for the other arm. For the cuts to the thighs, Frankie held the stick pointing down.

"Now for cut five." Clara raised her fake sword and brought it down toward Frankie's head. He rapidly raised his short and long stick crossed above his head, blocking the attempted cut.

They repeated the moves four more times before Clara called for Roddy to come on stage.

Sam and I followed and also went through all the moves with Frankie.

After an hour or more of practice, Clara called a halt. "We'll take a short break and then we'll run through Sam and Frankie's fight scene and finally, Andy and Sam's."

17.

CLARA PLACED US IN OUR POSITIONS FOR THE SWORD FIGHT. "As you know from your scripts, the fight scene happens in Act three," she said. "We'll only practice lines where there's fighting. The scene begins when dinner ends at Montague's house. Benvolio, that's Roddy, and Mercutio, that's Frankie, go to the square. It's a hot day and they fool around by the fountain. Just do your dialogue. I'll call out stage directions. The main action starts when some Capulets appear, including Sam as Tybalt." She motioned to Roddy.

It was amazing, I thought, the change in Clara when she was directing a play: no longer vague or acting vague and totally in control.

Benvolio: "By all that's bad. Here come the Capulets."

Mercutio: "I care not."

Tybalt: "I'll do the talking. Good day, gentlemen. A word with you."

Mercutio: "One word. That's it? How about a word and a blow?"

Tybalt: "I'm ready for that, if you give me occasion."

Mercutio: "Surely you could find some occasion."

"Sam, you move to face Roddy," Clara called out. "Frankie, when you respond to him, draw your sword."

Tybalt: "You consort with Romeo."

Mercutio: "Consort? If you make minstrels of us, don't expect anything but discords. Here's my fiddlestick to make you dance. Consorts indeed!"

"Sam is surprised and steps back," Clara interjected. "Roddy, you're worried the situation will get worse."

Benvolio: "Come on. This is a public place. Reason coldly or go somewhere private-like. Better still, go home. Everybody's looking at us."

"Sam, you step forward again, draw your sword and look menacing." Clara added, "Well done."

Tybalt: "Men's eyes were made for looking. I'm not moving for anyone."

"Frankie, you act as if you're going to make a thrust then lower your rapier and stick point in ground," Clara says. "Everyone relaxes, but then you come running in, Andy."

Romeo: "Benvolio, Mercutio!"

Tybalt: "Never mind. Here's my man."

Mercutio, "He's not wearing your uniform as far as I can see. If you think he's your man, you'll soon find out. When you lead us to the dueling field."

"Andy, Romeo's out of breath. Go to fountain and take a drink," Clara instructed.

Tybalt: "Romeo."

"Andy you turn and smile. Pretend to wipe water off your face."

Tybalt: "I'll say this to you. You are a villain."

"Sam, raise your rapier to challenge Romeo." Clara added, "Remember, he doesn't have a sword."

Romeo: "Tybalt, I have my reasons to excuse your behavior, but don't call me villain. I'm going to ignore you."

"Applause from the Montagues and boos from the Capulets," Clara said.

Tybalt: "Sir, this won't excuse your insulting behavior. Face me and draw."

Romeo: "I never insulted you. I love you more than you can imagine. So, dear Capulet…a name I hold as dearly as my own, be content."

"More applause," Clara interjected. "Seeing Sam ignore Andy's outstretched hand, Frankie steps forward."

Romeo: "Soon you'll know the reason for my love. Dear Capulet, please be patient until then."

Mercutio: "Romeo, how can you let him treat you like that. Hey, Tybalt, you're not leaving, are you?"

Tybalt: "What do you want?"

"Frankie, you draw your rapier," Clara said.

Mercutio: "My dear king of cats with your nine lives. I'll take one from you and beat out the other eight with a stick. Now, draw your sword by its ears or mine will be around yours before you know it."

Tybalt: "Well, sir. I am ready."

Romeo: "No, no. Mercutio, please put your rapier away."

"Frankie, this is where…." Clara grinned when Frankie adopted an absurd en garde position.

Mercutio: "Come, sir, your passado."

"Both sides laugh at the clowning, even Tybalt, when Mercutio falls back into the fountain," Clara said. "Except for Romeo."

Romeo: "Benvolio, help me. Draw, knock their weapons down."

"Benvolio's laughing too much to do anything," Clara said. "This is when Romeo runs in front of Mercutio. He pushes Tybalt away, not seeing the rapier thrust that has struck Mercutio. We need to practice this move. No dialogue until we get it straight."

We spent ten minutes going through the motions with Frankie and my right sides to the audience. Frankie was a few inches closer to them. Sam faced me and thrust his stick between my left side and arm. We were positioned so that the rapier would miss Frankie where the audience wouldn't be able to see it.

When Clara was satisfied, she said, "Action."

Romeo: " Mercutio, stop! Tybalt, please stop—"

I felt a sharp pain in my side. "Ouch! What the hell were you doing, Sam? That hurt."

"Sorry, Andy." Sam smirked. "I was trying to go under your arm. I missed."

Clara came up to the stage. "Sam that was uncalled for. If you won't be serious, I'll get Harold to do the part."

"Sorry, Aunt Clara. It was a mistake," Sam said contritely, yet the barely suppressed smile showed otherwise.

I saw it as an attempt to show he wasn't apologizing.

"We'll take a break," Clara said. "The scene continues with Tybalt and his friends walking away. Romeo is relieved, not realizing that Mercutio is mortally wounded. Benvolio accompanies Mercutio home. We'll do that part of the scene another time. Come back in ten minutes for Romeo and Tybalt's fight scene."

Sam pulled a packet of cigarettes out of his pocket and headed outside. Roddy followed him.

Clara waited until they were gone. "You all right, m'dear?" she asked.

"Sore." I rubbed my side. "I didn't see it coming."

"Tricky bast…" Frankie caught himself. Clara didn't approve of swearing. "Want me to do something?"

I'll be ready next time. Should have been then, I thought. "No…thanks. I can handle him."

"Sticks is one thing," Clara said quietly. "What about rapiers and daggers? We use what we have, real ones."

Might as well tell them. "I've had some training in Japanese sword fighting…kendo."

"I seen kendo in a movie. You're a real samurai." Frankie adopted an exaggerated pose with his sticks held horizontal in front of his chest "Swoosh, swoosh." He swept the air. "You just lost your head."

"More the defensive side. Like judo, get your opponent off balance."

"You ready to continue?" Clara called out over her shoulder as she went toward the door.

"Sure."

Frankie was sitting out front as an audience, and Roddy and Sam were waiting off-stage, when I went to the front. Clara spoke. "We'll start the scene where Benvolio rushes up to Romeo."

Benvolio: "Oh, Romeo, Mercutio's dead."

Romeo: "This is only the beginning. Where will it end?"

Benvolio,: "Tybalt's coming."

"Andy, this is where you spot Tybalt," Clara interjected. "Pull Benvolio's sword from its scabbard."

Romeo: "Tybalt, Mercutio's dead and one of us is going to join him."

Tybalt: "It's going to be you."

"Up to now, you've been brandishing your rapiers, but at more than two sword lengths apart," Clara said. "Now come together and each try a cut like you practiced: one of you to the shoulder and the other to the thigh. Then a point to the chest and, in parrying, both lose your weapons."

"What then?" Sam asked.

"Wrestle for a bit before your friends rearm you."

"I can do that." Sam stuck his tongue out at me. He faked a thrust before withdrawing his stick and striking at my right shoulder.

I parried the blow and struck him lightly on his right thigh.

Sam's face contorted and he rushed at me swinging wildly. I sidestepped and hit him on the butt.

"Sam, Andy, stop!" Clara shouted.

Sam ignored her and came at me, slashing at my head.

I ducked under his arm, stuck a leg in front, and pushed as he went past.

He tripped and dropped the short distance off the stage, landing on his side with a loud thump. Sam scrambled to his feet, swearing, "I'll get you, Ferguson!"

Frankie and Roddy restrained him.

Clara came over. "Sam, if you're going to act like that, I'll get someone else for the role."

Sam hung his head. "Sorry," he muttered. "He's no right to be on island taking our women."

"That's no business of yours," Clara said firmly. "Promise you'll not do that again."

"Suppose not."

"Shake hands on it," Clara said firmly.

I walked to him and held out my hand.

Sam hesitated before reaching up and shaking it, trying to crush my fingers with his abattoir-toughened grip.

"Let's try the scene again," Clara said. "We'll do it in slow motion and I'll call out instructions for each move."

We practiced for half an hour, with Sam visibly straining to control himself, before Clara stopped us. "Good enough. We'll finish the scene. Tybalt dies. Romeo runs away. The Governor, Harold, is called and joins the Montagues and Capulets. The Governor exiles Romeo." Clara handed out the parts. "I'll play Lady Capulet. Frankie, you're the Governor, and Andy, you play Montague."

When we finished the scene, Clara announced, "I'll be rehearsing the whole play in evenings next week. Sword fighting scene with rapiers on Saturday." She handed each of us a sheet of paper with handwritten instructions. "These show when and where you need to be prepared to attend."

I glanced at the paper, seeing I'd be rehearsing every night, except one.

"What happens on Thursday?" I asked.

"Act four. You're not in it," Clara replied.

On Wednesday, I'd be rehearsing scene three in Act three with Rose. Something to look forward to.

When we got home, Clara motioned for me to go into the kitchen. She went outside and returned with the base for my mask. The metal petals had been hard-soldered to form a rough hemisphere with a nosepiece and holes for the ears and eyes. All the edges had been bent back and soldered so there were no sharp regions.

"That's real neat," I said.

"We'll try it on, m'dear," Clara said. "Tell me where it's too tight." She placed a cloth on my head and gently pulled the helmet down.

"It's a bit tight on the ears, and here on the back of my head." I pointed to the spot.

Clara marked the metal with a pencil and removed the helmet. "I'll fix those and finish the mask Tuesday."

"When will I start using it?"

"Next Saturday, when we rehearse fight scene with rapiers and daggers."

Given what Sam had tried to do, I thought, probably a good idea.

18.

Saturday night was movie night in Portloe. Rose was still tending to Artley's mother and I met her at the village hall. After the mandatory cartoon, the show would be The Wicker Man, a 1970s British horror movie. When we sat down, Rose surprised me by saying she'd seen it in England with Johnny Trevenna. I didn't like to be reminded that they had dated, and held my breath before turning to what I hoped would be a more pleasant subject. "Oh, I see. Did you enjoy it?"

"Johnny liked the film, said it reminded him of Roseland."

"How so, and how about you?"

"Pagan rites, human sacrifice, fooling a foreigner. A little too horrific for me." She leaned over and kissed me on the cheek. "See what you think."

The movie had me hooked from the opening credits. A police sergeant investigates the disappearance of a young girl on a remote Scottish island. He is appalled to discover that the islanders worship pagan Celtic gods and practice pagan rites on May Day. In a strange way, I could understand the connection to Midsummer's Day and the appeal to Johnny.

The sergeant sees photographs of the harvest festival with a young girl as the May Queen. When the island's leader explains that the islanders honor the festival to ensure a good harvest, the sergeant worries that the young girl may be used as a sacrifice to placate the gods.

I began to sweat, seeing the parallel to Roseland's previous female infanticide, lack of women, and need for the sexual relief on Midsummer's Day.

I clasped Rose's hand. "I see where this is going," I whispered.

She smiled. "You sure?" she said with a raised eyebrow.

In fact, I didn't anticipate the ending. When the sergeant finds and frees the girl, the islanders chase them. The girl is willingly caught. She is not the sacrifice…he is! The islanders bundle him into a Wickerman cage on a pyre and set it ablaze. I shivered.

When the lights came up, I was conscious of the many faces staring at me. "Who picks the movies?" I asked.

"Three members of the Seythan," Rose replied. "Let me think. Today it's Elizabeth Gay…Daisy Quick…and either Arthur Nancarrow or Johnny. They rotate."

As far as I knew, none of them was in my corner. "Do you think this was a warning to me?"

"Andy, don't get paranoid. This film must have been ordered last year, before the new Seythan was in place."

We walked to the bus. "You're right. I guess I'm worrying too much," I said, without much conviction. "When will I see you again?"

"Tomorrow, then Wednesday night for rehearsal, Romeo." Rose put her arms around me and gave me a passionate kiss. "Juliet can't wait."

"Good. Oh. Then, do you know who between Arthur and Johnny was a selector?"

"I'm not really sure…."

The rest of her reply was lost in the noise of the bus starting up. A few days without seeing her. Not good but I was resigned to it.

A bright moon shone through patchy clouds illuminating the countryside on the way back to Veryan. After we passed the school, we came to a field. I noticed the wood pile that was being built up for Guy Fawkes Day. I felt cold and took a deep breath, holding it while I calmed down.

After I fell asleep, I had nightmares about being a flaming Wickerman on top of the Guy Fawkes bonfire.

***

"Do you think Isaac will allude to the *Wicker Man* in his sermon?" I asked Clara at breakfast, in the hope that his sermon might give me a clue as to whether he was the Head Masker.

Clara fiddled with her toast, smearing on butter before answering. "Hard to tell. He likes to lay a trail of clues…like detective story. You might find message in there somewhere."

At chapel, armed with that vaguely helpful clue, I waited impatiently for the hymn and psalm to finish. I'd asked the same question of Mary and Rose, who sat beside me. Their responses had been noncommittal.

Isaac went to the lectern. He placed his hands flat on it. "Last night I saw a film that in some ways reminded me of our island… The Wicker Man." He leaned forward, grasped the front of the lectern and, sticking out his jaw with his gaze on me, said, "A naïve foreigner who comes to a remote island pays with his life for interfering. This story reminded me of the time when the pharaoh of Egypt, fearing the increase in the population of the Hebrews…foreigners in his land, issued a decree, 'Drown all Hebrew boy babies at birth.'"

His focus moved to Clara. "But Yocheved, recently delivered of a child, placed her newborn boy in a caulked wicker basket and hid it in the reeds by the River Nile." As he emphasized wicker his gaze shifted back to me.

"All becomes well when the cries of the baby draw the attention of one of the pharaoh's daughters. She adopts the child and calls him Moses, saying, '"Because I drew him out of the water."'"

If that wasn't an allusion to my arrival on the island, what was?

Lost in my thoughts, I didn't resurface until Isaac said, "And what then became of this Moses…? He tended sheep." Isaac paused as if to say this was significant.

I glanced at Rose.

She shrugged.

"On Horeb, the mountain of God, Moses and his sheep came upon a burning bush. The angel of the Lord appeared from the bush, unharmed. Curious, Moses approached. God spoke from the bush and told him to lead the Israelites out of Egypt."

I nudged Rose. "Is he trying to tell me something?"

"Shh." Rose turned away.

I remained distracted until Isaac's final words. "Guy Fawkes Day is fast approaching. Our bonfire is not a burning bush. Its flames can harm you. Please keep your children, and people unaccustomed to our celebrations, at a safe distance. Amen."

No question, he'd directed the warning at me. Message received.

I had thought the basket was made from reeds. I now wondered if Isaac had invented the wicker construction, and I hadn't met any Israelites on Roseland. It remained unclear to me if Isaac was Head Masker. "I'm still confused," I whispered to Rose.

"You're not alone."

I had lunch with Mary and Rose. Afterwards, Rose and I went for a walk before practicing our lines for the upcoming scenes in the play.

At four, Mister Thomas appeared to take Rose back to Portloe to check on Young Artley's mum.

19.

I DIDN'T SEE MUCH OF CLARA, OTHER THAN AT MONDAY night's rehearsal, until Tuesday at noon when she came home early from the library. I was reading my part for the next rehearsal when she appeared, carrying the metal armature of my mask. I followed her into the kitchen. She asked me to try the mask on, and made final adjustments with pliers and a hammer to improve the fit. In the next step, she attached some small contoured pieces of wood with screws from the inside, explaining that these were a part of shaping the head to fit the image she wanted to create. The final step at this stage involved gluing in thin padding. Holes drilled around the rim then allowed her to sew in a cloth lining.

The helmet was a tight fit.

"Not too tight is it?" she asked.

"Snug, but comfortable." I handed her the mask.

Clara smiled in a way that seemed to imply she'd received a pat on the back. "Andy, go out to shed, there's a bundle of old newsletters. Please bring it in."

When I returned, she was mixing a white powder and water in a bowl. The label on a box on the table read 'Wall Paper Paste'.

"Tear paper up." Clara took a news sheet and tore it up to show me she wanted about half-inch strips.

For the next hour, I watched in fascination as she dipped successive strips in the paste and applied them to the mask, leaving holes for the eyes and mouth. The mask now had a forehead, brow, Roman nose, rounded cheeks, mouth, and a cleft chin. We set it aside to let the papier-mâché dry over the stove.

Late in the evening, Clara decided the mask was dry enough to for the next step. She painted the mask with exaggerated skin tones and a garish smile that appeared to be saying, "What the hell is the world doing to me?"

Finally, when the paint had dried, she topped off the whole affair with a dashing brimmed green hat with a jaunty feather.

"Thank you," I said, putting the mask on. The fit was perfect.

Clara held a mirror in front of me.

"It's wonderful." I said. "Juliet will love it."

***

That evening, we rehearsed scene four of the second act, in which Romeo has received a message from Tybalt saying something to the effect that he's going to trounce him with a sword. Romeo is too love sick to take him up on it and meets with Mercutio and Benvolio, who doesn't know of Romeo's love for Juliet. Mercutio takes the opportunity to tell dirty jokes and make fun of Juliet's nurse when she appears. Finally, Romeo manages to takes the nurse aside. He asks her to find an excuse for Juliet to visit the Friar so they can get married.

Frankie had a fine time hamming it up with the jokes. He accompanied the line, "Tis no less, I tell you, for the bawdy hand of the dial is now upon the prick of noon," with such a vigorous motion of his right hand that Clara stopped the scene and warned him to be less obvious.

I did fine up to the point when I was supposed to say, "Nurse give my regards to Juliet. I…." Suddenly, I felt scared that I would not see Rose again and there would not be a marriage. My chest tightened and I didn't complete the line.

"We'll take a break," Clara said, obviously having seen my discomfort. "Andy, a word with you about the rest of this scene." She led me to a quiet corner and we sat. "What's the problem?"

"Can you really fix it so that Rose and I get married before the Seythan meets?"

Clara looked away. "It won't be easy." She turned back to face me and took hold of my hand. "You have to trust me…regardless of what happens."

I wasn't comfortable with her use of regardless, given the games she played on me in the past, but didn't see another option. "Okay."

"Ready to try again?"

"Yes."

This time we completed the scene.

***

After a difficult night's sleep with recurring nightmares of being led by maskers toward a distant bonfire, with Clara by my side repeating, "You have to trust me," I overslept and made myself breakfast. Worried about having a mental block on my lines, I wrapped my sandwich in a sheet from the island's newsletter, and took it, my water flask, and my script to the rookery. Bundled up to handle the gusts of a cold wind, I practiced my lines to an audience of inattentive auks. An occasional gull or skua would swoop close to check whether my presence meant food, or maybe they came to warn me off.

As always, being with the birds was therapeutic and I returned home in the afternoon in a much better frame of mind. Clara got home from the library looking flustered. "I'm running late. Seythan needed something done." She seemed to be more distracted than usual and muttered to herself as she fixed our supper, starting with the thick cheddar cheese sauce of one of my favorite cheese recipes, Welsh Rarebit.

Refreshed from my time at the rookery, and feeling in a feisty mood, I tried to needle her. "Has the Romeo and Juliet play reappeared in the library yet?" I asked.

"What?" She stopped spreading the sauce on a slice of toast "No m'dear, it's not there. I thought I told you."

"You did?" She didn't appear concerned. *Try to get her off-balance again.* "What's happened about my library card?"

"It hasn't been approved yet." Clara placed the rarebits under the grill for a minute.

"By the Seythan? Why not?"

A sly smile flickered briefly. "Been busy with play, haven't given it to them yet."

"When will—?"

"I hope you will be all right this evening," Clara said firmly, the dithering act gone as she preempted any further questions. "Rose will be there."

Give up on the library card, shoot. "I spent all day practicing my lines. Remind me which scenes we'll be rehearsing."

"Scenes three, four, and five in third act," Clara recited, ticking them off on her fingers. She served up the rarebits. "Now eat up. We've got to get to hall."

Rose was already there when we reached the hall around six-thirty. Rose came over and kissed me, holding on while she asked, "Are you doing okay?"

"More or less. I've been practicing my lines. I miss you."

Rose gave me another kiss, more passionate this time. I was half expecting Clara to utter the timeworn lines, "Get a room." Instead, she said, "We need to get things set up."

Rose helped Clara and me clear the stage of tables and chairs that had been used for some other meeting. We had nearly finished when the sound of footsteps echoed from the hallway.

Rose released me with a final kiss on the cheek. "I need to fix my makeup," she said, and went to the back of the stage.

I turned to see Elizabeth Gay enter with Johnny Trevenna and Charlie Gay. Elizabeth immediately cornered Clara. From their facial expressions, it seemed to me that Elizabeth was trying to persuade Clara to do something.

Clara smiled sweetly and acted as if she didn't understand.

The one-sided argument stopped when Harold Anthony rushed in at seven-fifteen, and apologized breathlessly for being tardy. By now it was getting late and Clara turned on the lights, but only over the stage—a reminder that electricity was a scarce commodity on the island.

"Good," Clara said, stepping away from Elizabeth. "Now we're all here, we can rehearse scene three."

This scene had Romeo visiting the Friar, unhappy that the prince has banished him to Tristan—Clara's version. The Friar is sympathetic but tells Romeo he's lucky, it could have been worse. Juliet's Nurse arrives and arranges for Romeo to visit Juliet that night before leaving for Tristan. Harold stood in for Cap'n Artley as the Friar. He surprised me with his stage presence, and managed a fair approximation to the Captain's way of speaking. I succeeded in completing my role in the scene without fumbling my lines.

After we finished a second run through, our small audience gave a brief round of applause.

"Very good," Clara said, beaming.

As Elizabeth, Johnny, and Charlie went to the stage for scene four, I overheard Elizabeth say, "Ferguson should follow Romeo's example and leave. He's probably the cause of the problem with my plants."

I wondered what she was talking about, but forgot to ask about it when Johnny snorted and made a soothing comment, which I couldn't quite make out. Charlie shook his head.

In this scene, Capulet, Penseythan Capulet, and Paris, the suitor for Juliet's hand, meet. As she had indicated at our first meeting, Clara had reversed the roles of the Capulets. When Penseythan Capulet—Elizabeth—told Paris she was sure that she could persuade Juliet to marry him, she was looking at Rose...

Lady Capulet: "Sir Paris, I'll talk to my child and she will do as I say. There's no doubt about it. I'll visit her in her room right now."

Elizabeth spoke with absolute confidence. Good acting but surely directed at Rose and me.

I glanced at Rose. Her lips were pursed. I patted her knee.

"She's a mean…" Rose whispered.

I was about to reply when Clara called out, "I'd like to try it again, please. Elizabeth, this time would you make your determination to have Juliet accept Paris a little clearer."

Elizabeth's face tightened. "What are you—?"

"I'd like to do it again," Johnny Trevenna said, touching her lightly on the arm. "I don't think I captured how… er… Paris feels."

Elizabeth's expression relaxed. "If you'd like to."

That was thoughtful of him, I thought. "Nice move."

"He's not as bad as you think," Rose whispered.

Maybe not.

When they had repeated the scene, sounding little different from the first time, Clara ushered them off. "Scene five. Actors on stage." She motioned for Rose and me to join her.

"When you're ready," Clara said, moving to the back of the stage.

Juliet: "Do you have to go? That was a lark not a nightingale, who sings to me every night."

Romeo: "It was a lark heralding the morn. See the light touching on Brown Willy's crown. I must go and live or stay and die."

No sooner did I complete my dramatic line with my hand on my heart than the lights flickered.

Rose suppressed a quick grin and continued the scene.

Juliet: "No day-light but some meteor to guide you on your way to Tristan. No need to   leave. Please stay."

Romeo: "If you will have it so, I am content to be put to death. I'll admit it was a meteor we saw. It isn't day. Let us talk."

Juliet: "I am wrong. It is the lark I heard. A changed voice in my head confused me. The light increases. I plead with you to go."

Romeo: "A light to contrast with the dark of our troubles."

My point was emphasized when the lights in the hall went out. Rose came close and held onto me. I glanced around. Strange, I thought, the lights in Veryan were visible through one of the windows.

"Electricity's gone off," a voice said, sounded like Charlie Gay's.

"No," I replied, realizing what had happened. "Someone's opened the breaker for the hall."

A strange scuffling sound followed and the lights came back on. Six masked figures in garish clothes blocked the door. I'd seen their like before on Guy Fawkes Day. All men, I was sure of it.

"Romeo, you should listen to Juliet," a tall one said, his voice muffled by the mask. "Leave before something bad happens to you."

I wondered who would respond. I didn't think it should be me.

Johnny Trevenna surprised me by stepping in front of them. "This is not the place for confrontation," he said. "We all heard your message."

The masked speaker started to move forward, but a hand tugged at his arm. He joined his hands together in a gesture that brought a fleeting image of Isaac Nancarrow, although the manner of speech didn't seem the same "We'll leave. But don't you forget, Andrew Ferguson. Rose is not for you."

"Thank you, Johnny," Rose said, not letting go of my arm.

"It's getting out of hand," he replied.

At that moment, the lights went out briefly. When they came back on, the Maskers were gone.

Johnny appeared about to say more when Clara chipped in, "We can finish this scene tomorrow. You'll not be needed, Andy." She turned to Rose. "Can you be there?"

"Yes, I—"

The sound of the front door banging against the wall caused her to stop.

Arthur Nancarrow rushed in. "Sorry I didn't get here in time to warn you," he gasped. "Working in store. Saw maskers crossing green…. Had to wait 'til they left."

Any doubts I'd had about whether Isaac or Arthur might head the Maskers went away. Most likely it was Isaac, although the masker who'd spoken didn't seem quite to fit the bill. Something I couldn't put my finger on nagged at my subconscious.

On the way back to Clara's house, I commented to Rose, "That was all a bit weird. It looked staged."

"I agree. Right now, a lot of things are."

After we'd kissed goodnight at her front door, she said, "Ask Clara what she thinks."

As soon as Clara came in, I did.

"Maskers are strange," was all she would say as she scuttled up the stairs.

20.

AT BREAKFAST ON THURSDAY MORNING, I TRIED TO GET CLARA to talk about the previous night's incident. She made only vague comments and obviously didn't want to discuss it, leaving for the library as soon as we finished eating. Not feeling like going over my lines again, I washed up and went to Jacob's farm. The two pits had been completed and he'd installed a plastic sheet to act as a seal between them. His version of a cover lay on the ground next to it. I scanned the contraption carefully. He'd attached beaten-up pieces of tarpaulin—sewn together and sealed with some kind of tar paper—to a metal framework that appeared to be scaffolding. Hadn't he heard my comment about corrosion?

Jacob answered my question when he emerged from the barn. "Metal bits go on outside." His expression carried the implication he wasn't stupid.

"Very good. Did Morley deliver the second set of equipment?"

"In barn."

I followed him into the building, and he pointed to where the second pump, scrubber, generator, and boiler, still mounted on their shipping pallets, piping, cables, and controls were laid out on an earthen part of the floor. Next to them was a large tank, recently painted white, I guessed.

"Navy surplus," Jacob said. "Morley told me where to get it."

"Great. I was wondering about that," I said. "Now, you don't have a shed or lean-to like Morley does to put these in. You plan to set them up in the barn?"

"No point in wasting money. Barn'll do fine." He gestured at an area inside that had been cleared of farm equipment since the last time I'd visited, and now had a rectangular patch of concrete. "Right there. Had enough cement to get that done."

I scanned it quickly. He'd gotten it right. The area was by the wall nearest the pits and large enough to take the equipment.

"Checked what Morley had," Jacob said smugly.

"Nice job." Now to business. "Can Roddy or Frankie help me put it together?"

"Roddy. He's out with pigs."

I assumed that meant I'd have to fetch my assistant and set off.

Roddy was back to scooping pig crap into a wheel barrow. He seemed relieved when I told him we'd be starting on setting up the digester equipment in the barn.

I led him and his barrer back to the farmyard. "Where's Frankie?" I asked over my shoulder.

"Clara's got him doin' something."

I wondered if it was connected to the appearance of some maskers, but decided not to pursue the subject.

After Roddy had fetched tools from a small shed abutting the farmhouse, we did a trial layout of the components. We then decided on the best place to put the pipe through the wall and rearranged everything. By lunchtime, we had mounted the pump, scrubber, generator, and boiler on the floor and turned to the piping. It was then I discovered that Morley had not sent the fittings for joining them together nor the instructions; in my enthusiasm to get on with the job, I hadn't done my homework. Stupid. I decided to stop the work and make a list of all the steps necessary to complete the system.

"I need to go see Morley and get the pipe fittings and instructions," I said. "If you can find a paper and pencil, I'll work on a check list. There may be other things we'll need."

I started back to Clara's with a few scribbled notes. Poor Roddy returned to shoveling manure.

Well before I got near the gate where Frankie had dumped Sam on the ground, I saw that I had company; the Nancarrow brothers were waiting for me. For a moment, I considered backtracking and finding a different route home. "Hell no," I muttered to myself. In daylight with no surprise, like when they'd ambushed me in the store, I reckoned I could handle them. First check they don't have anything that could be used as a weapon, I decided. Continuing on at a steady pace, I felt comfortable in the knowledge that with my track time at college, I could always outrun them if necessary.

Before I reached the brothers, Sam pushed the gate open and held it. Sandy remained standing in the middle of the track to his right.

"Morning gentlemen," I called out. "No masks today, I see. Does your dad know you're here?"

The brothers exchanged glances. "None of your business," Sandy snapped.

"I'm coming through," I said, my heartbeat speeding up. "Don't try anything stupid." I held my right hand up in a karate stance, crouched slightly in preparation to kick, and headed to the left of Sandy.

"We can kill a pig and cut it up in twenty minutes," Sandy said, as I edged up to him. He pulled a long knife from behind him and held it up. The blade showed red streaks.

"Stick with pigs," I said. By now, I was nearly in front of him. "I'll break your arm before you can use that thing."

My ruse worked. Sandy slashed at me high up to avoid my hand. I ducked and kicked him in the crotch, jumping sideways and backing away as he doubled up.

Sam had started to swing the gate at me, but stopped when his brother fell in front of it. "You'll never marry Rose," he shouted, his face twisted with frustration.

I didn't wait for further debate and ran all the way back to the library in Veryan. Clara was in the office reading when I went in. "I was at Jago's," I gasped. "Nancarrow brothers tried to attack me again."

"Shouldn't have done that," she said hesitantly, a strange look on her face.

For a second, I wondered if it hadn't been in some script she'd spawned.

"I'll deal with it." Her voice was now firm. She stood and brushed past me.

"Can I borrow your bike? I need to go see Morley."

"Certainly, m'dear," she said on reaching the front door. "Best you get out of Veryan until I've talked to Isaac."

"Is he…?" My attempt to ask whether Isaac was Head of the Maskers fell on deaf ears. When I closed the library door, Clara was halfway to Nancarrow's store.

I made a sandwich and headed for Morley's farm. I told him about the items I'd need to complete Jacob's system and he agreed to send them over. I had the impression he was itching to tell me something. "Got time for a cuppa?" he asked.

"Sure."

My impression was confirmed as soon as we were seated. "I had a grand idea," Morley said, looking pleased with himself.

"Please tell me."

"Sewage from most of Portloe is sent through pipe out to sea. Same thing in Veryan."

I saw where he was going, but held off preempting him telling me his grand idea.

"Jacob and I both have tanks on wheels for spreading stuff. We could collect it and put in with manure."

"Good idea, I think...." A mental image of dirty water gushing into the sea flashed in front of me. "Isn't there a lot of liquid?"

Morley smiled, obviously having anticipated my question. "Thought of that. We'd build tank and only collect sludge, like with septic tanks."

His mention of tanks reminded me of what I'd seen in the quarry. "You know there's some large open tanks in the quarry that might work if we put them in the ground."

Morley beamed. "You're right. I saw them, but was looking for closed tanks."

I thought of something else. "You'd need to remove sludge after the sewage digests. I could come up with an approach."

"Yes, and have cover to stop smell." He took a sip of his tea.

"How many people are connected to the systems?" I asked, adding, "It can't be that many...I mean, that row of houses with Clara and Mary have septic tanks."

"Don't think so, Andy, but you're assuming our outhouses aren't connected. We use water from rivers to flush 'em out…regular like."

I hadn't thought of that. "So, how many?"

"About a half of buildings."

"I'll assume that means half the population, and do some calculations."

"Good. Do it soon. I called Martha and asked for a time to speak to Seythan. They'd have to fund everything. Called Jacob, too." Morley shrugged. "He's interested, but wants to know whether he'll have to pay for electricity…. That Jacob."

"Great idea." I thought for a moment. "You know, you could send electricity back to your respective villages. I could calculate what percentage would be appropriate."

"Fair swap, eh." Morley beamed for a second until his face turned serious. "You'd have to work with Johnny, you know."

Somehow, after what he'd said the previous night, I didn't worry about that prospect so much. "I can handle it."

His mention of Johnny reminded me of the nasty comment Elizabeth had made the previous night. "Have you heard anything about Elizabeth Gay having some problem with her plants?" I didn't add what she'd said about me.

Morley scratched his head. "Vaguely. Something about tomatoes."

"Should I offer to help?"

"Best not," he said. "Stubborn woman. Doubt she'd accept it."

"You had any problems?"

"Don't grow tomatoes. Peas and beans is my specialty."

"Let me know if you do have a problem."

"Will do. Now you better get on home before it rains."

I cycled back to Veryan, happy that Morley had come up with a way to make my contributions to the island more valuable.

That evening, I accompanied Clara on the bus to the hall in Portloe for the first rehearsal of Act four. The venue had been chosen because it was easier to get to for most of the cast, and Rose was still spending much of her time in and around that village. It was the first occasion I'd been on the stage in the hall and was surprised to find that there were rooms to the side in addition to a large area behind where the backdrop for the play would be. Various props were stored there, including a dais on wheels, which I guessed would stand in for the balcony. The first scene in Act four was the awkward one in which Paris, who assumes Juliet will marry him, meets with her. It was hard not to hear the undertones in Johnny Trevenna's words and the not-so-subtle rejection from Rose as they played their parts. Nevertheless, the evening passed without incident. The actors had very few stumbles, and Clara showed her delight by initiating a round of applause at the end of scene five. Rose gave me a passionate kiss in front of everyone before I boarded the bus.

"That'll show them," she whispered and unclasped her arms from around my neck.

"Sure as hell showed me," I replied with a grin, choosing not to wipe her lipstick off my face. "Good night to you, sir," I said to Johnny, who was close by.

He gave a wry smile. "You have the advantage for the moment, Romeo." He bowed slightly.

***

On Friday, I went to Jacob's to work on the digester. In my absence, Roddy had mounted and connected the tank to collect the methane.

"Nice job," I said, admiring his handiwork.

"Frankie helped me."

I spent most of the day helping Roddy complete the pumping, scrubber, and wiring.

Not wanting to risk meeting better-prepared Nancarrows, I took a circuitous path back to Veryan.

That evening, I joined the rest of the cast in Portloe to rehearse the final act of Romeo and Juliet. The evening passed without incident. I sat with Clara on the bus going back to Veryan.

"We're rehearsing the fight scene tomorrow afternoon with rapiers and daggers," she said as the bus went by the growing pile of wood for the Guy Fawkes Day bonfire.

My heart rate increased. "I haven't forgotten." Her reminder in turn made me think of my most recent encounter with the Nancarrow brothers. "Do you think Sam will try something stupid?"

Clara turned to face me. "Better not. I spoke to Isaac about it." Her face turned serious. "Either way, it wouldn't hurt for you to be prepared. Frankie's comin' by after breakfast. You and he can practice defense."

"Thanks." I suppressed the thought that, maybe, if Sam tried something, I'd attack him.

21.

WE LEFT CLARA'S HOUSE EARLY ON THE MORNING OF SATURDAY, October 11. At her request, I carried my mask. I'd expected that she would have Frankie train me in the village hall. Instead she led Frankie and me out the back door across the fields to a concrete pad by the edge of the Bodmin River. For once, Frankie didn't play a game he normally enjoyed—loping off forward and back as if he were a hunting dog—he carried the rapiers and stayed abreast of us.

The early morning mist had cleared and only a wisp of cloud remained at the summit of Brown Willy. I scanned the concrete and the remains of a wooden dock that stuck out into the river.

"Used to be small hut," Clara said. "Housed fishing equipment for my father-in-law. Now put on your mask."

The minute I had the mask on, I understood why she'd been so insistent that I bring it. My vision was impeded by the nose and the bulge of my cheeks, and my neck felt stiff.

Frankie gave me a rapier and Clara handed us the daggers. "Take up your positions two sword lengths apart," she said. "Andy, try practice moves copying Frankie."

We spent twenty minutes acting out thrusts, slashes and parries before Clara told us to move into fighting distance. There, we went through the sword fight scene I'd have to repeat with Sam that afternoon.

Frankie threw in a few crafty moves that caught me by surprise the first time he tried them.

After I'd dealt with one of these moves, Clara called out, "I think you're ready, Andy. Don't want to tire you out."

I viewed myself as fit, but this was a new kind of exercise and I was happy to stop. I bowed to Frankie. "Thanks. I think I can handle anything Sam's going to try."

"Just watch *you* don't try anything...." Frankie snorted. "Hurt Sam and you'll be answering to Isaac."

"Frankie, that's enough," Clara said in a rare voice of authority.

We headed home in silence with Frankie acting in his dog role.

***

"Shouldn't fight on an empty stomach," Clara said, handing me a plate of fried fish and chips.

Used to the eating ritual, I took the vinegar bottle and sprinkled some on my food, following with a light dousing with salt and pepper. "Do you think Sam will be a problem?"

Clara shook her head. "No. I spoke to Isaac about his behavior. He'll be a good boy."

I wasn't totally convinced but kept it to myself and concentrated on eating.

We finished the main course and had apples for dessert.

As we washed up, Clara said, "You need to know something. Next Tuesday, we're going to Tristan."

"We?" I said in surprise.

Clara smiled. "You and Rose."

"Rose told me she'd be going there to help Tristan's doctor." I hoped I knew the reason I'd be going with her, but…. "Why me? To get married?"

"That's the plan." Her face took on a crafty look.

She's up to something. "Why are you telling me now?"

"This afternoon in hall, I'll tell Sam any more rehearsals will have to wait 'til I get back from Tristan." She handed me a plate to dry then motioned at me with a finger. "Most important you act surprised."

"Got it." Maybe we could fool my enemies.

Clara had been correct. Sam and I practiced the sword fight scene without incident.

In fact, he even muttered, "That went well," when we finished.

It was then that Clara said, "Sam, don't forget, next rehearsal won't be until I get back from Tristan."

"What?" I exclaimed.

Clara suddenly took on her vague and catty persona. "Andy, didn't I tell you?"

I shook my head. "I don't think so."

"Oh, dear." Her hands fluttered. "Next rehearsal's when Frankie and I get back from Tristan. We'll be helping Rose do her annual doctoring."

"I knew Rose would be going. I didn't know you'd be with her. Then you'll be gone more than two weeks?" I asked, taking a surreptitious look at Sam.

He appeared puzzled.

"Leave this Tuesday, back Thursday thirtieth. Midday I hope,"

Clara replied. "You all practice your lines. Dress rehearsal's that Thursday night. Performances, Friday night, Saturday matinee and night."

"What'll I do for food while you're away?"

"Mary'll take care of you."

"Okay, I guess."

"There's some of us could take care of him," Sam muttered, giving me a glare.

Apparently, Isaac's words with Sam hadn't had much effect. "Do you think Sam bought it?" I asked when we were back in Clara's house.

"Bought what, m'dear?"

"That I didn't know you were going to Tristan and that meant I wouldn't be going."

A smile flickered across Clara's face. "I certainly hope so."

***

Sunday, I went to chapel with Rose. Isaac's sermon started with a passage from the Marriage at Cana and changing water into wine. He continued with muddled analogies to making a purse from a sow's ear to electricity from manure. At the end, I wasn't clear whether he was recommending all these actions or condemning them. Given that the pub was attached to his store, I assumed his intent was to recommend. His conclusion was a prayer for the safe passage of those going to help people in need on Tristan. That part was clear. I squeezed Rose's hand. She turned and smiled at me.

After chapel, Clara and Frankie joined me for lunch at Mary's house. I waited impatiently while the others beat to death interpretations of Isaac's sermon. What I wanted to hear about was how they'd get me on the boat without the Maskers finding out. An unusually secretive Rose hadn't wanted to discuss it, saying that everything was in Clara's hands.

Finally, Clara raised the topic. "Rose, tell us about your plans for getting to boat on Tuesday."

"Mr. Thomas understands he'll pick you and me up at six-thirty and take us to Portloe."

Wait up. "What about me? Does that mean I'll have to go down the cliff to get in the motor boat?"

Rose and Mary looked quizzically at Clara.

"That was my first idea." Clara tilted her head. "Wasn't sure it'd work. That's how Andy came on the island. Maskers might be waiting." She shifted in her seat. "Frankie's going to be on boat. He won't be there to help Andy climb down. Too dangerous."

"So, what do you want me to do?"

Clara's eyes twinkled. "You leave early and go out back and make your way to Guy Fawkes field near schoolhouse."

"And wait to get picked up?"

"Yes." She looked at me expectantly.

Clever plan. Was anything missing? I mentally ticked off a list: my clothes and shaving stuff would fit in a backpack; I could try out the route in advance; and…. I couldn't think of anything else…except…the crew. "Isn't Sandy Nancarrow one of the crew? Won't he be a problem?"

"Thought about that," Clara said. "Cap'n agreed not to take him. That's why Frankie's going."

"Won't Sandy be suspicious?"

"Cap'n already told him. Sandy said it wasn't a problem, he and Sam were expecting a pile of work at abattoir."

That all sounded good. I was beginning to think Rose and I really would get married soon. "Bless you," I said.

Late in that evening, Rose took me in her arms and kissed me at the front door. Finally pulling back and clasping my face in her hands. "Whatever happens, remember I love you and we will be married."

I returned to Clara's, warmed by her words.

22.

At five-thirty on Tuesday morning, Clara let me out the backdoor. With my backpack securely strapped on, I scrambled over the low wall at the end of the garden. Despite a morning mist, a faint moon glimmering through scattered clouds provided sufficient light for me to reach the north end of the field without tripping. From there, I worked my way east along the hedge to where I could see the stile and gate into the next field. I stopped and listened. Hearing no sound, I proceeded to the stile and clambered over it to avoid the inevitable squeaking had I opened the gate.

Walking slowly and stopping to check for any signs that someone was watching, it took me about fifty minutes to reach the field where the pile of wood and other combustibles were waiting for Guy Fawkes Day bonfire. A light wind was blowing from the west and I didn't detect the faint smell of gasoline until I'd edged my way around to near the metal gate in the hedge by the road. I had the idle thought the odor was odd, but was soon distracted by the sound of an approaching car. It had to be Mr. Thomas going to pick up Clara and Rose.

Twenty-five minutes later, I heard the sound of the car returning and went to the gate. The Lagonda's headlights lit up the road. A crackling sound behind me caused me to turn.

I watched in horror as the pile of wood erupted into a mass of fire and smoke. "Oh, shit!" The skeletal outline of a man appeared briefly on top of the pyre before it vanished in flames.

I froze at the sight of what had been a Wickerman. A mistake, I realized, as figures wearing a variety of animal masks emerged from the smoke and bore down on me. Too late, I tried to climb over the gate but rough hands pulled me back, threw me face down, and held me on the ground.

I managed to twist my head to where I could see the gate. The Lagonda came to a stop and I heard a door open. The sounds of an argument continued for many minutes, a man's voice I didn't recognize and Rose's prominent among them. I couldn't make out what they were saying. The argument stopped suddenly and I heard footsteps.

Rose knelt down beside me and stroked my head. "I'm sorry, Andy," she said. "I have to go. That's the only way they won't hurt you. Don't try to follow." She bent close and kissed the back of my head, whispering, "Clara says it's for the best."

Shortly afterward, the car started up and drove off. The hands that had held me down let go. I waited a minute and gingerly got to my feet. Four maskers remained. One stepped forward. His vulpine mask leered at me in the flickering light from the bonfire. The mouth was a red gash that showed jagged teeth. I could not decide if it was Isaac.

"Why the Wickerman?" I asked.

"Warning to stay away from Rose," a gruff voice replied. "Next time you could be in it."

"How did you know I'd be here?"

The mask tilted. The masker clasped his hands in front of

him. A gesture I'd seen in the chapel. No rings, I noticed. "Clara told us," he replied. "Take him away. You know what to do." He walked off and disappeared behind the still-burning bonfire.

"Don't try anything," a snarling rat's face said as they led me down the road to Veryan.

I was too confused and distressed to think of fighting back. Was this all a part of one of Clara's games to make a fool of me, with Isaac a part of it? But Rose had said, "Clara says it's for the best?" What did that mean? I didn't know what to think.

When we reached the square, it was light enough for me to see my destination. The stocks were back. Sure enough, the masked men placed me in them and left.

I sat, hunched forward with my wrists and ankles clamped by the stocks' wooden bars, and brooded about my fate. In my despondent state, I even asked myself whether Rose had been a party to the game. Her comment about Clara could mean she knew what was going to happen. I recalled what Rose had said that Sunday night: "Whatever happens, remember I love you and we will be married." So, maybe Clara did have a plan to get us married, but I couldn't imagine what the hell that might be.

My situation became more miserable when the wind picked up and rain pelted down. I bent forward and closed my eyes. The water still dripped down my neck, saturating my t-shirt and even reaching my underpants. I wanted to cry, but by that time, I had become angry and worked up fanciful schemes to get back at the Maskers. When that palled, I wondered when someone would notice my plight. The answer came about half-an-hour later.

"How on earth did you end up here?"

I looked up and saw Arthur Nancarrow's concerned face.

"Maskers."

Arthur produced a set of keys and unlocked the padlocks that held me down.

I massaged my wrists and ankles and, with Arthur's help, got to my feet. We headed for Clara's house. "How did you manage to get the keys?"

"Getting store ready," Arthur said. "Looked out window and saw you. Keys were in Seythan House.... What did you mean by maskers?"

"I was supposed to go to Tristan with Rose. I got intercepted."

"You two were going to get married?"

"Yes. Clara arranged it."

"How did Maskers find out?"

I was about to reply that Clara had told them, but... "I don't know."

The bus rolled into the square and parked by the store as Arthur, holding my arm, helped me hobble to reach Clara's house.

Mary's door opened and she appeared. Catching sight of us, she raised a hand to her brow and called out, "What happened?" She came toward us.

"Maskers," Arthur replied. "Put Andy in stocks. I just let him out."

Mary stopped, a bewildered look on her face. "But...." She glanced across the green. "I'll tell someone to let school know I'll not be in 'til later." She ran over to the bus.

Arthur seemed inclined to stay at Clara's front door, but Mary shooed him away. She eyed me. "Andy, you're soaking. After you've changed come to my house...backdoor. I'll make you breakfast."

I dropped my backpack on the floor of the kitchen, tore off my clothes, and dumped them on the stone floor. *Dealing with them can wait.* Upstairs, I dried off with a towel and put on fresh clothes.

When I reached Mary's kitchen, she sat me down. After making a cup of tea, she went to the stove. "Eggs and bacon?"

"Please."

"Cut yourself bread and butter." Mary put two bacon strips in a frying pan. "Now, tell me the whole story." She broke eggs into a saucepan and added milk, a pat of butter, pepper, and salt.

I got the bread and butter and explained about the bonfire, the Wickerman, and the Maskers.

Mary stopped stirring the eggs for a moment. "How did they know? Clara was convinced she had them fooled."

"I asked a masker, their Head I think, that question."

Mary looked at me quizzically.

"He said Clara told him."

"That don't make any sense." Mary put the bacon on a plate and ladled on the eggs.

"I agree. But Rose told me that Clara says it's for the best."

"I wonder what Clara's up to." Mary shook her head from side to side. One of a very few times I'd seen her look frustrated. "They'll be gone for two weeks. What to do?"

I ate a piece of bacon with bread and butter and toyed with my eggs. "So, there's nothing for me but to wait."

"You can come and stay with me. I'll get your old room ready."

That sounded better than being alone at Clara's, but I didn't want to put Mary at risk. "Are you sure?"

"Yes," Mary replied in a firm voice. "And there is something I *can* do. Go to radio station and call the Captain. He can find out what really happened."

Encouraged, I quickly finished my breakfast and had a second cup of tea.

23.

I WATCHED MARY TAKE HER BICYCLE AND HEAD OFF FOR THE
school. Alone in the house, I slumped on the sofa and closed
my eyes, temporarily damming the tears that had welled up. My
chest ached and I hugged myself. *Damn. Damn. Damn*—like
Charlie Brown when Lucy pulled the football away. *So close and
then to fail.* I tried to comfort myself by visualizing Rose, but the
images rapidly became ones of Clara. Had Clara been fooling me
all along? Some weird game to make up for her unhappy past?

On my previous stay on the island, I'd heard how Clara had
fallen in love with John Nichols, son of Penseythan Agnes Nichols. When Clara was chosen to be Queen, the Penseythan arranged that the King would not be her son but Pete Quick. Her
rationale was that Clara and John, being second cousins, were
too closely related. I recalled that in North Carolina, first cousins were allowed to marry. I concluded that Agnes was just being nasty.

The couple tried to hide until after Midsummer's Day, but
were caught. John was placed in the stocks during the time that
Clara was in the large Round House servicing Pete and six other
men. John ran away after they released him and drowned himself
in the lake on top of Brown Willy. Although Clara's marriage to
Pete had been a good one, she never completely recovered. Com-

pounding my concerns was the constant thought that she was Johnny's aunt.

I tried to persuade myself that surely she couldn't be getting her revenge through me. This rationalization turned out to be an unsuccessful endeavor. I had no choice but to wait and see what Mary found out. That was all I had to hang on to.

I considered what to do next, and went back to thinking about Morley's suggestion to collect sludge from the sewage systems. I went to Clara's and brought back a notepad and pen, along with essentials for staying at Mary's.

As I considered using anaerobic digestion of sewage, my primary problem was remembering the relevant numbers for human output. I did a back-of-the-envelope calculation. One number that kept coming to mind was one hundred grams per day per adult on a high-fiber diet. I noted, crap = 100 grams/day.

I studied the ceiling. Now, was that wet weight or dry weight? I thought about my own experience and decided it had to be dry weight. But was the island's diet high-fiber? They seemed to eat pretty well. I concluded they probably met the estimate.

Now to the question of how much energy it might contain. Again, a number surfaced. This time about 30 gigajoules per metric ton for coal. Poop, not nearly as dense, couldn't be as good as coal. I settled on 20 gigajoules per ton. With a perfect efficiency of conversion to methane and production of electricity, that implied 0.28 kilowatt-hours per day per person as an absolute maximum. I went for a more conservative number, 0.2.

Now to reality: most of the islanders weren't connected to the sewage systems, and while it might be possible to transport more material from septic tanks, I wasn't sure that was realistic—therefore, assume half of the islanders, about 250 people; conversion to electricity would at best be around 15 percent plus some heat for the sewage. In total, the electricity production might reach fifteen kilowatt-hours per day for the island. Not bad, since I'd estimated 40 for Morley's system and 20 for Jacob's. As I finished the calculation I suddenly understood how best to do it.

I sat back and closed my eyes, returning to my previous morose state. A knock on the door interrupted my attempts to think only about happy times with Rose. I opened the door to find Arthur. He wore his white store-coat instead of the jacket I'd seen him in earlier.

"Quiet time at store," he said. "Just came to see how you were doing." His face showed concern. "Would you like to talk?"

I'd been hasty in considering Arthur as a possible Head of the Maskers. Isaac appeared, more and more, to be the candidate. This was not a good subject to raise with Arthur. I pointed to a chair. "Have a seat."

I picked up my notes. "Morley Thomas had an interesting idea for the digesters." An expectant look encouraged me to continue. "Add sewage from Veryan and Portloe."

Arthur scratched his head. "Does that mean we won't discharge it anymore? I've heard say best fishing is near outlets in sea."

"Yes, but what I plan will still put most of the nutrients into the effluent. I just want to collect the sewage in tanks, digest it and send the methane to Morley's and Jacob's farms to add to what the manure produces."

"Very clever, Andy. You'll make more electricity."

I nodded.

"How much are you talking about?"

"An additional twenty-five percent," I replied.

I waited while Arthur mulled over my plan.

"You said add tanks. Who's going to pay?"

"Morley says that the Seythan would have to fund everything. He's going to talk to them…" Of course, Arthur was a member. "Y'all."

"You'd pump the gas, so there'd be electrics involved?"

"Yes. I'd need Johnny Trevenna's help."

A smile flickered briefly before Arthur said, "Interesting."

"Will you support it?"

"I'll have to hear what you, Morley, and Jacob have to say." He noted points on his fingers: "Who pays what, cost of electricity, who gets electricity, where tanks could be put. And so on. If you don't mind, I'll talk to Isaac about it."

The mention of his brother reminded me of what had happened earlier that day. "Do I need to talk to Isaac, too?"

"About your plan?"

"No. About what happened this morning."

A strange expression crossed Arthur's face. Bewilderment? Concern? I couldn't tell. He shook his head from side to side. "Don't see what good that would do. I'd better be going. I'll let myself out."

After Arthur had gone, I went over what he'd said. Did it mean Isaac wasn't chief honcho of the Maskers or that talking to him wouldn't help? I needed fresh air and decided to cycle to Morley's and tell him about my calculations.

***

I scanned the fields for signs of Morley as I cycled down the track to the farmhouse. Seeing no one, I rested my bike on the wall by the front door and knocked.

Hilda appeared. "If you're looking for Morley, he went to the quarry. You should be able to catch him there."

This was a good break because we could check out possible components for the sewage treatment approach. "Thanks," I said, climbed on my bike, and sped off to Portloe.

The village was built into a narrow valley and straddled the Fal River: river being a somewhat grandiose name for a modest size stream. I hadn't paid much attention before to the river, but this time I noticed how pipes at various places diverted water into each house, and that a large pipe ran along the river bank. I guessed this was the sewer. About two-thirds of the way down the main street, a bridge crossed the river and accessed the road to the quarry, which I reached a few minutes later.

I found Morley making measurements on one of the large tanks I'd seen on my previous visit.

"Think it'll do?" I asked.

Morley looked pleased to see me. "This is right convenient, Andy. I think so. How are you getting on with your calculations?"

"Done. I reckon we can get about fifteen kilowatt-hours from the two systems…probably ten here, and five in Veryan."

Morley's face scrunched. "That's another quarter each, when you add to me and Jacob."

"Yes. Another thing is, I realized it made more sense to ship the methane to your farms rather than use it on site."

"Right clever, Andy. This will help the island tremendously. I've got news, too. Seythan meets this Saturday and I'm on the agenda."

"Wonderful. Do I need to say anything?"

"Probably better to let me do talking. Give me your calculations and sketch of what you plan."

I was happy to do that, not wanting to risk getting into an argument with Elizabeth Gay. "How about Johnny Trevenna? Do I need to talk to him?"

Morley's brow furrowed. "Again, better not. Wait 'til later."

No problem for me. "Fine."

We spent the rest of our time before I returned to Veryan getting information on the tanks, piping, and pumps.

When I arrived home, Mary was in the kitchen preparing dinner.

I didn't go through the normal pleasantries. "Did you get hold of the Captain?" I asked, impatient to find out anything about what had happened to me.

Mary turned to look at me, her normally smiling face somber. "Artley talked to Clara about letting the Maskers know where you'd be. All she'd say was that she had to do it."

"Does that mean she's been playing Rose and me along all this time?"

A faint smile appeared briefly. "Hard to say with Clara. She's deep. My advice is to keep the faith."

Easy for her to say. The ache in my chest returned. "I guess."

24.

I HAD ATTENDED ONLY ONE MEETING OF THE SEYTHAN ON MY first visit to Roseland, and it hadn't been a happy event. They'd sentenced me to jail and to spend Midsummer's Day in the stocks: with me believing that Rose was the Queen and Frankie Quick the King. This late spring day, Saturday, October eighteenth, was way better. I wasn't in the hot seat. But a feeling of apprehension settled over me at the sight of the long table with a cloth draped down to the platform on which the table sat.

The members of the Seythan glanced at me when I entered the room: Elizabeth Gay, Jacob Jago, Arthur Nancarrow, Martha Nancarrow, Daisy Quick, James Thomas, Johnny Trevenna. Behind them, photographs of earlier Penseythans stared at the assembly—the oldest set being faded sepia prints. Ominously, the photo of the previous Penseythan, Jane Trevenna, loomed behind her son, Johnny.

I dipped my head to acknowledge the Seythan, then scanned the five rows of seats that faced the platform, spotting Morley in the second row sitting with Harold Anthony. Why was Harold here? I was glad I'd put on my going-to-church outfit, because nearly everyone was wearing their Sunday best.

The committee's reaction to my entry had led many in the audience to turn and see what was happening, Morley among them. He motioned for me to join him and Harold.

"They're likely to ask Harold to run the numbers," Morley said by way of explaining Harold's presence.

"Happy to go over them with you," I said.

Harold smiled and was about to say something when Martha called the meeting to order.

The first item on the agenda was the budget, presented confidently and precisely by Harold. I was seeing a different side of him. As far as I could tell, the island was running a surplus because of above average revenue from the lobsters and other seafood sold to South African distributors.

The next item was a written statement from James Thomas criticizing those who had willfully set the Guy Fawkes wood pile on fire. The Seythan voted unanimously in support of Martha Nancarrow's condemnation of this wasteful act. Arthur was appointed to organize a drive to rebuild the wood pile. No discussion of why it had happened or who did it, I noted. It suggested that even the Seythan was wary of taking on the Maskers.

With that proposal settled, Martha motioned for Morley to come forward. "Morley Thomas has a proposal for us relating to how we handle sewage. Let me remind those without septic tanks that we pipe your sewage out to sea from Portloe and Veryan."

Morley moved to a lectern that faced the committee. He placed our notes down before reading from them. "Thank you for giving me this opportunity to make a proposal to Seythan. As most of you know, er...particularly Jacob... Well, Jacob and I have installed digesters for manure to produce gas and use it to make heat and electricity." He turned and pointed at me. "Young Andy there has helped us."

Morley scanned his notes. "Er, well, it seemed to me we could add sewage to the mix, and Andy has done some calculations."

Daisy Quick, her narrow face showing more irritation than normal, raised her hand. "What's this got to do with Seythan?" she asked, her tone of voice harsh.

Morley stared for a moment. "It'll mean extra electricity for all the island, Daisy. Another fifteen kilowatt-hours a day beyond the sixty Jacob and I will produce. Now, Jacob and I expect to sell half our electricity so this would add fifty percent to that. I'm hoping Seythan will see fit to provide the start-up funds."

Daisy raised her hand. "You talk about more electricity but—"

"Daisy, if you don't mind, let's hear the proposal first," Martha said firmly. "Morley, please continue."

Daisy pursed her lips and glanced across at Elizabeth, who mouthed what appeared to be "patience."

I wondered how much of Daisy's concern was that she didn't like the proposal and how much was my involvement in it.

Morley shuffled his notes nervously. "We don't have all the numbers yet, but I can say what we have in hand, and what we plan." He glanced at Martha.

She nodded. "Give us what you have."

"First, we'll need to dig holes to put tanks in…two in Portloe, and two in Veryan. They'll be on the line of the present sewage pipes. We don't need to buy tanks…there's four in quarry that'll do just fine." He paused again.

The committee remained silent. The only sound came from

Elizabeth's pen scratching as she scribbled furiously on her note pad.

"We'll make covers temporary-like, and when we see it's working we can order proper ones," Morley said. "We found enough piping to run collected gas to Jacob's digester and to mine. We'll put on scrubbers to clean gas later. We found pumps in quarry. That leaves installation and electrical stuff. For that we need Johnny's help, and he's agreed to sit down with Andy and complete the whole design." Morley looked up. "That's about it."

Daisy started to raise her hand again but stopped when she saw Elizabeth signaling to the Penseythan.

"You have some questions, Elizabeth?"

"Comments and questions." Elizabeth glanced at what she had written. "Let me summarize what I understand. Your two digesters are expected to deliver sixty kilowatt-hours of electricity a day…" She raised her eyebrows. "As yet not demonstrated?"

Morley and I had anticipated the comment and he quickly said, "No, ma'am, demonstrated with my digester."

Elizabeth's face tightened. "But not with Jacob's." She held up a hand to indicate she didn't want a response. "Assuming his also works, you propose to add another quarter from household sewage. In total, forty-five kilowatts to be distributed to the island's system." She scanned her notes. "My understanding is that without any of this electricity, the island consumes some five hundred kilowatt-hours daily. Thus the additional electricity from the sewage would add at most three percent." She put the notes down and stared at Morley. "That doesn't sound very cost effective."

This was something I'd worried about and had prepared an answer for Morley.

I couldn't see his face but I knew Morley was smiling when he responded, "Electricity shuts down at nine every evening. That three percent, fifteen kilowatts-hours, means one hundred and fifty watt-hours for each household…enough to keep lights on for another hour. Five hours when you add in what Jacob and I will provide."

Elizabeth pursed her lips for a moment. "Then the issue will be the cost of this electricity. Can you give me a number?"

Morley shook his head. "Not until Andy and Johnny have got together and completed the design."

Elizabeth turned to face the Penseythan. "Then I move we table this until such a number is provided."

Martha Nancarrow glanced around at the committee. "Before we vote on that, I would like to hear any other questions or comments."

Arthur Nancarrow raised his hand. "I think it's an interesting idea and I would like to find out how all the committee feels about it. I move we have a show of hands on who agrees with me and who doesn't."

He's supporting us. More evidence he wasn't head of the Maskers, I concluded.

"Do you agree that we need the costs before making a decision?" the Penseythan asked.

"Yes."

"Then I would like a show of hands before voting on Elizabeth's proposal." Elizabeth's grunt echoed around the room. "Those in agreement with Arthur please raise your hands."

Jacob Jago, Arthur Nancarrow, and Johnny Trevenna each waved a hand.

"Those not in agreement?"

Elizabeth Gay and Daisy Quick indicated their disagreement.

"I believe James Thomas, like me, is unsure." Martha glanced at James. He nodded. "I counted three generally in favor, two not, and two unsure. We will now vote on Elizabeth Gay's motion to table this proposal until we receive information on all the costs. Those in favor?"

All the Seythan members raised their hands.

Martha Nancarrow counted the hands. "I see we're all in agreement. Morley, please arrange to provide the financial information at next Saturday's meeting." She made a note. "I don't believe there's any other business." She glanced around. None of the Seythan reacted. "Thank you for attending."

I wasn't surprised that Morley's younger brother, James, had not been supportive. Hilda had hinted that the two didn't get on well. She indicated the problem centered on Morley inheriting the farm and all of the land, with James and his wife ending up as caretakers for the Trevennas.

Morley returned to his seat. "Johnny thought this might happen. He can't meet now. Got to go somewhere. He'll come to farm tomorrow afternoon. All right with you?"

"Sure. I'll work on some numbers."

On my way back to Mary's house, I noticed Johnny Trevenna going into Nancarrow's Store with Arthur. It looked like Arthur had helped get Johnny's support. Interesting.

25.

I WENT TO CHAPEL WITH MARY, NUMBERS FOR THE NEW PROJ-
ect swirling around in my brain. Isaac's sermon was a drone in
the background.

"What did you think Isaac meant?" Mary asked as we walked
to her house.

"No idea. My mind was somewhere else."

"Rose?" Mary took my arm. "She'll be back for you."

"Of course," I replied without thinking. Most of the time, certainly, she was on my mind. "Well, honestly, I was thinking about
the new sewage plant and the fact that I have to discuss it with
Johnny Trevenna."

Mary pulled away and punched me on the arm. "Sewage
plant! Wait 'til I tell Rose." She laughed. "You should have listened to Isaac. I think that's what he was going on about when he
mentioned Hercules cleaning out the Augeian Stables."

***

After a lunch of fish and chips, and treacle tart with cream, I
headed off to Morley's. On turning into his track, I spotted a
figure just short of the barn…Johnny. I took a deep breath.

I cycled up, got off my bike, and leaned it against the fence.

Johnny came forward and held out his hand. "I wanted to apologize for all things that happened to you. It went too far. I should have been smarter." His face seemed to show a genuine concern that I'd reject the apology.

I'd always imagined that the first time we met, I'd slug him. I'd even considered how to do it. I hadn't back at the rehearsal because I knew it would only make matters worse for Rose. Now I was faced with making him a friend. Again, I thought of what Rose would want. "Accepted." I shook his hand. "Thank you for doing that. I've been thinking about the costs. Not an easy task and wouldn't have been helped if we'd been at odds."

We started toward the barn.

"You do understand that I always believed Rose would be for me." Johnny turned and smiled ruefully. "It took a long time to sink in that she wouldn't."

We walked toward the barn. Fine for the King to say. "What about Midsummer's?"

Johnny grunted and continued walking. After a minute, he said, "Nothing I can do about that. Like Rose, I'll not go against traditions."

I fought back the urge to reply, 'Like your mother wouldn't stop female infanticide.' "I guess I understand." A sudden image came to mind—Jane Trevenna tumbling over the cliff to her death. I'd killed her. "Your m…mother…I'm sorry," I stuttered.

"When I heard she was gone…at first I wanted to kill you," Johnny said. "Then Cap'n Artley explained what happened. I guess you had no choice."

Further discussion was eliminated by Morley coming to greet

us. "I've shown Johnny the final plans. We're both ready to work."
He led us into the kitchen. Susan was next to the stove, pouring
hot water into a teapot. She turned and smiled. Her brown hair
was tied up with a blue ribbon that reflected the color of her eyes.
She wore a tight sweater and a short skirt. For Johnny's benefit,
I suspected.

"Hilda's gone to Portloe," Morley said by way of an explanation. "Johnny and I have worked up some designs." He pointed at
the diagrams on the kitchen table.

We sat down and Morley pushed a sketch in front of me.
"Here's what I think we need for Portloe." He indicated a spot
near the sea. "This is where we'll put the tanks. Ground's rocky,
I don't think we can bury them. Maybe half underground." He
glanced at me.

"Fine, as long as they're downhill of the last connection to the
sewer," I replied.

"Right. Now, we'll run the gas pipe alongside the sewer
through the village," Morley said. "No need to bury it until last
mile and a half through my fields."

Susan interrupted our discussion by placing a plate near to
Johnny. "Biscuits…Rich Tea."

"Thanks," he said, not looking up. "Makes sense to me." He
reached for the plate.

"Why don't you tell us about the electrics?" Morley said.

Johnny stuffed the rest of a Rich Tea biscuit into his mouth
and placed a circuit diagram in the middle of the table. "We won't
need to run any wires to the tanks before you install the scrubber.
It makes sense to install the pump at the farmhouse. The main
addition will be a system to match the output from the farm to

the hydroelectricity from the dam on the Fal. The dam's just upstream from the village and only a mile or so from the farm."

"What will this system involve?" I asked.

Before Johnny could reply, Susan appeared with a tray. Morley cleared a space and she set it down on the table—a teapot, mugs, spoons, milk, and sugar. "I'll be Mum," she said, using the common British phrase I'd heard before. "Milk first?"

We all nodded. She added milk and then poured tea into the mugs. She picked up one and leaned across Johnny so that the bulge of her breast in her sweater touched his shoulder. "Johnny, would you like me to sugar it for you?"

Johnny shifted sideways and grinned at her. "I think I can handle it."

Susan pouted. "I'm sure you can," she said.

"We need to get on with business," Morley said, shooing her away with his hand.

Johnny added sugar, stirred, and took a sip with another biscuit before continuing. "Transformer to match output of the two generators…Morley's has lower voltage than at dam. A circuit to decide levels of current required from each generator to match the load." He smiled. "One great thing about both sources is they can store energy; hot water in one case, gas in another. Wind power would be harder to fit in."

"Do you have a cost estimate, Johnny?" Morley asked.

Johnny shook his head. "Only approximate. High voltage cable from farm to dam will be a big part of it. I'm trying to track down if we have anything on the island. I checked and there's a good enough transformer in the quarry. I can cobble together controls that will do 'till I get one from mainland."

"So, how much?" I raised an eyebrow.

"At a guess, forty thousand pounds including labor."

I did a quick sum in my head…ninety thousand dollars. Shit. "I'd hoped it would be less." I turned to Morley. "What about the manual labor for tanks and pipes?"

"Five to ten thousand depending on whether we run into a problem." Morley glanced at us. "That only includes temporary covers. What do you think?"

"We're talking about fifty thousand pounds." Johnny sighed. "Jacob's system will be about the same. So, one hundred thousand pounds in total. It won't be an easy sell."

"Agreed." Morley frowned. "I need to tell Martha about the cost. She can decide who to pass on the information to before next Saturday."

"Wait," and "Hold on," came simultaneously from Johnny and me.

"You first," he said.

"We need a contingency."

"Right on," he said. "At this stage, I recommend twenty percent, mainly for the electrical part."

Morley glanced up at the ceiling. "You want me to tell her a hundred and twenty thousand?"

"Yes," we replied in unison.

"So be it."

We talked about our proposal for another hour, with Johnny giving a more detailed breakdown of his costs that Morley could use if necessary.

Morley walked with me to my bicycle, leaving Johnny with Susan. "She fancies him," he said.

"I could tell. I hope it works out." I climbed on the bike.

"So does Hilda...and me." Morley patted me on the back. "And we hope Clara can fix you up, but it's hard to tell what she's doing."

Given she'd told the Maskers about her plan to get me with Rose to Tristan, I didn't have much confidence in that. "Hmm," I muttered and rode off.

***

The next week, I spent most of my time working with Johnny and Morley refining the design and laying out the various tasks for completing the Portloe part of the new plant. It was a welcome break from brooding about Clara and my situation with Rose. Reluctant at first, I came to accept that Rose had been right when she talked to me on the bus; Johnny was not the jerk I had believed, but an intelligent, decent man.

The following Saturday, I watched as Morley, armed with a more detailed proposal, appeared before the Seythan for the second time. During his presentation, Elizabeth Gay made numerous notes.

When Morley had finished, the Penseythan asked for questions.

Elizabeth immediately raised her hand.

Martha pointed in her direction. "Elizabeth, you have the floor."

"As I understand it, each system of yours requires funding of some fifty thousand pounds. For this investment we will get fifteen kilowatt-hours a day." She paused, seemingly for effect. "I suppose that if we add in the additional amount of thirty that the two farms will supply, this might be viewed as forty-five kilowatt-hours a day." She consulted her notes. "That means that over a year, the island would receive sixteen thousand, four-hundred and twenty-five kilowatt-hours. Assuming that we had to pay back the capital at ten percent per year... and I must thank Harold for providing this information, the cost of electricity would be approximately one third of a pound per kilowatt-hour." She dwelt over saying the number. "This is far higher than we pay today. I apologize to Morley and Johnny for recommending against something they have obviously worked hard to achieve, but the proposal makes no sense."

She couldn't bring herself to mention me. The mean old.... Oh, hell, what was the use?

"Thank you, Elizabeth." Martha raised her hand as if to caution the Seythan. "We should remember that our electricity is heavily subsidized by the British government's overseas development funds. Are there any other comments...Johnny?"

Johnny shook his head.

"In that case, I call for a vote. Those in favor?"

Jacob, Arthur, and Johnny raised their hands.

"Those opposed?"

Elizabeth, Daisy Quick, and James Thomas raised their hands.

Martha smiled. "A tied vote, so it comes down to me. There is something I didn't tell you because I wanted to get a clear understanding of where you all stood."

"What?" Elizabeth expostulated.

"After Morley had briefed me on the numbers, I had the same

reaction as you, Elizabeth. Then I thought about how we could achieve the goals, because I believe the new approach to handling the sewage will improve the environment and add to our own energy supply... I radioed our governor on St. Helena and told him about our situation. He assured me that he will ask for development funds from Britain, and believes we should certainly receive at least ninety percent of the total. With those funds, the cost of electricity would be acceptable. Note also that the money would provide employment. I therefore vote in favor."

"This is trickery," Daisy exclaimed. "You should have told us in advance. I move that we delay any decision until these...these imaginary funds appear."

"Proposal heard," Martha replied. "I offer an alternative, which is that we commit to a first phase in Portloe, connecting to Morley Thomas's plant, which is already in operation. We delay the Veryan phase until the funds arrive and Jacob Jago's system is operational." She glanced around. "Are there further comments?"

Daisy glared. Elizabeth, head down, made notes. Jacob started to raise a hand then stopped.

"First we vote on Daisy's proposal. Those in favor."

Daisy raised her hand.

"Those opposed." The rest of the Seythan, with the exception of Elizabeth, raised their hands.

"One in favor," Martha said. "Five opposed and one abstention. The motion fails. Now, I ask for a show of hands for those in favor of committing to the Portloe phase, and delaying the one in Veryan."

The vote had five in favor and, not surprisingly, two opposed.

"The motion passes and the Seythan authorizes funding in the amount of fifty thousand pounds for the Portloe project." Martha pointed at Harold Anthony. "Harold please provide what is necessary from the general funds to the island's work crew and John Trevenna."

"Yes, Penseythan," Harold replied.

"Are there further comments?" Martha looked around. Nobody on the Seythan responded. "Then that concludes the meeting. Our next meeting will be on Saturday, November fifteenth, when we will discuss the Midsummer's Day festivities."

My elation at our success evaporated rapidly as images of King Johnny with Queen Rose flashed through my head. My previous hopes that Clara would solve our problem had been dashed by her betrayal of me to the Maskers.

My reverie was interrupted by Morley. "Why such a glum face, Andy?" he said. "We won."

"It's great. I was just thinking about other things."

"Oh, you mean Midsummer's? Clara will find a way. Hilda's convinced of it."

"I hope you're right."

26.

On Sunday, I declined Mary's offer to go to chapel with her. Instead, I made lunch and took it, my water bottle, and binoculars to the auk rookery. Watching the auks and their mating rituals took my mind off my troubles for an hour or more. When unpleasant thoughts began to resurface, I headed up Brown Willy. The sky was clear except for scattered clouds drifting in from the west. I stayed to the eastern side of the mountain to avoid the cold, blustery wind as I climbed to the summit and sat.

Roseland lay before me basking in the sunlight. Through my binoculars, I watched the congregation leave the chapel. Time for lunch. After demolishing my sandwich, I munched on the apple and drank some water. A nap followed and, when I woke up, I spotted activity in the Guy Fawkes field. Farm carts were lined up in the road and men were busy recreating the pile of wood and other combustibles. I wondered if anyone would add a Wicker Man. Maybe that nasty game was over. I hoped so.

Scanning further afield, I studied Portloe and the area by the sea that would house the tanks. Monday I would go there to help in their installation with Johnny Trevenna and Morley's son, Nicholas. Johnny had dispelled any thoughts that my role would be supervisory. "Be prepared for hard work," he'd said.

***

When I cycled down the track from Portloe on Monday morning, I found Nicholas Thomas digging a hole with a crew of three men. I skirted a trailer carrying one of the surplus tanks, some round logs, and what appeared to be a block, tackle, metal tripod, and slings. Tire marks from the tractor that had pulled the trailer were still visible in the dirt. The crew was preparing the downstream pad on the slope where the sewer pipe, mounted on supports, funneled down to the sea. There, we would not have to dig deep holes to position the tanks below the pipe. Today the sea was calm and a faint whiff of sewage permeated the site.

Nicholas's pickaxe looked like a toy in the hands of this giant of a man—Morley Thomas on steroids was the impression he gave me. Called Nicholas, not Nick, I'd learned: a tribute to his intimidating size, I guessed. Johnny stood among the men. Dressed in overalls and sturdy boots, he was busy shoveling out the dirt and rocks unearthed by the others.

"Grab a shovel," Nicholas said, when I'd laid my bike on the ground. I removed my parka and joined them.

The dimensions of the tanks were ten by ten foot square, and seven foot high. The hole was already two foot deep, but I could see that it had reached a rock layer in a couple of places. Johnny had explained that to go into bedrock would require explosives. While shoveling, I studied the slope and estimated that a similar hole above us could hold the second tank and still have the sewer pipe tilted down so gravity could keep everything flowing.

After another hour of shoveling, Nicholas called a halt. "Reckon, we've done enough digging," he said. "Five minute break." He pulled a pipe from the pocket of his overalls and lit it.

I sat down with Johnny and took a swig of water. While the day wasn't warm, the sun was shining and I'd worked up a sweat. "How far do you think we'll get today?" I asked.

"Probably get the one tank in. Er...," he replied. Heaving a sigh, Johnny turned to face me. "Look, the Seythan isn't going to vote you to be King. It'll be me."

"I know."

"Sorry."

Any further discussion was stopped by Nicholas, back in the hole, calling out, "We'll clean up pad and move tank."

It took another hour to level the pad to Nicholas's satisfaction. We then manhandled the trailer to just above where the second tank would sit. After erecting the tripod with its block and tackle, Nicholas attached the slings, allowing us to winch the tank off the trailer. We then pulled the trailer up the slope. Two of the crew laid wooden rollers on the ground, blocking the lowest roller with rocks. We lowered the tank onto the rollers. Three of us kept the load from sliding down the slope, while the fourth crewmember knocked out the rocks. Like a tug of war team being dragged across the line, we let the tank travel gently down to the pad. The remaining man moved rollers in front of the tank when they became free. Finally, the tank rested on the rollers on the pad.

Concentrating on not making a mistake, I stopped fretting about Johnny's statement and wishing that Rose would get back from Tristan as soon as possible.

Finally, we reassembled the tripod, block, and tackle, lifted the tank, removed the rollers, and lowered it to its final resting place. By now the wind had picked up, dissipating the sewage odor.

"Lunch break, lads," Nicholas gasped, his chest heaving from having taken much of the load. He recovered a bag from near the trailer, sat on a ledge facing away from the rest of the crew, and unloaded bread, cheese, and a bottle of pickles onto a cloth on his lap.

I sat down by him and unwrapped my ham and lettuce sandwich. "How long do you think this will take?" I asked.

Nicholas took a bite of bread, cheese, and pickle and played with his beard. "Should get first section of down-pipe in today. Tomorrow, second tank and finish connecting tanks. If all goes well, Wednesday and Thursday we'll lay in your gas pipe."

He ate some more of his lunch. His expression indicated to me he was wrestling with something. "Painters'll come and coat inside of tanks with ship's anti-fouling paint. Best I could come up with to hold back corrosion. Next Monday, we'll reroute sewer pipe into tanks." He paused and drank from a thermos.

I decided to wait and see if he'd tell me about it, and took a bite of my sandwich.

After tapping out the residue, he refilled his pipe, lit it, and took a few puffs. "Midsummer's," he said. "Not good what Seythan's up to." He looked out to sea.

I waited.

He turned back toward me. "If Rose weren't going to be Queen, it would be Susan, likely."

Taking another bite, I raised an eyebrow.

"From what I hear, Johnny's lost Rose to you. Susan would be a good match for him."

That's what Hilda had been after. "I agree. From what I've heard, she's a smart girl… But I don't see how that's going to happen unless Rose and I can get married."

Nicholas took a long drag on his pipe, blowing the smoke away from me. "Clara's going to fix it, isn't she?"

I drank some water while I worked up a response. "That's what I thought, but I expect you know the Maskers stopped me going to Tristan, and…" No point in telling him that it was Clara's doing.

"Heard that." He patted me on the shoulder. "She'll come up with something, my mum says." He stood. "Back to work." He collected his belongings and put them in the bag.

"I'm counting on it," I said without much conviction.

***

The schedule Nicholas had described turned out to be correct, and Thursday morning, I was with the crew laying the gas line alongside the sewer pipe in the creek at the upper end of Portloe. In this section, the water burbled over a rocky bed and no tendrils of grass licked the edge like upstream. I held up a section of gas pipe so that Nicholas could weld it into the line.

With the St. Just scheduled to return from Tristan, my mind wasn't on the job, and I wondered idly who lived in the cottages with corrugated iron roofs that bordered the River Fal.

"Andy, hold your end higher," a deep voice said.

I raised the pipe to make it level. "Sorry. I was daydreaming."

"Don't worry. Rose'll be here soon." Nicholas chuckled and turned on the welding torch.

In fact, I had to wait impatiently until mid-afternoon to hear the sound of the St. Just's horn as it rounded the Dodman Point.

"We can manage without you, Andy," Nicholas said. "Off you go."

"Thanks." I cycled to the harbor, trying to give the impression I wasn't frantic to get there, and arrived in time to see the St. Just negotiating the narrow passage between the rocks to the jetty. The Penseythan, Arthur, and Mary were in a group on the dock. I joined them, trying to appear relaxed and hoping I wasn't too sweaty from laboring.

The tops of the tanks we'd installed were visible across the water. I pointed, and said to the Penseythan, "See what we've already completed."

Martha got a brief glimpse before the St. Just's wheelhouse blocked the view. "Wonderful," she said. "When do you think you'll be finished?"

"Nicholas says the plumbing will be done next week. Johnny's still working on installing the controls. What with rehearsals and the play coming up, then Guy Fawkes, he thinks another week or maybe two."

She eyed me. "You two getting on?"

Good question. If she'd asked it a few weeks earlier, it would have been difficult to answer. "Yes. We work well together."

"Good."

Further discussion stopped when the boat bumped against the dock and Frankie jumped off the prow, holding a mooring rope. He tied it around a bollard and returned to catch a second rope launched onto the dock from the stern by Young Artley. My attention was soon diverted by seeing Clara and Rose emerge

---

from the wheelhouse. Rose smiled and waved. Clara's face was expressionless.

Frankie lowered a gangplank and helped his mother disembark. She walked steadily toward the Penseythan. Rose started after her.

I passed Clara on my way to Rose.

"I hope you've been studying your lines," Clara said. "Dress rehearsal's tomorrow."

I'd been too distracted to bother, and was in no mood to let her know I hadn't. "I'll be there, ma'am."

Any feelings of unhappiness disappeared when Rose appeared. I started to apologize. "I came straight from working on—"

Rose ignored my attempt to explain my disheveled appearance and came into my arms. We kissed and hugged for so long that when we stopped and glanced around, everyone else had started to leave—Mary on the Captain's arm, Clara talking animatedly to Arthur, and the Penseythan chatting to Young Artley. Frankie followed, zigzagging from side to side, mocking the way they walked.

Rose gave me one last hug and heaved a sigh. "I'm sorry," she said. "Clara tried her best, but the Maskers weren't fooled by your attempt to confuse Sam Nancarrow. And they picked up on Sandy not being chosen for the crew. They worked out what she planned."

"All very well," I said bitterly. "But the Maskers kidnapped me to prevent me going to Tristan. Their leader said that Clara had told them."

"What?" Rose shook her head. "You've got to trust Clara."

"But she told them."

"Do you believe that?"

"I don't know what to believe…. Your mum's been looking after me. I guess with you home I'll have to go back to Clara's."

"Sorry, but yes." Rose hugged me again. "Look, my car's here. I've got to go. Do you need a ride?"

"No. I biked. Can I see you this evening?"

"Probably not. Cap'n Artley got a message there are folk I need to visit."

"Tomorrow?"

"For sure. At dress rehearsal," Rose called over her shoulder.

I watched as she, Clara, and Frankie got into the Lagonda and drove off. Mary and the Captain were walking to his house near the port. I cycled back slowly, worrying about how I could face Clara.

27.

CLARA WAS NOT AT HOME WHEN I ARRIVED IN VERYAN. NOBODY locked their doors on Roseland, and it was a simple matter to gather up my belongings and move them from Mary's back to Clara's house. By now, it was approaching five in the afternoon. I assumed that Clara would be back by six to prepare supper at her usual time. To while away the hour, I sat in the living room and went over my lines.

A scuffling sound from the kitchen alerted me to the fact that Clara had returned using the backdoor. I found her there, peeling potatoes. A large fish with fluted tail rested on the draining board of the sink.

She glanced up when I came in. "Been at Frankie's," she said.

I'd had plenty of time to think about what I'd say to her when she returned. Going over various subtle ways of asking her what the hell she was up to. They all went out of my head when the moment came to confront her. "Why did you tell the Maskers I'd be in the Guy Fawkes field?" I asked, my voice rising angrily.

Clara placed the potatoes on a cutting board and sliced them carefully. "Will sauté potatoes be all right?" she asked sweetly. "With this nice fish Frankie caught as we were coming into harbor…and green beans." She glanced at me, her face showing no reaction to my outburst.

"The night I was waylaid by maskers, their leader told me you told him where I would be," I said quietly.

"I wonder why he would say that," she said sweetly.

I realized that we were in for another game like she'd played when I tried to get a copy of Romeo and Juliet. No point in fighting her. And she was my only hope. "Do you have another plan for Rose and me to get married?"

"Getting married isn't a simple matter, m'dear…. Now, can you get me the fileting knife from the drawer?"

I did, and she turned her back on me and began to prepare the fish.

End of discussion. I gave up on trying to fathom whether the masker had lied to me. "If there's nothing else I can do to help, I'll get back to studying my lines."

"That would be a good idea." She removed the fish's head with one sharp whack.

Over dinner, we talked about her trip to Tristan. Clara spoke gushingly about what Rose had accomplished. She asked me about the new sewage plants. I read until lights out, and went to bed with a dull ache in my stomach from brooding about whether Rose and I would ever be married. Despair kept me awake for what seemed like hours.

***

After breakfast, I cycled to Portloe, wearing a knapsack containing my lunch, water, script, and the clothes Clara and I had agreed to for my role as Romeo. I joined the crew and helped to complete the gas line to Morley's digester, finishing just before five-thirty at Morley's farm. Hilda insisted I have supper with them. After a rushed meal, I arrived at the Portloe village hall at six-thirty.

Rose was already there, wearing my favorite, long white dress, gathered up under her bust with a blue ribbon. Her hair was up and she wore minimal make-up. She looked gorgeous and I wanted to give her a kiss, but she motioned me away. "Everybody's been waiting for you, Romeo. You need to get changed."

I had just enough time to put on my costume to join the other actors backstage for final instructions from Clara for the dress rehearsal.

"Have you all brought your masks?" Clara asked.

I held the mask she had brought me and would put it on later. The others held up their masks, with Anthony holding up two. "I have two," he declared proudly, "for my roles as the Governor and Paris. Would you like me to show which is which?"

"No, m'dear, we can save that as a surprise," Clara replied with a faint smile.

"What if I have to stand in for an additional role?"

"In that case, use the mask of the person who is unable to perform or one of your two."

"But what—?"

"Harold, enough for now," Elizabeth Gay snapped. "It's nearly curtain time, and I have a question. I believe that I know my lines well, but there may be some less experienced." She glanced at me. "Who will be providing cues?"

"Thank you, Elizabeth for raising my next point," Clara said sweetly. "I will, when I am not onstage. Otherwise, it will be Harold. I believe he has learned the entire script."

Harold beamed. "Indeed I have. Would you like me to give an example? Pick a scene."

"Thank you, Harold, that won't be necessary," Clara said. "If there is nothing else, I will go out front now and give the prologue."

Clara walked onto the stage and parted the curtain to face the audience. I glimpsed a packed house. Clara had explained that because we'd only have two performances, it was necessary to allow all the islanders to see the dress rehearsal. The murmurings and scuffling noises stopped and to the silent hall, she said, "Our story takes place on the fair island of Verona. There, a long-standing feud between the families of Penseythan Capulet and Lady Montague turns violent. Two unfortunate young people are caught up in this maelstrom of conflict and commit suicide, ending the feud. Our players will enact this story of a doomed love, and will make up for whatever I have left out of this prologue."

Though nervous at first, I worked my way through the first act without fluffing my lines.

Harold showed a commanding presence as the Governor in the first scene of that act. He impressed me with his change of character, mask, and voice when he came on as a servant in the second scene.

A murmur from the audience accompanied the kiss I exchanged with Rose in scene five. Whether it was the fact that we kissed or the awkward meeting of our two masks, I couldn't tell. After our scene was over, Juliet talked to her Nurse, and asked who I was.

When the Nurse returned, she said, "His name is Romeo…a Montague and the only son of your family's greatest enemy."

Juliet said to herself, "The man I love turns out to be the son of the man I hate. Oh, what a monstrous fate it is to fall in love with such a foreign man."

When Rose uttered the word foreign, the audience gasped and I heard a few giggles. Martha Nancarrow, who was standing next to me, patted my arm. "Don't worry about it," she whispered. "You're not the only one who'll be the butt of Clara's little jokes."

I grinned nervously, wondering what the reaction would be to the balcony scene, which was coming up in Act II, Scene II. But the audience was quiet as I stepped down from the stage and faced the small raised area where Rose stood for the balcony scene. A smattering of applause followed our exit.

Backstage, I took a drink of water and prepared mentally for the next acting test, the marriage in what I now knew to be Clara's highly-modified sixth scene. I had survived the scene with Juliet's Nurse, Clara, finding out about my plan to wed Juliet. Then I'd listened as the Nurse informed Juliet of the plan.

Now, I waited impatiently in the wings with the Friar, Captain Artley, to go on stage and wed Juliet. At last, Rose and Clara left the stage. Stagehands went on and rearranged the set, and the Captain and I donned our masks and entered. The face on his mask resembled a sea lion with extravagant whiskers, and he wore a cowl over it.

When Friar Lawrence uttered the words, "Let the heavens be thrilled with this holy act, and nothing unfortunate follow it," I thought about my failed wedding attempt and froze.

"Amen, amen," Harold said from off stage, reminding me of my lines.

From then on I had no trouble. Rose entered and we completed the marriage ceremony, exchanging rings, and finishing by signing the papers with a quill pen. I wrote Romeo Montague with a flourish. Rose gave me a sideways glance, penned Rose Pascoe, and removed her mask.

Someone backstage, Frankie, I suspected, yelled out, "Go on, kiss her."

I didn't need any encouragement and removed my mask. This time, we kissed passionately. Someone wolf-whistled and a few in the audience clapped.

Rose whispered, "I love you, Andy."

For a moment I felt married. But Captain Artley didn't have that power. "I wish this were real," I replied.

"Patience," she said as we exited. There we handed the rings for Clara to keep until the following performance.

A ten-minute break followed while the stagehands rearranged the set for the fight scene in Act III. I had stayed out of Sam Nancarrow's way. Now, following the exchange in which Benvolio failed to persuade Mercutio to stay out of trouble, Sam, as Tybalt, and I entered from opposite sides of center stage. Mercutio then challenged Tybalt, who killed him. My pulse rate increased as it became my turn to fight.

Sword fighting with the mask on was trickier because of the reduced vision. Nevertheless, Sam and I did a passable job following the instructions we'd received. That is, up to the point when Sam failed to parry my thrust and I hit his shoulder. "Oops," I exclaimed without thinking.

Upon which, Sam raised his rapier up and ran at me, striking down at my head. Caught by surprise, I only managed to protect myself partially with my rapier and dagger. His sword hit me on the top of my head, cutting through my jaunty cap and bouncing off the metal skullcap with a tinny noise.

Slightly dazed, I fell sideways to one knee. Sam's momentum caused him to trip over my outstretched leg and fall off the center stage. The audience roared with laughter, apparently assuming this was another of Clara's little jokes. Men in the front row helped Sam back up and we finished the scene more or less as planned.

With Tybalt lying dead on the stage, Benvolio dragged me away, and told the governor what had happened. Penseythan Capulet wanted Romeo to be executed, but instead the governor fined him and ordered him into exile.

Clara took my torn cap as I left the scene. "I've got my sewing kit," she said. "I'll see what I can do temporary-like…after I've had a word with Sam. What he did was uncalled for."

"He thought I hit him deliberately," I said. "Don't be too hard on him."

"Suppose so." Clara pursed lips made it clear she wasn't convinced. I joined some of the cast out back to cool off.

Clara succeeded in making a tolerable repair by the time I returned to the stage in the third scene. From then on, the play went smoothly. At the end, believing that Juliet was dead, I took poison, and Juliet killed herself with my dagger. A thoroughly miserable ending, I thought, as it contributed to my general feeling of unhappiness. Rose, obviously sensing my mood, took my hand as we joined the cast on stage for a final bow, and we received a round of applause.

After the curtain fell, Clara told us she wanted to get together the next morning to go over a few things before the afternoon's matinee. As soon as he'd finished, the Captain came over and shook my hand. "You did right well, Andy," he said, then turned away and coughed into his hand. Further rasping coughs followed.

"You all right?" Rose asked. She didn't wait for a reply. "Go get Mum," she said to me. "I need to check on Cap'n Artley."

I found Mary in the audience and brought her backstage. The Captain was slumped in a chair. Rose said, "We'd better take him home. I'll get my medical kit from the car. See you tomorrow, Andy."

They were gone before I could say anything. Clara came up and patted me on the shoulder. "You came by bike?"

"Yes."

"When you get home I'll make you a nice cup of cocoa, and we can talk about tomorrow's performances."

Wonderful. Just what I needed. "Thanks." As I was leaving, I saw Isaac Nancarrow take Sam aside. I heard angry words. Sam hung his head and shuffled his feet. Could Isaac be telling him off again because of his attack on me? *Interesting.*

28.

Saturday, November the first, I boarded the bus with Clara and we headed for Portloe. I noticed that the Guy Fawkes bonfire pile had reached its previous height and there was no sign of a Wickerman. Thank God. Maybe the Maskers had given up on intimidating me now that there appeared to be no possibility of my marriage to Rose. I wondered why she was still optimistic about Clara coming through with a solution.

Sam Nancarrow got off the bus before me and waited to one side. When I got off, he motioned for me to come over to him. "Sorry for last night," he said. "I lost my temper. It won't happen again."

Isaac must have really reamed him out. "Understood," I said, holding out my hand. We shook and he didn't try to crush my fingers. "I'll try to be more careful, too."

Clara spent a couple of hours that morning rehearsing what she felt were rough patches in our previous night's performance.

After lunch, we dressed for the two o'clock matinee. The Captain surprised me by showing up.

Clara asked if he was up to it.

"I'll give it a try," he replied in a hoarse voice.

The Captain manfully survived all his scenes, even surprising me by signing the marriage certificate with his real name after I had penned Romeo Montague and Rose, again, had written Rose Pascoe. As we left the stage, she nudged me in the ribs. "Next performance, use your real name," she said.

Might as well. "Okay."

The play went more smoothly the second time. Sam and I managed to complete the sword fight without incident. This was to the disappointment, I suspected, of the audience, which included the island's children, who must have heard what happened in the dress rehearsal. Nevertheless, at the end, they were very appreciative, calling us back twice and clapping louder when Rose and I stepped forward. It showed the island's kids weren't as concerned as some of the adults about having a foreigner among them.

This time, I didn't have time to brood about my situation because immediately after the performance, women from across the island brought in food, cold meats, Cornish pasties, salads, and fruit pies. I joined the cast in eating supper. After a while, I noticed something. "Where's the Captain?" I asked.

"Mum took him home, "Rose replied. "She won't let him do another performance. Harold will play the Friar."

"I wonder what accent he'll use."

Rose chuckled. "Your guess is as good as mine."

In fact, he did sound different when, wearing the Captain's mask, he married us. The scene was marred by banging noises off stage at the end of the wedding ceremony, drowning out the part where the Friar says, "Do you, Romeo, take this woman…" "and do you, Juliet…" When he said, "Does anyone have just cause and impediment," some wag in the audience shouted out, "Paris does." But the words, "I therefore pronounce you to be man and wife," were uttered without interruption. I wondered what the remaining members of the Seythan, seated in the front row, felt about it.

This time, I signed Andrew Ferguson to Juliet's Rose Pascoe. Rose surprised me by removing her mask, motioning for me to do the same. When I did, she came into my arms and gave me a flamboyant kiss. Some of the audience stood and cheered. Out of the corner, of my eye I saw Friar Harold sign his name with a flourish. We exited with the Friar brandishing the marriage certificate.

"What accent was that?" I asked Rose.

"Don't know exactly," she replied. "Sounded a bit like Tristan folk. That Harold is a character. Let's ask him." We glanced around to see Harold's back as he scuttled outside.

"I'll go check." Before I could move, Rose put her arms around me and kissed me again.

To my surprise, the kiss was passionate, and she ground herself against me, not holding back like she usually did.

"I love you," she said. "Don't worry, everything's going to be fine."

When I managed to disengage, I asked, "Do you know what Clara has planned?"

She seemed about to say something, but hesitated. "Not really, but I bet it's really clever, and you'll like it," she said with a grin

"I needed a breath of fresh air." Harold's voice interrupted my response. He held the Captain's mask out. "It's uncomfortable. Did I do all right?"

"You were perfect, and we loved the accent," Rose said.

Harold beamed. "I went to Tristan once when I was a teenager. Thought I'd give it a try."

"Will you stick with it?" I asked.

"Don't know. Maybe I could do American accent, like you."

Rose raised her hand. "Wouldn't that confuse the audience?"

"Suppose so. Another time maybe."

"Set's ready. You're on," Clara said, handing me my rapier and dagger and giving me a shove toward the stage. I put on my mask and went in to face Sam. We fought in a gentlemanly fashion and then I slew him—just like Shakespeare ordered.

Harold came back as the Friar in various scenes and as the Governor and various servants. He succeeded in varying the accents in a consistent manner: Tristan for the Friar, and upper class English for the governor.

When the play was over and we had taken numerous bows, I walked out with Rose, hopeful we would have time together since Mary would be remaining with the Captain. *No such luck.* She gave me a quick peck on the cheek. "I'm going to check on Cap'n Artley," she said. "I should be able to get back tomorrow in time for chapel. See you there." She headed down the street to the Captain's house.

"The path of true love never runs smooth." Clara's voice came from behind me.

"So you think there's a solution, then," I snapped without thinking. "Like with Romeo and Juliet."

"Of course, m'dear," she said. "It all went very well. They did get married, you see."

"And then died. Wonderful."

"I'll make you a nice cup of cocoa."

"What I need is a brandy. I'm going to the pub."

"I don't think it will be open. Come on, we need to get on the bus."

Damn. Damn, and double damn.

29.

ROSE ARRIVED LATE FOR CHAPEL, SLIPPING IN BESIDE ME AFTER the second psalm.

"How's the Captain?" I whispered.

"Much better. He's gone back to sea…said the air would do him good."

"Where to?'

"Cape Town. There's a load of lobsters to sell and goods to pick up."

"So that's why Frankie's not here?"

"Yes."

I was about to ask another question when a couple in front of us turned and glared.

We joined in singing "Abide with me." Shortly afterward, Isaac started his sermon. I wasn't sure I followed what he was saying because I was thinking about the Captain's remarkable recovery. Glancing around, I noted Sam sitting with his mother. *No Sandy.* He must have gone back to crewing on the *St. Just.*

Isaac said something about the marriage at Cana and turning water into wine. Not clear whether he thought that was good or not…probably not good business for a publican. I partially suppressed a giggle. Rose elbowed me and gave a quizzical look. I grinned self-consciously.

The pastor then switched to fighting and quoted passages from the Bible: "Fighting is condoned if the opposition is evil and the cause is good; but true believers are not to fight each other but strive for peace." He was looking at Sam. "And, we are not to fight the government but are to submit to its laws and customs." Seemingly said to me.

"Don't go against the Seythan," Rose said.

"Message heard."

The service finished with yet another rousing rendition of "Onward Christian Soldiers."

After the service, members of the congregation congratulated us on our performance; also heaping praise on Clara, who hovered in the background. She invited Rose and me back for lunch, where I helped by peeling and cutting potatoes for chips to go with fried fish.

As we were finishing a delicious plum pie, Clara said, "I hear Mary's going to remain at the Captain's house."

How did she hear?

Clara tilted her head and looked sideways at me. "Rose'll be on her own."

"What are you suggesting?" Rose asked. Her voice didn't show concern.

Where are they going with this?

"Now Frankie's gone, I like having the company, but you young people should be spending more time together."

Does Clara think I should move in next door? I decided to stay out of the discussion and glanced at Rose.

Rose smiled. "I do want to be with Andy, but Clara, people would talk. We have to wait until we're married."

"Romeo and Juliet were married three times in the past two days." Clara scraped the last bit of pie off her plate.

I couldn't hold back. "In a play, not in real life," I blurted out.

"Better than nothing," Rose said. "You and I can't live together. I have my position to think of, but we should spend more time together. After we've washed up, we'll go for a long walk, then home and do a puzzle." She grinned conspiratorially.

Not exactly what I had in mind. Suddenly, the reality of our situation hit me; in two Saturdays from now, the Seythan would meet to pick the Queen and King. "And wait for Seythan to decide our fate."

"You give up too easily," Clara stated. She finished her pie. "I'll do washing up. You two go for your walk." She winked at Rose, who winked back, took my hand, and led me down the corridor.

I had the idle thought I might be participating in another of Clara's plays. "Thanks, Clara," I called over my shoulder.

We worked on a new puzzle for a couple of hours: Romeo and Juliet's wedding, as far as I could tell. In between finishing the edges and filling in the walls of the chapel, we engaged in some heavy petting. Finally, Rose heaved a deep breath and straightened her clothes. "Let's go for a walk."

I'd hoped for more, but didn't want to spoil what had been the closest we'd gotten to having sex. "Sure."

It was a balmy afternoon and we went to see the auks, and then strolled along the cliffs toward Trewince, returning as it was getting dark. Rose still seemed convinced we'd get married. On when and how, she was uncommunicative. She repeated that Mary and the Captain planned to get married and we'd live in Mary's house. When we got back there, Rose closed the front door and pointed at the coffee table. "You get started on the puzzle. I need to change."

I sat and stared at the pieces of Clara's new creation. *Obviously, this was a set up. But for what?* Rose was moving around upstairs. I ignored the distraction and started on finding the pieces of the man and woman. I'd located maybe half of them when I heard Rose coming down the stairs.

"Andy."

I looked up. Rose stood a few steps up beckoning to me. She wore a diaphanous nightie, back lit by the landing light, and nothing else. She didn't wait for me but turned and headed back up, the image of her sexy slim figure forever etched in my brain.

I now knew how the rock hopper males felt when they heard their mate's call to them on their return to the nesting ground. I shoved the table away, spilling the puzzle onto the floor, and ran to the stairs. Rose had reached the top and was turning toward Mary's room.

"Mum's bed is bigger," she said.

I had to ask. "Why now?"

"I'm tired of holding off. You're not the only one who's been frustrated. I want you to be the first. I'm not going to wait for the Seythan to act."

I had held off sex for so long, I didn't bother to think further about why Rose had chosen today. "Not just the first time, but many more," I said on reaching the bedroom. Rose lay provocatively on the bed. Words from a favorite musical of my dad's *Little Me*, about a farm boy dancing for the first time with a real live girl, came to mind. After many years, I had worked out that it was a signal to my mom of his intentions that night. As I hastily stripped, feeling slightly silly, I warbled a few bars.

The accumulation of frustration for over two years made me an impatient lover and I screwed up, literally, our first time—not enough foreplay—and I could tell it was uncomfortable for Rose

The second time, some hours later, was gentle and loving and, to my relief, far more than sexual: a feeling of being one with a woman. The kind of love, which I'd come to understand, existed between my mother and father. Afterwards, we slept in each other's arms until faint light filtered in around the edges of the curtains. We managed a third time before Rose pushed me out of bed. "You'd better go out the back way, Andy."

"Okay. Will I see you tonight?"

Rose patted my backside. "Now that you've learned to pace yourself, I hope so."

I wanted to ask her why she had slept with me, but decided not to spoil the moment.

When I crept in the back door, Clara was in the kitchen sipping a cup of tea.

"You're up?" I said.

"Lot of noise last night," she replied. "Couldn't sleep."

I'd forgotten how sounds went through the thin common walls. "I wonder what that was."

"Hmm." Clara went to the stove. "Expect you'll want a hearty breakfast."

I wolfed down the eggs, bacon, and fried bread.

When I'd finished, she said, "Charlie Gay came by late last night. He wants you at band practice for Guy Fawkes. Five in village hall."

"Okay. But first I've got to go to Morley's and help Johnny with the new sewage installation."

***

Arthur Nancarrow greeted me when I entered the hall. "You did well in play," he said. "Nice wedding, too. Harold made a fine Friar."

The state of euphoria I'd sustained since the previous night dissipated. "Pity he wasn't a real priest."

A faint smile flickered briefly. "You can't win 'em all," Arthur said, patting my arm.

"Apparently not." I wanted to ask him how he'd vote in the Seythan when they chose the King, but I thought I knew the answer. Even a friend like Arthur wasn't going to buck the system. We joined Charlie's wife Petunia, their son Roddy, and the rest of the band.

At that point, Charlie called us to order. "Seeing as we're all here, Roddy, hand out the music, please. I'm changing the order this year. To start will be *Starry Gazy Pie*, followed by *The Saints*, then *The Oggy Man*, and *Heartbreak Hotel* always goes down well with the teenagers…good bouncy tempo. We'll finish with the *Imperial March* from *Star Wars*. I'd wanted to have the new material Andy ordered, but it hasn't arrived yet. Hopefully, it'll be on the *St. Just* when it returns from Cape Town."

After we'd moved all the chairs to the side, we practiced for three hours. We tried marching in the confined space but stopped when Jacob complained his arm still bothered him and he couldn't maneuver the big drum without hitting someone. At the end of the session, I went back to Clara's. There were no lights on in Mary's house. I hoped Rose would be back later so I could sneak over.

When I opened the front door, Clara looked up from her knitting. "Rose left message." Clara tilted her head, and continued to knit while eyeing me with a faintly amused look on her face. "She's is staying with Mary in Portloe. Clinic tomorrow. Would you like some cocoa?"

I tried not to show my disappointment. "Thanks, but no. I've got to get up early to go to Morley's and help Johnny."

30.

AFTER WORKING MONDAY, TUESDAY, AND WEDNESDAY THE fifth of November, Johnny and I, and a couple of Nicholas's crew, completed the electrical part of the new Portloe sewage system. Johnny rigged up a recorder to keep track of the electrical output from Morley's farm on an hourly basis. Now, all we had to do was wait to see how it performed.

I cycled back to Veryan, feeling good. I stopped by the gate to the field where the Guy Fawkes event would be held. Islanders were already busy setting up stalls around the edges. A couple waved to me. I scanned the pile of wood. A typical figure of Guy graced its summit but not a Wickerman frame. Maybe that meant the Maskers had given up on taunting me. I sped away, anxious to see if Rose had returned so that we could go to the celebration together.

Mary came to the door when I knocked. She wore the costume I'd seen at previous such events: a long white dress with a purple belt, a folk-art necklace, and garish makeup—a Druid priestess in full regalia. "Rose is getting ready," she said. "Come back when you're dressed."

Back in my room, I put on the band uniform that Mary had stored for me, slung my trumpet across my back, and on a whim took my mask.

Rose greeted me at Mary's house, her face also heavily made up. "Don't try to kiss me," she said, backing into the living room. "You'll look as if you've been attacked by a zombie." Her low-cut white blouse and high-waisted red skirt added to the impression of a Victorian whore.

"I'll wait 'til later," I said, attempting a wink that must have degenerated into a leer.

"Dirty old man." Rose chuckled. "You're out of luck," she whispered. "Mum won't go back to Portloe until the Cap'n returns."

"Foiled again." I tried not to show my disappointment.

Mary emerged from the kitchen, stopping the discussion. "We can go now."

It was dark when we reached the Guy Fawkes field a half-hour later. Most of the islanders were already there. Illumination was provided by lights strung along the hedges and on the booths. Small fires were being used to grill sausages and fish. The booths were doing a roaring trade selling Cornish pasties and other pies, beer, cider, and soft drinks. I left my mask under the cloth-covered table from which Hilda Thomas sold slices of cake and joined the band.

Charlie Gay waited until we were lined up and raised his hand. We launched into the music *Starry Gazy Pie* and marched around the bonfire pile. Not the coordinated march of an American band on the grid of a football field, but a reasonably well-organized stroll, in which I quickly learned to stay out of the range of the larger wind instruments and Jacob's huge drum. We transitioned to *The Saints* and *The Oggy Man*, before coming to a halt in front of a raised area on which Martha Nancarrow and the Seythan stood. In the same style as Mary, the women wore Druid priestess-like costumes and heavy makeup. The men wore naval hats and chains with what I knew to be cricket whites.

Martha intoned the speech I'd heard on previous occasions. "We are gathered to celebrate the foiling of Guy Fawkes's attempt to disrupt the rule of Britain. In doing so, we remind ourselves of the need to be ever vigilant in our efforts to maintain order on our own island. God save the Queen!"

"God save the Queen!" the crowd chanted in unison.

We played the British national anthem. The islanders sang with emotion.

Beside us, someone prepared a torch and handed it to Martha. She walked over to the woodpile, saluted, then turned and plunged the torch in. Flames tore through the pile. It was then that I noticed my mask perched on the Guy's head. The fabric and papier-mâché was gone in seconds, leaving the shiny metal helmet. Some in the crowd oohed in surprise.

I soon forgot about that apparent threat, as our band celebrated by playing "Heartbreak Hotel" and then, finally, "The Imperial March" from Star Wars. As we marched away, maskers emerged from the crowd and pranced around the fire. Women with witches' masks and extravagant costumes joined them. The band went to the beer stall for a few rounds. Roddy tried to get me to alternate beer and cider. I'd been that route before and become nauseated. Saying no, I went to find Rose. She and Mary were away from the crowd and involved in an animated discussion with Martha. Rose waved me away. I wondered if they were discussing the upcoming Seythan meeting. My stomach ached, less from fear of what might happen than from hunger, and I went to get a pasty.

The steak, onion, potato, and swede pie soon filled the void and I moved on to the next requirement: a need to handle the pint and a half of St. Austell's best. I scanned the crowd to check for groups of maskers who might cause me a problem. Seeing none, I parked my trumpet by the beer stall and went to the lower end of the field to relieve myself.

Two men in masks joined me before I finished the task. I zipped up and turned to discover that two more men had moved in behind me. One of them wore a vulpine mask with jagged teeth. He had led the group when they'd burned the Wickerman. Arms grabbed me and I was frog-marched through a gap in the hedge.

"You are not wanted on the island," the Head of the Maskers said, his face hardly visible away from the bonfire. "We don't need you and your newfangled ideas about farming. The old ways have treated us fine and will into the future."

I remembered something my father had said about diseases spreading rapidly in the modern world, and couldn't resist a comment. "Why are you so sure? What about crop diseases? You an expert?"

"Fucking foreigner." The words from behind me were accompanied by a blow to my side. I doubled up in pain.

"Forget about Rose. You will never marry her. Take the next boat home. This is our last warning."

A second blow caused me to drop to my knees and I threw up. The maskers were gone when I managed to stand. I made my way through the hedge and walked slowly back toward where I'd seen Rose.

She met me half way. "You all right?" she said taking my arm.

"Not really. Maskers gave me another warning. I need to sit. Water would be good."

Rose helped me to the nearest booth and they gave me a camp chair to sit on.

"Back in a minute." She returned with a bottle of lemonade. "Sorry, will this do?"

"Thanks." I sipped it slowly.

A couple of minutes later, Clara turned up. "I saw maskers follow you down field. What happened?" she said.

"Why didn't you warn me?"

Her face took on a shifty look. "Men's area. Couldn't…. They say anything?"

"Told me to get off island and forget about Rose…. I'd never marry her."

As I'd come to expect from Clara, a faint smile flickered. "No worse for wear then?"

"Bloody sore," I said loudly, causing nearby people to stare. The effort hurt and I bent forward.

Rose rubbed my back. "Calm down, Andy."

"All's well that ends well."

When I looked up, Clara was gone. Her comment had sounded cheerful. I couldn't understand why. Did she really believe Rose and I would get married?

Rose helped me walk home and I went to bed.

***

The following morning, I cycled slowly over to Morley's farm to help Johnny with the wiring for the pump. Over the next days, with a break for the weekend, we finished the system and started it up. During this time, anxiety about the upcoming Seythan meeting began to dominate my waking hours. In spare moments, when I couldn't see Rose to calm down, for therapy I sat and watched the auks.

31.

On Saturday the fifteenth of November, Rose and I walked to the Seythan house. I tried not to show that my legs felt weak. We entered and sat three rows back. I studied the Seythan members trying to read what each might be thinking. *Waste of time.* They were chatting idly among themselves. Johnny noticed me and waved. Arthur smiled. Elizabeth looked up and stared. I half-raised my arm and fluttered my fingers. Her face took on a hard look and she turned away. My heart raced.

Rose must have sensed my discomfort, for she took hold of my hand and squeezed. "It's going to be fine," she said quietly.

"God knows how," I replied without thinking.

"You have to have faith in Clara."

I glanced around. Where was she?

Rose studied the room. "Not here…." She frowned. "I guess it's all up to me."

I wanted to ask what she meant, but Martha called the meeting to order.

"We have two items to discuss," she said. "First we'll hear from John about progress with the Portloe sewage work. I asked Nicholas Thomas to give the presentation, but he's working on something and declined. Harold will follow with details of the budget. I remind the committee that we have to decide if we have enough information to proceed with the Veryan job. John, your report please."

I'd hoped they would get the business of King and Queen over first. *No such luck.*

Johnny Trevenna picked up a notebook and some loose sheets of paper, went to the lectern, and faced the committee. "The final touches on the mechanical work were completed on Monday the third. Since then, I've been working with Andy Ferguson on the electrical components. That work was completed four days ago on the eleventh. I don't have a lot of data yet, but yesterday evening the electrical output was up by ten to fifteen percent over the case with no sewage gas. Andy and I estimate it will take a month to get the accurate numbers."

Elizabeth Gay raised her hand. "Penseythan."

"You have a question?" Martha asked.

"Two. First, how did you obtain the numbers? Second, I recollect we were promised a twenty five percent increase, which frankly, in any case, I believed to be inadequate for the expenditure." She turned to look at Martha. "And that was regardless of where the funds came from."

Johnny nodded his head. He and I had expected these questions. "Thank you for anticipating the additional information we had prepared. As to the first, I set up a recorder that keeps track of the electrical output every hour. I took the average over the two days before we started the gas flow from the sewage tanks. The ten to fifteen percent is the increase observed over the following two days. As to the level, Andy calculates that it will take a number of weeks for the anaerobic sewage treatment to reach maximum output...." He paused as if having finished, then added before anyone could interrupt, "In fact, the hourly output shows a steady rise." Johnny collected up the loose paper and handed a sheet to each member of the Seythan. "I've plotted the hourly readings, I apologize that it's hand-written, but you can see the progress we've made."

Martha studied her copy. "Impressive. Any other questions or comments before we hear the budget numbers from Harold?"

Elizabeth glanced at Daisy Quick. I suspected they'd planned more queries. Daisy shook her head.

"I think it looks good," Jacob Jago said. "And I hope the Seythan will see fit to get started on the Veryan system."

"Thank you, Jacob. We will take that up after the budget. Harold."

Harold went to the lectern with a pile of notes.

Martha raised an eyebrow. "Just the summary, Harold, please."

Harold's shoulders slumped slightly. "The work came in on budget," he said. "Electrical a little more than anticipated. Mechanical work a little less because of availability of surplus equipment." He straightened up.

"He's going to give a lecture," Rose whispered.

"You see, there were four tanks and sixty-four lengths of piping, which is four times four times four, and four—"

"We understand, Harold," Elizabeth snapped. "There were a lot of fours. What is your point?"

Rose chuckled. "She shouldn't have asked."

"Elizabeth, I'm glad you asked. In some cultures, the number four is unlucky. It's called "Tetraphobia." Fortunately, we don't suffer from it, but in Japan, four sounds like the word for death. Elevators may not show a fourth floor, and—"

"As you say, we don't believe in that superstition," Martha said. "I understand you have a handout with the budget?"

Harold's shoulders slumped again and he collected up eight pieces of paper, which he handed out.

"Thank you, Harold. Now I would like us to consider whether to proceed with the Veryan stage. Is the committee satisfied that we've seen enough information to go ahead?"

"Yes," Jacob said.

Daisy waved her hand vigorously. "No. I want to see the full twenty-five percent achieved before I'll support it."

"A show of hands from those who believe we're ready."

Jacob and Johnny indicated yes. Arthur hesitated before raising his hand.

"Those against?"

James Thomas, who had remained silent to that point, spoke. "I congratulate Johnny and Nicholas for coming in on budget, but I agree with Daisy. We should see Portloe working at full level first."

Daisy and Elizabeth each raised a hand in support.

"A tied vote." Martha studied the table. "While I am sure we will eventually receive government funding, it hasn't come yet. I am going to go with being cautious. We will discuss Veryan next month. Thank you John and Harold for good presentations." She pushed one set of notes to the side. "Now to Midsummer's Day."

I attempted to breathe steadily. Rose squeezed my hand. "Have faith," she said.

"How? Where's Clara?"

"Don't know."

Without Clara coming up with some magical logic as to why I should be King, I couldn't see how it could work out well.

Martha gaveled the table to quiet the audience murmuring, which had grown in intensity. "The order of business is to select the King and Queen for Midsummer's Day. We will start with the King. In lengthy discussions across the island, over the last seven or eight weeks, I winnowed the candidates down to two: Andrew Ferguson, nominated by Clara Quick and others, and John Trevenna, nominated by Elizabeth Gay and others. I call on Clara to give the qualifications of the first nominee." Martha glanced around the room. "Is Clara here?"

"I don't think so," someone called out from the back of the room. "She was, but left a few minutes ago to check on something at home."

Martha sighed. "That makes it very awkward. "

Clara had deserted me. The whole thing had been another of her games. "Why?" I said more loudly than I'd intended.

Rose put an arm around me. "There's a reason."

"We'll return to Andrew," Martha said. "Elizabeth."

Elizabeth stood. "We have known John all his life. He is a Roselander, not a foreigner, a fine young man and son of a Penseythan who guided us through difficult times. The island has paid for his education and he will serve us as our expert in the electrical area for many decades. There is no one more worthy of playing the role."

"Eloquently put." Martha's lips compressed. "I'm not sure how to handle this. Can someone else speak up for Andrew?"

The murmuring rose up again. Finally, I heard a chair scraping as someone stood. I looked around. It was Charlie Gay. "I don't know what's happened to Clara," he said, "but I know what she and I and many other islanders think about young Andy. I've known him through the band for many years. He's a fine young man, an asset to the band, and an asset to Roseland because of his training in agriculture." Charlie hesitated. "I'm not supposed to say this, but it doesn't matter that he's a foreigner. He and Rose are in love and they would have been married if certain people hadn't interfered." He sat.

The murmur became a roar as people argued about what he'd said. Martha, who appeared to be tearing up a sheet of paper, let the hubbub die down before using her gavel again. "Thank you, Charlie, for your eloquent support of Andrew. This is a very awkward situation and I am going to start with a secret ballot so I can understand what the Seythan thinks." She passed out a small piece of paper to each member. "Write your choice on the paper and hand it back to me."

The Seythan members took their time responding. Martha collected the answers and studied them. "Four in favor of John Trevenna, two for Andrew Ferguson. My vote will not affect the answer. John Trevenna will be King.

Johnny looked at me and raised his hands in supplication. I shook my head. "I expected it," I mouthed.

Rose put her head on my shoulder. "I don't think Clara could have changed that vote."

On thinking about it, neither did I.

"We will now discuss the Queen," Martha said. "Again, I winnowed the proposals down to two. Rose Pascoe, nominated by Mary Pascoe and others...."

I hardly heard the mention of Susan Thomas. Mary was in it, too. What the hell was happening?

"Mary, will you come forward. Is Mary here?"

Rose stood. "No. My mother asked me to speak in her place. In the simplest terms, I cannot be Queen."

A stunned silence was followed by a clamor of people asking why. Martha had to gavel five times before it was quiet enough for her to say, "Explain your statement."

Rose held out her hand and pointed at the wedding ring I'd placed there during the play. "Because I am married to Andrew Ferguson."

The silence was broken by Elizabeth Gay. "When?"

"Two Saturdays ago. You were a witness."

Elizabeth rose to her feet. "What nonsense is this? Are you referring to that marriage in *Romeo and Juliet*?"

"Yes."

"You're claiming that Harold Anthony had the authority to marry you?"

"No."

Everyone turned to look at Harold. He stood. "I wasn't the Friar," he said, grinning.

Martha raised her hand. "Then who was?"

"The Reverend Thomas Martin from Tristan." Clara's voice came from the back of the meeting room, where she stood with Mary. Everyone turned to stare. "And Mary and I were the witnesses, as were most of you."

"Do you have a signed marriage certificate?" Martha asked.

Rose opened her purse and removed a document. "Here."

"Please bring it up to me."

Rose complied.

The Penseythan studied it. "This appears to be legitimate. I will need to consult with the Reverend Martin to confirm its validity."

She pointed at Rose and me. "If this turns out to be a hoax, there will be consequences for you and other perpetrators." Her arm swung round to point at Clara. Following the gesture, she said, "In the circumstances, since we need to choose a Queen, I propose we appoint Susan Thomas pro tem. All in favor." She raised her hand.

Daisy, Elizabeth and James hesitated, but soon followed after Jacob and Johnny, smiling broadly, raised their hands. Arthur sat staring blankly at the audience.

"Arthur." The Penseythan's voice rang out through the hushed room.

Arthur raised his head. "Sorry, I was taken aback." He raised his hand.

I felt as dazed as Arthur looked. Obviously, for the past weeks, I had been jerked around by Clara's plot. She had always planned to betray me to the Head Masker. Then he would be convinced she'd given up on getting Rose and me married, and not realize that the marriage would take place in the play. *Wait up.* Everyone on the boat must have known about the Reverend Martin. That meant the Captain, Young Artley, Frankie and, *God dammit,* Rose. I turned to face her.

"Yes, I knew." Rose took hold of my hand. "The only way Clara would help was if we all agreed to tell you nothing. She was concerned you would give it away. You had to look miserable. I'm sorry."

Mixed emotions raged in my mind. On the one hand, I felt like an idiot and wanted to strike out at the people who'd made a fool of me. On the other, I was elated that at last Rose and I were married. "I should have guessed when you slept with me." I leaned over and gave her a quick kiss.

Rose grinned. "Thank Clara. I wasn't sure about it. She said she was worried that in frustration you'd do something stupid."

I sat quietly for moment, thinking about everything that had happened. *The library card?* "What was all that business with the library card?"

"Two reasons. First, it was all a game because she didn't want you to see Shakespeare's play." Rose chuckled. "It doesn't have a marriage scene. And second, underneath was a backup marriage license in case signing for the marriage during the play got messed up. Also, it was to protect against someone destroying the certificate that Martha has."

I remembered a comment from weeks earlier. "Because Martha and the Head of the Maskers may be too close?"

"I don't know where you heard that. Best forget it."

Any further discussion was prevented by a stream of people wanting to congratulate us. When the last one had left, I looked around for Clara. She was standing with Mary at the back of the room, a smile on her face.

"Clara," I said when Rose and I reached them. "Thank you. I should have had more faith." I put my arms around her and hugged. Another thought struck me. "Why do the ceremony in the play? We could have met the reverend on the boat."

Clara held me away and smiled a gleeful smile. "And take away the fun of doing it in front of them all?" She then uttered the words I'd heard on my previous stay on the island. "You played your part very well." Her eyes twinkled briefly. "Now I have to let you go. I'll miss your company."

I hadn't thought about that. "I'll miss you, too."

"Don't get carried away," Mary interjected. "You're only moving next door. As I promised, I've transferred the house to Rose. I'm moving out today."

"Will you and the Captain get married?"

"Soon as he returns from Cape Town."

"Wonderful."

"By the way, I'm staying with Frankie tonight," Clara said and pointed a finger at Rose and me. "You two can make all the noise you like...and don't worry about Mrs. Edwards on the other side." She chortled. "She's deaf."

With those encouraging words bringing a smile to our faces, Mrs. Rose Ferguson and I started our married life.

32.

Rose and I settled into Mary's old place, our new home. We went to chapel on the Sunday following the Seythan meeting. Isaac's sermon had a theme of marriages. We decided that he was giving us his blessing but, as always, his allusions were confusing and we may have been wrong. Many in the congregation congratulated us, and when we reached our front door, we found a pile of presents.

"I'll write the thank-you notes," Rose said. "You can sign them."

"Bless you, my child-bride," I said without thinking, receiving a sharp jab in the ribs.

"Now help me carry them in."

***

The next morning I woke late, feeling warm and relieved that the months agonizing about Rose were over. I heard the sound of the Lagonda entering the square as I reached sleepily across the bed. Rose was already up, and when I got downstairs, she was at the front door.

"See you later," she said. "I'm going back to Portloe."

Somehow, Rose being away for her work didn't concern me as much now we were married. I rushed over. "I'm going to cycle over to Morley's the get Douglas to telegraph my parents about our marriage." I imagined my mother's reaction. "Hope Mom can handle not being there. Will you be back for dinner?"

"Yes. I've left instructions on the kitchen table." She gave me a peck on the cheek and was gone.

I really am married, I thought, *and it feels good.* My breakfast of tea and toast with strawberry jam was interrupted by a knock on the front door. I opened it to find Frankie, his normally smiling face serious.

"There's problem," he said.

Knowing what was expected, I led him into the kitchen and made him a cup of tea.

"There is?"

Frankie took a long swig of tea. "There's blight hit plants," he said. "Our potatoes got problems."

I had a vague recollection of Elizabeth bitching about some problem. Also, Morley had indicated the issue was with tomatoes. But he hadn't seen any signs with his plants, and I'd forgotten about it. "Just potatoes?"

"Tomatoes, beans, and more."

"What are the symptoms?"

"Spots, blotches, wilting. All sorts."

I thought hard about a course I'd taken on plant diseases, and wished I'd had my *Westcott's Plant Disease Handbook* that the Maskers had dumped in the sea. *Please God let the replacement be on the boat.* "It could be many things. Can you show me something? I'll come with you right now."

"That's not all." Frankie put down his cup. "Some people are saying you're responsible."

"What? How?"

"They say disease came from States. Equipment you shipped to Morley was contaminated."

"That's absurd. When did your problem show up?"

"Started a few weeks ago while I was on Tristan. Came to head yesterday. What with play and everything, I didn't want to bother you before."

"Where can I best see the damage?"

Frankie headed for the kitchen. "Quick farm."

I followed him out the back door and over the fields to the north of where we'd celebrated Guy Fawkes Day. Even from a distance, I could see the splotchy, yellow patches on the leaves of a potato crop beyond the metal gate in a field a couple of hundred yards short of the Quick farmhouse, a sprawling, single-story building with a corrugated iron roof. We went up to the gate beyond where the ashy remains of the Guy Fawkes bonfire covered the grass in an untidy pile.

"I can see enough from here for the moment," I said. "I don't want to risk spreading it."

"Do you know cause?" Frankie asked.

"Not good news," I said. "It looks like alfalfa mosaic virus."

"What can we do about it?"

"I don't want to say too much without my disease book. I'm hoping it'll be on the boat." I studied the potatoes and tried to recall what Westcott's said. "From memory, and don't quote me, precious little to cure it. If I'm right, the contaminated plants might have to be destroyed."

At that point, a memory came back to me. "How about tomato plants on the Gay farm?"

"Ruined," Frankie replied. "Miss Elizabeth's the one spreading the rumors."

"Anyone else?"

"Dunno."

I tried to recollect the order of the dates I'd heard something. Elizabeth's snide remark had been at play rehearsal, week of October fifth, likely Wednesday the eighth. At that time, Morley hadn't had any plant issues. The Quick potato problems had occurred after October sixteenth when Frankie went to Tristan. *Interesting*. I needed to go find out about the state of Morley's peas and beans. But first I would check if there were any useful books in the library. "I'm going to see Clara. Find some other books on agriculture."

When I reached the library, Clara was busy or pretending to be busy filing returned books to their allotted places. "Where do you keep books on agriculture?" I said.

She stared at me for a moment. "You might try the A-shelf," she said hopefully. "Anything in particular?"

"Plant diseases."

"P or D might be better." She glanced away. "Might not do you any good. I think Elizabeth Gay has the one you're looking for."

"How long has she had it?"

"I'd have to check sign-out book."

"Would you do that, please?"

Clara got to her feet and went to her desk. She opened a book on the table and started leafing through it. "Here it is... October ninth."

So Elizabeth knew about the problem back then. *How?* I concentrated on remembering everything that had happened prior to that date, eventually recalling an off-the-cuff remark of Young Artley about maskers nearly dumping plants for Elizabeth along with my belongings. They were a likely source of the disease. She knew it and was trying to shift the blame to me. I'd have to be very careful. This situation could damage my image as the island's agricultural expert—a person to be consulted if there were any problems in that area. "Would you ask her to return the book?"

"I'll try, m'dear." Clara's expression and tone of voice changed. "Tell me why you need it all of a sudden."

"Frankie says that Elizabeth Gay's spreading a rumor that the equipment I shipped to Morley brought in a disease affecting her tomato plants."

"I think I may have heard something about that, but I've been so busy with play and getting you and Rose married, it slipped my mind. What do you plan to do?"

"I suspect the disease was carried by ornamental plants for Elizabeth that came in on the *St. Just* with me on September seventeenth. Then spread to her tomato crop by October eighth and showed up on the Quick potatoes sometime after October sixteenth. I'm off next to see if Morley has had any signs of the disease. He hadn't earlier." I had a thought. "Could you find out who else has a problem and when they detected it?"

"You believe the disease is spreading east, with the wind being in that direction most of the time?" Clara smiled. "I think I could find out without arousing suspicion."

Smart woman. "Yes, and if I'm right and it is alfalfa mosaic virus, it would be carried by aphids blown in that direction. But I need a book that spells this out. I'm hoping that Dad has shipped me one and it'll be on the *St. Just*.... I'd better get going to Morley's. Can I borrow your bike?"

"Certainly, m'dear." Clara returned to filing.

***

Morley wasn't visible when I cycled into his farmyard. I went to the front door and knocked. Hilda opened the door. She held a mop and could have been the British World War II land-girl I'd seen in one of my father's old National Geographic magazines, with a scarf over her hair, a brown shirt and dungarees.

"Morley's in Portloe," she said. "Elizabeth Gay called a meeting of farmers to discuss this blight that's hitting everybody."

Damn the woman. "You've had problems then?"

"Yes, 'bout week ago, Morley noticed white patches on beans and then peas. He was going to tell you, when Elizabeth contacted him."

"Can you show me?"

Hilda put down her mop and led me past the barn to where rows of peas and beans were laid out.

Before we reached the plot, I could see that the plants were stressed: yellow dots on the beans, streaking on the stems and leaves of the peas, and wilting. From memory, I suspected it could be the mosaic virus. "Has it affected the yield much?"

Hilda scratched her chin. "Beans not too much. Peas when pods are discolored, I reckon."

"I'm waiting for my book on diseases. Hope it'll be on the boat. I think I know what it is, but I don't want to guess unless I have to."

"Right to be cautious. Would you like a cuppa?"

"Sure." I wondered why Elizabeth had held her meeting in Portloe rather than Veryan. As we returned to the house, I concluded it might be to draw attention away from the direction in which the disease had spread.

The reason for inviting me in became clear as soon as we were seated with tea and slices of a delicious sponge cake. "Morley and I are real delighted Clara fixed for you and Rose to get married. Susan is, too."

This was about Susan. "How does she feel about being Queen?"

Hilda chuckled. "A bit nervous about the you-know-what."

I knew what—sex with Johnny Trevenna. "I guess somebody's given her advice."

"I was queen once, and talked about what I did." Hilda gave a lopsided smile. "Martha kindly volunteered, too."

"I'm sure she'll do just fine."

I didn't want to spend much more time on this topic, and was saved by Morley's return.

"Saw your bike," he said. "We need to talk."

"Elizabeth's plotting something?"

"Yes. She wants to blame you and me for bringing disease in on equipment you sent me." He made himself a cup of tea. "Trying to get Martha to hold special session of Seythan to discuss it."

"Like a Salem witch trial?"

"Suppose so." Morley's face showed no understanding of the allusion.

"When?"

"It'll have to be a Saturday." Morley went over to a calendar hanging on the wall. "Either next Saturday, the twenty-second, or the twenty-ninth."

I did a quick calculation. The *St. Just* had left for Cape Town on the second, stopping at Tristan to let the Reverend Martin off. They should be back well before the twenty-second. Nevertheless, I didn't want to risk it. "Can you persuade Martha to delay to the twenty-ninth? I need a book that should be coming on the boat."

"I'd need a reason."

"You would like to attend but...." I couldn't think of a reason. "Is there something needs to be done on the farm?"

Morley scratched his head. "I'll try and think of somethin'."

He didn't sound particularly helpful. "Is there a possible issue with your herd?"

"I could talk to Isaac," Morley said.

Why Isaac? I must have looked puzzled because Morley continued, "He's closest to vet on island."

Interesting. The reverend butcher with the abattoir also doubled as a veterinarian.

"Failing that, maybe Clara could," Hilda said.

"I'll talk to her." Relieved at having two activities to undertake, I took my leave and headed for the radio station.

***

Clara wasn't in the library when I got back to Veryan, nor was she at home. I hoped she was out checking where else the disease had occurred. An optimistic feeling enveloped me as I returned to what was now my house. Settled on the sofa, I made notes on what I knew about the spread of the disease. A quickly sketched map with locations and dates of occurrence gave visible clarity to the location of the first outbreak—the Gay farm. The direction of the transmission was consistent with the prevailing winds from the west and infection by insects, likely aphids.

Rose came in as I finished a set of notes. "Have you heard?" she said.

I held up my analysis. "Yes, and I've worked out what happened." I explained my conclusions.

Rose sat next to me and studied my map. "Makes sense. Do you have back up from some authority on plant diseases?"

Damned good question. "No. Elizabeth Gay took out the only book in the library, but I'm hoping my new agricultural books will be on the St. Just."

"That Elizabeth." Rose sighed. "She just won't give up. I wish I understood why she has it in for you."

"I'm a foreigner."

"Suppose that's it. Other than this," she pointed at my notes, "what else are you doing?"

"Morley's going to see if he can get the Seythan meeting delayed to give me more time to prepare…find out about other outbreaks. I tried to find Clara to ask for her help. Other than that, it's waiting for the boat."

"We'll work it out," Rose said, giving me a hug and pressing against me, hinting of another exciting night in bed.

33.

ON A BLUSTERY WEDNESDAY, THE SOUND OF A DISTANT HORN signaled the imminent arrival of the St. Just. Rose was working and Clara kept me company on the dock. I stayed in the back of a crowd of islanders eager to collect their goods. Women restrained their children from getting to near the edge.

A cheer went up when the boat appeared around the point and made its turn into the narrow passage through the rocks and past the lobster pens. Young Artley, at the bow, and Sam Nancarrow, at the stern, stood ready to toss the mooring ropes to men prepared to secure the boat to the bollards.

Captain Artley angled the boat in and then applied reverse propellers with a turn of the rudder to bring the St. Just to a stop against the dock. As soon as the boat was moored, the crowd surged forward. Clara and I held back.

Young Artley, Sam, and various helpers unloaded the cargo, and islanders departed with their treasured belongings. After a frustrating wait, Captain Artley worked his way through the remaining crowd. He was holding a package and looked troubled. "Andy," he said. "This is your music, I think."

"What about my books? Did they get to Cape Town?"

He scowled. "Yes. There was another large parcel from your father. I know we loaded it but…Young Artley searched high and low. He couldn't find it."

Oh shit. It had to be Sandy Nancarrow. When would they leave me alone?

Before I could ask, Clara spoke up. "Did you ask Sandy about it?"

The Captain scanned the horizon. "Yes. He couldn't explain it."

"I'll speak to Isaac," Clara said. She turned on her heels and went to the waiting bus.

Was that clear proof that Isaac was Head Masker or merely that as Sandy's father, he might be able to make Sandy divulge what he'd done with my books, much as he'd got Sam to apologize for the sword incident? I still couldn't tell. Either way, I didn't care as long as I got them back. And what if Sandy hadn't "mislaid" them?

I had to wait until Thursday night for a partial answer when a knock on the front door interrupted my dinner with Rose. I went to the door and found Young Artley clutching a large package wrapped in brown paper.

"I got an anonymous message," he said. "Package was hidden behind tanks we use to transport lobsters. I hope it's what you need."

I quickly tore off the wrapping. An envelope with a letter from my parents was the first item I came across. In it, they expressed delight at my marriage and said that they still planned to come in January. I set the letter aside and scanned the books, which were in a box, spine up. Scanning them, I soon found *Westcott's Plant Disease Handbook*. "Thanks a million. Exactly what I need." I clasped Artley's hand and shook it vigorously.

"Glad to be of help," he said.

I had a sudden thought. "Can you check the manifest for cargo on September seventeenth? Find out what plants Elizabeth Gay had shipped to her."

Artley looked puzzled for a second. "Will do. She ain't going to like it." A joyous smile spread across his face. "Say hello to Rose. Need to get back to help Patsy with the kids." He was gone.

I left the box on the table in the living room and went to the kitchen to get a knife, meeting Rose in the hall.

"You can finish eating first," she said gently, taking my arm. "The books will still be there."

After dinner, I studied Westcott's and confirmed my belief that the disease was alfalfa mosaic virus. Two ornamental host plants, ornamental peppers and pachysandra, appeared to be good candidates as carriers. I hoped they would show up on the *St. Just's* manifest.

Rose kissed me on the back of the head. "I'm going to bed," she said. Her tone of voice carried an invitation.

I wanted to go with her, but worries about the next Seythan meeting held me back. "I need to finish this. I'll be up soon as I can."

After checking my other books for further information, I added to my set of notes. Around nine, I followed Rose to bed.

***

Friday lunchtime, Clara dropped by with information on other places to which the disease had spread and when. The most recent sign of the virus was on a row of beans Douglas Billing had planted by the radio station. Clara informed me that Charlie Gay had called band practice for that evening in the Veryan village hall. After she left, I made notations on my map. To my eyes, the source of the infection was clear. Now all I needed was evidence from the manifest.

Following a hastily eaten dinner with Rose, I walked over to the hall.

Charlie greeted me at the door a worried look on his face. "I don't know what's come over Elizabeth," he said. "She's always been stubborn, but this is ridiculous. She's not speaking to Clara and can't accept that you are here to stay with Rose."

I didn't want to divulge my plans to counter her and merely said, "I think I can handle the situation."

Charlie looked relieved.

"This will make you feel better." I handed him the new sheet music. "It's John Williams's music for the movie *Superman*."

"Thank you, Andy." He beamed with delight. "Best wait for next rehearsal. Give members time to practice their part."

He ushered me into the hall. The rest of the band was waiting.

"New music from States, courtesy of Andy," Charlie said. A smattering of applause followed his announcement. He set the music down on the stage. "Tonight we'll practice for Midsummer's. *Floral Dance* of course, *Lamorna* and *Oggy Man* during interval. Later I'll fit in one of the new pieces. *Can you Read my Mind* is right pretty."

We practiced until eight, when I went home. Rose was in the kitchen going over reports on her patients.

"Cap'n dropped by and left this note," she said, handing me a sheet of paper.

I scanned it and read, "Ships manifest for Wednesday, September seventeen included a pachysandra and ornamental peppers for Mrs. Elizabeth Gay." It was signed *Captain Hartley Billing*. "Bingo," I exclaimed. "One of those is likely culprit."

Rose indicated she needed to continue working. Relieved that I now had all the pieces to explain the alfalfa mosaic virus outbreak, I went to bed and soon fell asleep.

***

The Seythan convened at ten on Saturday morning. I sat with Rose, Frankie and Morley. I held my copy of Westcott, and a sheaf of notes with copies of the map, which Rose and Clara had helped me make. Clara, Cap'n Billing, and Mary were two rows back.

The Penseythan called the meeting to order. "We have three items of business. First is the question of the legitimacy of the marriage of Rose Pascoe and Andrew Ferguson. I have talked by radio with the Reverend Martin. He confirms that, while it was an unusual ceremony, he did marry them during the final performance of *Romeo and Juliet*. If there are no questions, I will move on to the second item, funding of the new sewage system in Veryan." She paused.

Elizabeth Gay studied some papers in front of her. Daisy Quick pursed her lips.

"No questions. Good.... Seeing that matter is settled, I call on

John Trevenna to present the data on the Portloe sewage set up."
Martha turned to Johnny. "You may remain here."

Johnny passed out a sheet of paper to each Seythan member.
"Here are the numbers for electricity production from the new
system," he said. "As projected, the kilowatt-hours eventually increased by about twenty-five percent over what Morley Thomas
gets from the manure."

Daisy raised her hand. Martha motioned for her to speak. "It
seems strange to me that you would get exactly what you predicted."

Johnny nodded in acknowledgment of the question. "Thank
you for asking. Let me clarify. The average is about twenty-five.
The lowest was twenty-one and the highest was twenty eight percent."

Daisy pursed her lips again.

"Are there other questions or comments?" Martha glanced
around. "If not, let me add that I have heard from the governor.
He assures me that funding will be coming for up to eighty percent of the cost of the two installations. I would like a vote now
on whether to proceed with the one in Veryan. Those in favor?"

Jacob Jago, Arthur Nancarrow, the Penseythan, James Thomas, and Johnny Trevenna raised their hands.

"Those opposed?"

Daisy and Elizabeth shook their heads.

"Five in favor with two abstaining. The motion passes." Martha made some notes. "Now to the final item. The disease that has
infected many crops on the island. Elizabeth Gay introduced this
topic and wishes to comment on the problem. Again, Elizabeth,
please remain up here while you speak."

Elizabeth Gay stood and stared at me. She picked up her notes and read, "On September seventeenth, a shipment of equipment from the United States was delivered to the farm of Morley Thomas. Since that time there have been outbreaks of what I believe to be the alfalfa mosaic virus." She held up a book, which I guessed was the one from the Veryan library. "I cannot prove it but, based on the chapter on crop diseases, the evidence suggests that the disease came in on that equipment." She pointed at me. "I propose that the shipper, Andrew Ferguson, should be held responsible and pay for the damages." She sat down, her expression triumphant.

Martha sighed visibly. "Before we hear a response from Mr. Ferguson, do any Seythan members wish to comment?"

Daisy Quick, Johnny, and Jacob raised their hands.

"Daisy?"

"This just shows the problems we get when we allow foreigners to meddle in our affairs. Many of us have not forgotten what that Russian Pavlov did to Petunia. And—"

Martha cut her off. "Daisy. This is not the time for that discussion. Johnny?"

"Precisely for that reason, we should hear what Andy has to say. He is the…our expert on agriculture."

"Jacob?"

"I agree."

"Mr. Ferguson, please present your information."

Thank you Johnny and Jacob. Up to that moment, I had been nervous. Now, knowing I had support and Elizabeth had nothing substantial, I stepped confidently up to the lectern. I held out Westcott. "This book has been an authority on plant diseases since 1950," I said. "I have been around the island and looked at numerous affected-plants, and I agree with Mrs. Gay. The problem is the alfalfa mosaic virus. However, it is extremely unlikely that it arrived on the equipment I shipped." I glanced at Elizabeth Gay. "Much more likely is that it came in on a host plant or plants."

A worried look flickered across Elizabeth's face. She appeared ready to comment but didn't.

"In that regard, I have a note on the *St. Just's* manifest of September seventeenth from Captain Billing. It lists a shipment of pachysandra and ornamental peppers for Mrs. Elizabeth Gay." I held up Westcott. "Both of these plants are known hosts for the virus."

A murmuring erupted but quieted when Elizabeth snapped out, "That doesn't prove they were the carrier."

Martha motioned for her to calm down. "Please continue, Mr. Ferguson."

"I would like the committee to look at this map I have prepared, which shows the spread of the disease." I walked forward and handed the maps to Martha. She distributed them.

"The first time I became aware that there might be a problem was at a play rehearsal on October eighth when I overheard Mrs. Gay make a comment to John Trevenna and others about damage to her tomato"—I was careful to use the British pronunciation—"plants."

"This is ridiculous," Elizabeth muttered. "I have no recollection of any such thing."

"A day later, Mrs. Gay took out that book on plant diseases from the library." Elizabeth's head sank briefly. "The librarian can confirm that...and the book has not been returned yet."

Martha glanced at Johnny and raised an eyebrow.

His forehead wrinkled and, after a moment, he said, "I remember the conversation at rehearsal."

The murmuring increased briefly.

Thank you again, Johnny. That having been settled and Elizabeth having lost some of her credibility, I continued, "The next outbreak I heard about was from Frankie on the Quick farm's potatoes sometime after October sixteenth. Later, on November sixteenth, an outbreak occurred on peas and beans at Morley Thomas's farm. With the help of a number of people, I obtained the places and dates of other outbreaks. They are all shown on your maps. The arrows indicate the time spread of the virus from west to east. The disease is spread mainly by aphids, and I note that the prevailing wind is in that direction. I think the implication of this is clear."

Elizabeth stood and tore up her map. "It is clear indeed. My plants were shipped with your equipment and received the disease from that."

I had anticipated the response. "Such a transmission is highly unlikely. Anyway, I was on the boat. Your plants were delivered after my equipment was stowed in the hold. They were kept on deck by the wheelhouse and given to you before my equipment was unloaded. I'm sure the Captain could confirm that."

"Andy's right." The Captain's voice boomed out from behind me.

Elizabeth shook her head in frustration. "Does anyone accept Mr. Ferguson's self-seeking assertions?"

Martha looked relieved at having to make a decision on getting a vote. "Elizabeth has asked a good question. Who on the Seythan believes that Mr. Ferguson's assertions are unsupported?"

Elizabeth raised her hand. She stared at Daisy, who looked down and studied a fingernail.

"Who considers Mr. Ferguson's assessment to be well founded?"

Jacob, Arthur, James, and Johnny quickly raised their hands, supporting me. Daisy glanced at Elizabeth and raised hers. Martha followed suit, saying, "It seems a majority favor Andy Ferguson's explanation." She turned to me. "On behalf of the Seythan, thank you for your careful analysis. The question now is what to do. Please would you give us some advice?"

"Thank you, Penseythan and members of the committee. I regret to have to tell you that there is no treatment for this virus, and spraying the aphids is also ineffective. I know that some of you have already taken action to remove the damaged plants. That work must be completed. The plants should either be burned or, if you can guarantee high enough temperatures, composted. In some cases, the digesters at the Jago and Thomas farms might be used. As an added precaution, disinfect all tools and transport used. Finally, it will be necessary to get new seeds for all the crops. I recommend ordering them as soon as possible."

I paused to consult my notes. "One other thing. As you can tell from its name, the virus is normally found in alfalfa. My understanding is that this is not an island crop, so the actions I gave should be sufficient." I returned to my seat, pausing to add, "I'll be happy to help if any of you need me."

Martha looked around to see if any Seythan members wanted to comment. Most smiled in my direction. "In that case, thank you, Andy. I am now going to use my prerogative to hold a closed session to decide how to pay for this catastrophe. The Seythan's decision will be discussed in next week's public meeting. I declare this session closed."

I returned to Rose, who put her arms around me. "You were wonderful," she whispered.

"Good job," Morley said, patting my back. "You showed that woman."

"I think she knew her plants were responsible, and got scared," I replied.

"I got scared, too," a voice said from behind me.

I turned to see Daisy Quick.

"I'm sorry," she said. "That potato crop is a large part of…. I shouldn't have let Elizabeth persuade me. My comment on you being a foreigner and all. That was uncalled for. You and Rose make a fine couple."

I held out my hand. "No harm done. Let me know when you'd like me to drop by."

Daisy wiped a tear away. "Thank you. I will."

Late that afternoon, a knock on the door interrupted my review of Westcott so that I would be better prepared for possible future crises. At first, I didn't recognize the elderly man, though he looked familiar.

"Fred Gay," he said. "Is Rose in?"

Now, the family resemblance was obvious—Charlie's brother. Elizabeth's husband. "Rose, someone to see you." I returned to the sofa.

Rose emerged from the kitchen where she had been preparing dinner. "Fred, what can I do for you?"

Fred shifted nervously. "Elizabeth's not well. Could you come and see her….please?"

"Of course. Let me get my coat and kit. Andy, can you finish up in the kitchen?"

I wasn't really sure I could, but this wasn't a good time to equivocate. "Sure."

Rose returned over an hour later as I finished cooking the vegetables to go with the fried fish.

"What was the problem?" I asked as she closed the kitchen door.

"Nervous exhaustion and some kind of breakdown," Rose replied. "From the little she said, the Seythan gave her a rough time. She's a very proud woman and she felt humiliated. I gave her some pills to relieve the tension…." Rose's face showed concern. "Do you mind that I went to see her?"

"Not at all. It's your job. What she tried to do to me was stupid. Hopefully, this will put an end to the attacks on me."

Rose came over and we kissed. "Now everyone knows I made the right decision in marrying you," she said. "We can get on with our lives in peace."

"Right." I didn't voice my concern that the Head Masker, whomever he might be, could still try something to ruin our lives.

34.

SUNDAY MORNING FOUND ROSE AND ME BACK IN THE CHAPEL.
Elizabeth Gay, on Fred's arm, preceded us in. His head was up
as if daring anyone to say anything. Her gaze was on the ground.
But, when he started up the aisle to where they normally sat near
the front, I saw her jerk on his arm and guide him into a back row.

"Go ahead and sit down," Rose said. "I need to check on Elizabeth."

When she joined me, Rose whispered, "She's not quite there
yet, but I think she's recovering well."

Clara and Frankie sat down with us as Isaac went to the
makeshift pulpit and began the service. The topic of his sermon became clear following a lengthy waffle about harvests and
plagues: *The danger of bearing false witness.* He quoted passages from Proverbs and Exodus, adding that in ancient times the
penalty for a person who sought to harm another by lying was
to suffer the fate they had proposed. It wasn't clear to me whether he was implying that Elizabeth should now be considered a
foreigner and exiled or that she would have to pay for the crop
damage. I didn't wish either fate on her, and wondered what the
Seythan would come up with.

The final hymn was *Abide with Me.* When we were seated,
Isaac quoted a verse in his closing remarks:

"I need Thy presence every passing hour;
What but Thy grace can foil the tempter's pow'r?
Who, like Thyself, my guide and stay can be?
Through cloud and sunshine, Lord, abide with me."

Isaac emphasized 'tempter's power.' *Curious*, I thought and glanced at Rose.

She put her head close and whispered, "Isaac's implying someone got at Elizabeth."

"Oh."

We were halfway home when I heard rapid footsteps behind me. I turned to see Fred Gay.

He stopped and held his sides. "Whew," he said. "Long time since I ran. Mr. Ferguson, Andy, could you spare a minute to speak to Elizabeth?" He gestured to where she was standing to the side of the chapel.

"Certainly. I'll be home in a minute, honey," I said to Rose.

Fred stayed with me as I went to Elizabeth then, when I reached her, he continued on the path to their farm.

Elizabeth straightened up. "Mr. Ferguson," she said. "This is not easy for me, but I need to apologize. Somebody gave me bad advice. I should not have listened. Your analysis of what happened with the virus was correct. I should have acted sooner before it spread to the other farms. It was petty of me to use the situation to make your life difficult."

"I—"

She held up a hand. The imperious woman had reemerged. "I know what happened on the cliff two years or more ago, but I will never forgive you for causing the death of my good friend, Jane.

As to you and Rose, Jane and I had hoped…nevertheless, it was you Rose chose, and I believe that is a woman's right."

I hoped she would tell me who had given her the bad advice. The Head of the Maskers, I suspected. "Your apology is accepted. Can you tell me who gave you this advice?"

She steepled her fingers. "No. That would be unwise for both you and me."

Uncertain of the reception I'd receive, I had held off going to look at her tomato crop or the remains of it. "Can I help you deal with the damage to your crop?"

"That would be acceptable," she replied. A woman back in charge. She held out her hand. "From now on, we should work together. Monday morning then." Her statement sounded more like instructions, and she didn't appear to want a response. We shook and she left to join Fred, who was waiting by the bridge over the Bodmin River.

***

In fact it turned out to be convenient to make the visit as instructed. Nicholas and the work crew were scheduled to deliver the first of the tanks mid-morning on Monday. I arrived at the Gay farm at nine toting my lunch and a water bottle. The ornamentals I had seen before had been uprooted.

Fred met me at the door. "Thanks for coming. Elizabeth's gone to Nancarrow's," he said. "Let me show you the crop…or at least what's left of it."

The field of tomatoes was a mess, with wilted leaves and discolored and rotting green tomatoes. "As I said at the Seythan meeting, you need to burn all these plants. As to the *tomahtoes* you could collect them up and put them in Jacob's digester...if he agrees."

Fred's face crumpled slightly. "I'll talk to him. I've got a small cart I could put stuff in."

"Oh, and disinfect all the tools and the cart to protect against a future outbreak."

"Will do. What about next year?"

"Get new seed, and I'll be happy to help in any way I can."

Fred shook my hand. "Andy, I'm right glad you're here." He surprised me by adding, "You'll be a real asset to island." I guessed he hadn't been happy with his domineering wife's actions.

Progress at last. I wasn't happy that acceptance came about because of a major misfortune, but without it, my struggle would have continued. Fred and I agreed that I should come back after he'd talked to Jacob. I continued over the fields to the coast at the mouth of the Bodmin River to check on the potential site Nicholas had chosen for the tanks.

The set up by the river where the sewer pipe dropped into the sea was similar to that in Portloe. However, the slope was less severe and the river tumbled gently over the rocks. We would have to dig deeper holes than previously to take the tanks. Posts in the ground indicated where we would be digging. To the side was a tarpaulin. I lifted up an edge and saw picks and shovels.

Looking back up the river to see if the crew was on its way, I detected no one and walked the quarter mile to the rock hopper penguin site. The mating pairs had built their nests and were busily fending off intruders as they waited for the eggs to hatch.

I amused myself watching their antics for over an hour before the sound of a tractor penetrated the background noise. When I arrived back at the river, Nicholas, the crew, and Johnny had already started digging the bottom platform. I took off my parka and joined them.

By lunchtime, we had dug down more than two feet on both tank sites, hitting rock on the lower level. "We won't be able to go much further, lads," Nicholas declared. "It'll need explosives. I'll talk to Martha. Take a lunch break." He strode off up the track to Veryan.

"Martha has explosives?" I said to Johnny.

"Under lock and key in the Seythan House," he replied. "We don't have much cause to use them."

Sensible, I thought. The discussion turned to whether we had all the components for the new system. After lunch, we continued digging the upper platform until Nicholas returned in the mid-afternoon, carrying a sturdy canvas bag.

"Took time for Martha to remember where she kept the keys," he said with a grin. He fished in the bag and pulled out a hand drill and bit which he gave to one of his crew. "Bert, start the holes for the explosives while I have a bite to eat. Two holes should be enough for now. The rest of you keep on digging the other base."

Out of the corner of my eye, I saw Nicholas insert the explosives. He then ran wires back to an old-fashioned plunger device, bringing back memories of old Western movies I'd watched as kid. At that point, he called a halt. "I'm ready to blast," he said. "Get back about a hundred yards. There could be sharp flying pieces."

We retreated and watched while he connected the detonating wires, lay on the ground, and initiated the explosion. Immediately following a loud bang, a fountain of rocks and dust erupted from the lower platform. When the dust settled, we took the picks and shovels and cleared out the debris.

Nicholas measured the depth of the hole. "One more blast should do it," he said. "Two more holes please."

After the dust settled, we finished leveling the platform to Nicholas's satisfaction. We then placed the first tank on it, following the procedure with block, tackle, and rollers we'd used before.

The following day, Nicholas used the last three sticks of dynamite to blast out some recalcitrant rock, and we completed digging the second platform. "Good," he said, after filling in a form. "Nothing to return to Martha."

On Wednesday, we installed the final tank. That left running the gas pipe, installing the pump, and assembling the electrical components. The piping was installed by late Friday. We delayed completion of the electrics until Monday, because the Seythan was meeting Saturday morning to discuss what to do about the Alfalfa Mosaic Virus catastrophe.

***

The first thing I noticed when I went into the Seythan meeting was that Elizabeth Gay was seated with the committee. Did this mean that she had been absolved of all responsibility for having introduced the virus, not acting to prevent its spread, and slandering me? My question was answered immediately by the Penseythan.

After calling the meeting to order, she said, "In our closed session last Saturday, we came to unanimous agreement on the following actions relating to the Alfalfa Mosaic Virus. First, from now on, no plants may be imported unless they are guaranteed free of disease by the South African authorities. Second, we censure Mr. and Mrs. Gay for the delay in informing other farmers of the problems with their tomato crop. Third, we insist that Mrs. Gay apologize to Mr. Ferguson for making misleading statement about him." Martha paused to let the information sink in.

Poor Fred, I thought. *I doubt he had any say in the decision.*

Martha continued, "While the spread of the disease might have been inevitable, an earlier warning might have reduced the damage. As compensation, the Gay's will donate one third of next year's crop to be distributed across the island. Finally, I have spoken to the Governor, and he assures me that, as a British Crown Colony, we should be eligible for relief funds. He has authorized me to initiate the order of seeds. Captain Artley is prepared to pick them up in early December. Some late crops should be possible. The Governor will also arrange for delivery of some vegetables to see us through the next months." She smiled. "He couldn't guarantee what they might be, so have your cookbooks ready."

Following the meeting, I accompanied Johnny to install the electrical components and controls at the Jago farm. Later in the afternoon, with the work completed, I returned home to wash up and get ready for that evening's dance in Portloe.

35.

ROSE AND I TOOK THE BUS TO PORTLOE, JOINING CLARA, FRANK-
ie and Esther, and Martha and Arthur Nancarrow. Elizabeth and
Fred Gay were noticeable absentees. Sam and Jennifer Nancarrow arrived late. "Where's Sandy?" I asked Rose.

"Got a cold, I heard," she replied.

The band started off with the new musical numbers I'd given
them, acknowledging my gift before they began. Martha grabbed
me for the first dance: *I Will Survive.*

"Andy, thank you again for the music," she said as we gyrated.
"I think most Roselanders now understand how valuable you will
be to this island."

First I'd won over Daisy and Elizabeth, now this compliment.
For a moment, I felt good. Then, as I spun around, I saw the stage.
An image of *The Wickerman* movie I'd seen there flashed briefly.
"What about the Maskers?"

Martha's grip tightened. "They're my problem," she said firmly. "You concentrate on Rose and your work."

Certainly, they'd not done anything to me since Guy Fawkes
Day. I hoped she could handle them. "Wonderful," I said, not
very convincingly.

Rose took me for the next dance, a slow one: *The Rose.* She held me tighter than before we'd been married and moved against me suggestively.

"If that's a hint, can't wait 'til later," I whispered.

"What do you think?" she said with a giggle.

A variety of women asked me to dance, with Clara being the last one before the break. As we waltzed, she turned me to look at where Susan and Johnny were dancing. "They make a fine couple, don't they?" she said.

The two of them looked really happy. "Yes. You planned it all along, didn't you?" I drew back to see her face.

"Maybe," she said with a sly grin.

The air in the hall had become stuffy from sweaty dancers, an occasional smoker, and a lack of ventilation. At the break, Rose and I went outside for a breath of fresh air, joining Young Artley and Patsy. Patsy had just finished a long description of how entertaining her new baby was when a flash of light lit up the sky to the south-west of Portloe. A few seconds later, a loud bang reached us. A red glow followed. I thought hard about the sequence of events and soon worked out what it meant. "That was at Morley's farm," I said. "Likely his barn. We'd better check."

"I'll come with you," Rose said. "Someone may have been hurt. We can go past the clinic and pick up my medical kit."

"Let me get Martha," Artley added. "You stay here, Patsy." He didn't wait for her answer and rushed inside.

A number of islanders had already headed for the farm when Rose, Artley, Martha, Arthur, and I took the path across the fields. The moon peeking around scattered clouds provided enough illumination for us to find our way.

Some fifteen minutes later, we arrived at the farmhouse. Even from a distance, we had seen that the barn was ablaze. As we got closer, I smelled the manure that was now exposed because the cover had burned up. The first arrivals had joined Morley and Hilda in a vain attempt to put out the fire. They were now concentrating on preventing the flames from reaching the farmhouse by removing flammable material from between the two buildings and throwing water onto anything that couldn't be moved.

Rose and I joined in as soon as she had established that no one had been hurt.

Finally, the barn's fire burned out, leaving three of the walls standing with more than half of the roof still supported. I found Morley in the middle of a large group, everybody asking the same question: "What happened?"

Morley scratched his head. "Reckon digester blew up," he said.

"Do you think an electrical fault might have ignited the methane?" Arthur Nancarrow asked.

"Don't rightly know." Morley turned to Johnny, who was standing next to him holding Susan's hand. "What do you think?"

Johnny shook his head. "Doubt it. Andy and I checked all the pipes for gas leaks. Anyway, most of the electrical system is away from the methane. What do you think, Andy?"

In my gut, I had the feeling there was something fishy about the explosion. I went over in my head what I'd read in a review of digesters in the States. Certainly, there had been some disasters, but also they were always in mature ones. I recollected that accumulation of explosive concentrations of nitrates had been an issue in a different kind of system. That didn't explain what had happened here. *What to say?*

"Cat got your tongue?" Arthur muttered.

I picked my words carefully. "There have been cases in the States, but not in a new system like this. And they were a different set up in which nitrates and hydrogen sulfide caused problems. This system hasn't been around long enough for that. I would like to study this in daylight. Johnny, would—"

"I'll be there," Johnny said.

"Me, too." The large frame of Nicholas came through the crowd. His face had a grim look. "Just got here." He held up a large flashlight. "I'm going to have a look around." He headed for an area away from the barn and paced up and down, shining a light in front of him as he went.

"I'll help him," Arthur said and he darted off.

Morley, Rose, and I were about to join him when headlights lit up the track to the farmhouse, heralding the arrival of the Lagonda.

James Thomas got out. He ignored his brother and me, and spoke directly to Rose. "Elizabeth called. Isaac's not feeling well. Can you go see to him?"

"Let me get my kit," Rose said. "Andy, do you want to come with me?"

I wanted to, but knew I should stay. "Morley…Hilda, would it be all right if I spent the night so I can get an early start?" I asked.

"Certainly, m'dear," Hilda replied. "I'll make up a bed."

Clara emerged from the crowd. I had noticed her roaming around looking lost. "Can you give me a lift?" she said.

"Certainly," Rose replied. She kissed me and I watched the Lagonda leave.

***

The next morning, I got up as soon as light filtered around the curtain in the attic that had served as a makeshift bedroom. I stretched to relieve the aches from sleeping on an army surplus cot. When I entered the kitchen, Hilda was busy at the stove. Morley and Nicholas were already there. Nicholas was studying small shards of various materials on the kitchen table. He picked one up and sniffed it. Seeing me, he held it out. "Smell this."

I recognized the piece as a part of a pipe that connected the digester to the generator. A faint odor seemed familiar. Then it hit me. "Smells a bit like those rocks we cleared on Friday," I said.

Nicholas nodded. "Dynamite, but how did someone get it? I used all the seven sticks and detonators I signed for."

"You mean someone deliberately blew up my barn." Morley's face expressed disbelief. "Who would do such a thing, and why?"

Good question. "Maybe they were getting at me," I said.

"You mean Maskers, don't you, Andy?" Hilda said, coming to the table with a tray carrying tea essentials. Nicholas cleared a spot and she poured the tea.

"Yes. The latest business was blaming me for the plant virus. Elizabeth Gay apologized and implied someone had put her up to it. When I asked who, she clammed up. The Head of the Maskers has been after me from before I arrived. I've asked this before. Do any of you know who he is?"

"It's a well-kept secret," Morley replied. "Only a few older maskers know who they chose. Any of us could make a guess, but that wouldn't be fair."

Neither Sandy Nancarrow nor his father, Isaac, had been at the dance. And, apparently, both had been ill. I had been about to ask whether it could be Isaac Nancarrow, but decided it also wouldn't be wise for me to make a guess. A knock on the door interrupted another question.

Arthur Nancarrow opened the door and poked his head around. "May I join you?" He held out a canvas bag. "Here are the pieces I collected last night. I don't know if they're of any use."

Nicholas took the bag and emptied it on the table, then thumbed through it. "Nothing new," he said after a cursory glance.

Another thought struck me. "Could there have been a timer set to cause the detonation during the dance?" I said. "That would have allowed someone at the dance to have done it."

A puzzled look crossed Arthur's face. "Why do you ask?"

"It weren't an accident," Nicholas said. "Dynamite were used."

"How could anyone get their hands on dynamite?" Arthur said. "It's locked up. Only Martha has the key." He rifled through the remnants of the explosion. "Don't see any pieces of a timer mechanism here. Mainly bits of pipes, some material, and what might be parts of a generator."

"Right," Nicholas said. "It's light enough now. We can go back out and take another look."

We filed out and spread around what was left of the barn. Johnny joined me shortly afterwards. "It doesn't seem right, Andy. We checked. That system was gas tight."

"Nicholas believes dynamite was used."

Johnny had just been about to pick up a metal shard. He froze. "Head of Maskers still out to get you?"

"Reckon so." I knew that man had talked Johnny into beating me up. "You've met him, haven't you? Who is it?"

"Sorry, Andy. I don't know. He always wore a mask, kept in the shadows, and spoke through something that muffled his voice."

We searched in an ever-widening circle, occasionally dropping what we'd found on the ground near the farmhouse door.

After a couple of hours, Nicholas called a halt. "Reckon we've done all we can," he said. Let's lay it out and see what we've got."

We sorted the scraps into piles of similar material, seeing nothing exceptional until Johnny picked up a metal coil. "This looks like spring from a clock," he said, flexing it.

Spurred on by his find, we refocused our search, including going back to the scraps on the kitchen table. After another half hour, we had eight pieces that might have come from a clock.

"Someone could have rigged up an electric device using power from the generator with the hands of a clock used to trigger the detonation last night," Nicholas said thoughtfully.

"That means anyone could have done it," Johnny said.

"I think you're right," Arthur agreed.

Damn. That meant my assumption that it might have been Sam faking illness or Isaac couldn't be proved. "What do we do now?" I asked.

"Get Martha to check store," Arthur replied. "I'll cycle back and let her know you're coming." He went to his bicycle, which was propped up against the farmhouse wall.

"Thanks for your help," Morley called out as Arthur sped away. His shoulders slumped and I could see he was fighting back tears. He gestured at the devastated area. "What can I do?"

"We'll help you rebuild the barn," Johnny said quickly. "What about the digester, Andy?"

I surveyed what remained. "Pits are still there. We can make a temporary cover and I'll order a new one and replacements for all the parts that were destroyed. The sewage plant's still working." I pointed at the flame burning at the end of the broken pipe."

While the rest of the islanders continued with the cleanup, Johnny and I made an inventory of the parts we needed to order. With that job completed, we climbed onto a trailer, and Nicholas pulled it behind the tractor as he drove to Veryan.

36.

Rose and I were having supper when Clara arrived at the back door. Rose ushered her in and poured a cup of tea.

"What can you tell me?" Clara asked in an unusually abrupt voice.

"Dynamite was used and we found eight pieces of what looked like remnants of a clock, which suggest the explosion was set off by some timing mechanism," I said. "Nicholas was the one who worked out what had happened."

"Who found those pieces?"

I thought back to the morning. "Johnny found the first bit… then I think it was Nicholas, Arthur, and I don't remember who else."

"I saw you, Johnny, and Nicholas go into the Seythan with Martha."

"Yes, we were checking the store. Two sticks of dynamite and blasting caps were missing. The detonator and reel of wire were there." I paused. "The last entry was for seven sticks that Nicholas used up when we put in the tanks for the new Veryan sewage system."

"So they could have been stolen anytime?" Clara appeared to be musing to herself.

"I guess so."

Her head jerked up. "What?"

"I said you were right, they could have been stolen anytime."

"Of course." She drank some tea and glanced out the window. "Did Nicholas know how many sticks were used?"

"From the explosion damage, he thinks only one."

Clara's eyes closed. "I wonder what the Maskers' next target will be."

"So you think it was Maskers? I wondered about that."

"Of course, m'dear. Who else could it be? Morley's well liked."

I recalled something Hilda had said. "What about his brother, James?"

"There's animosity there, but surely he'd not do something like that, m'dear." Clara's face showed genuine surprise. "And how would he get his hands on dynamite or know how to set it off?"

"I've been tied up today with this nasty stomach virus Sandy and Isaac have," Rose interjected. "The culprit seems to be fruit that Sandy brought back from Cape Town. Do you know what else is happening about the explosion?"

"I talked to Harold," Clara said. "He says Seythan met in closed session. They'll do what they can to help Morley rebuild. Problem is, there's not a lot of money left in island savings account after building sewage plants, and setting some aside to buy seed for new crops. They're looking for donations…not just money, but also wood and roofing to repair barn."

"At the dance, Mum said the *St. Just* would go back to Cape Town as soon as possible to get the seed," Rose said. "What about a new generator and other stuff for the rebuilt digester?"

"It'll wait until he and Andy can give them a list. They'll do what they can."

"I'm going to send a message to Dad to get a new cover," I said, giving a rueful grin. "And that will about wipe me out."

Rose patted my arm. "It's the right thing to do."

***

Monday, the first of December saw Johnny and I back at Morley's farm assessing the damage and making a list of what was needed to repair the digester. Morley had already made a temporary cover for the two pits, and several islanders had dropped off building materials for the barn. Fortunately, some of the electrical equipment—the pump, controls, and recorder for the sewage system—had been spared. That left a need for replacements for the generator, boiler, scrubber, and controls for the digester, plus twenty feet of power line. We totaled up the cost and soon reached a few thousand dollars.

"I hope Harold can come up with the money," Johnny said. "I'd like to do it for less." He knocked on what remained of the barn's wooden door. "Maybe I can find some bargains, but I'll only have a couple of days in Cape Town to find them."

"For once, Murphy's Law won't screw you up," I said.

"Who's Murphy?"

I remembered that the British expression was different. "American for Sod's Law," I said.

***

Harold did manage to find the funds, and Johnny left on the *St. Just* at crack of dawn on Wednesday the third of December. Young Artley, Frankie, and Sandy were the crew for the Captain. The boat would not return until the nineteenth at the earliest, cutting it close for Johnny to be back in time for Midsummer's Day. I'd offered to go in his place. He'd thanked me, saying that he owed it to Susan and his future parents-in-law. He chuckled and added that, anyway, he would be able to get better bargains than me.

During the following week and a half, I monitored the Veryan sewage plant, happily watching the electrical output rise to what we had predicted. Most of the time, though, I spent helping clean up the virus-ravaged fields.

Occasionally, I would bump into Clara. As far as I could tell, she was still investigating the incident at Morley's farm. When I would ask her if she had made any progress, she would smile sweetly and give some answer such as, "More complicated than I thought," and, "We've never had something like this." Despite the lack of clarity, I realized that she might have worked out the answer.

The one comment she made that had me really worried was when she said with a serious face, "Be very careful, Andy. Some people you think are Rose's and your friends may not be."

Later, I asked Rose what Clara meant. "Maskers, mainly," she'd replied.

On the morning of Saturday the thirteenth of December, I was well received when I presented the electricity numbers to the Seythan. They asked me for a summary of progress in the cleanup. I told them it was going well, with most of the infected plants being burned. The damage to Morley's digester had limited the amount of material we could dispose of by that route. Nevertheless, some of the less affected fields would be ready to accept seeds for a second crop when the *St. Just* returned.

The afternoon found me at band practice preparing for the Midsummer's festivities. True to his word, Charlie had chosen the *Superman* song, *Can you Read my Mind* to play during the ceremony when Johnny and Susan would go before the Penseythan for some last instructions on their way. The remainder of the time, we would play *The Floral Dance* and the old favorites, *Lamorna* and *Oggy Man*.

Arthur came and sat with me during the break. "Made any more progress on Morley's barn?" he asked.

"I helped him build a new cover and we found and installed piping to replace what was damaged. Other than that, we'll have to wait for Johnny to get back."

"How about who did it?"

"Not my area," I said. "Leave things like that to Clara." I was about to add that I thought she might have an answer, but Arthur absently mindedly scratched his head, a sign he was nervous— about what?—and I merely said, "Ask her."

Our conversation then turned to progress with repairing the crop damage.

After the band had practiced in the village hall for an hour or so, Charlie announced that we would march the parade route, playing *The Floral Dance*. He took us down the road, under fair skies, to where the two small Round Houses bracketed the sides of the road into Veryan. From there, we marched and played our way back to the square, stopping for a final chorus or two by the large Round House. Jacob was fully recovered and seemed to have no trouble in handling his drum.

Charlie turned and faced us. "Right, lads, have a beer on me," he said and led us to the pub.

***

On Sunday, Rose and I joined Mary and Clara in the chapel. Isaac's sermon was focused on biblical stories about brothers. He started with Esau and Jacob, and Esau's unhappiness when Isaac blessed Jacob. I wondered if the preacher was referring to Arthur not being happy that he, the older brother, was the primary factor in their store. He then alluded to Joseph and his problems with apparently jealous or aggravated brothers. Who that referred to wasn't clear to me. But then he came to Cain and Abel, and he seemed to be addressing his remarks to Morley Thomas. "Is he implying something about James Thomas?" I whispered to Rose.

"I've no idea," she replied.

Isaac's finale was a quote—rewritten, I discovered later on by checking Rose's bible — from Matthew 18:15: "If your brother does damage to you, in private, tell him he was wrong. If he doesn't listen, tell him to talk to the leader of your community."

"Can you explain what he's getting at?" I asked Clara quietly.

"I think so," she said and turned away, making it clear she wasn't going to confide her understanding to me.

Mary came to our house for lunch and the conversation soon turned to the sermon. Mary finished a mouthful of fish. "I think Isaac knows something about who blew up Morley's barn," she said.

"I'm pretty sure Clara does, too," I said. "Are there other brothers we should consider beyond Isaac and Arthur, and Morley and James?"

Mary glanced at Rose, who shook her head.

"Then, assuming Morley didn't do the dirty deed, that leaves us with Isaac, Arthur, and James or someone they talked into doing it. And they had to have some way of getting the dynamite sticks." I waited for their response.

Both nodded, then Rose said, "By someone else, you mean Sam or Sandy Nancarrow?"

"Yes. Or someone we haven't thought of."

"I don't think it could have been Sandy or Isaac. They were really ill," Rose said. "And Sam and Arthur were at the dance."

"I heard you found remains of a clock," Mary said. "Does that mean whoever set it up didn't have to be there?"

"If it was a time-delayed mechanism, yes," I said.

Rose looked surprised. "You don't sound sure about that?"

"Johnny and I discussed it," I said. "I didn't tell you because it's just speculation. Johnny pointed out that bits of a clock were the only evidence for them being part of a trigger. We didn't find any other remnants that weren't part of the original electrics. He suggested that it might be a red herring, introduced to eliminate the possibility that someone used the island's magneto blasting detonator."

Mary gasped. "That would mean someone was able to steal the dynamite and use the detonator and return it later without being detected."

"Right, and the detonator plus the reel of wire to connect to the dynamite is not that heavy, but you wouldn't want to carry it for the eight to ten miles from Veryan to Morley's and back."

"You could use a bicycle," Mary suggested.

"Or the Lagonda," Rose said, a worried look on her face.

I hadn't wanted to raise that since James Thomas was Rose's chauffeur. "Unfortunately, that is a possibility. But it doesn't explain how whoever it was got into that storage shed by the Seythan House. He would need the key to remove the stuff and to return the detonator. Which reminds me, we checked, the detonator was there on the Sunday morning."

Rose served up potatoes and cabbage. "Let's eat up before this gets cold. We can think about who would have access to the key."

After we'd cleared our plates, Rose placed an apple pie for dessert on the table. "All the Seythan material, including that key, is kept in a safe in the Seythan House," she stated firmly. "The only people with access are members of the Seythan."

"That doesn't mean they'd all know how to open the safe," Mary interjected. "I've seen it. You'd need to know combination. Obviously Martha knows. Then Arthur is another candidate." She paused, looking thoughtful. "Of course, James Thomas worked for Jane Trevenna when she was Penseythan. He might know."

"That makes him the most likely because he has both motive and possible opportunity," I said.

Rose shook her head. "I know he's gruff and that can put people off, but he's been very supportive of me. I can't see him doing it…at least not alone. There has to be somebody else."

"Head of Maskers?" I asked. "James Thomas might be a masker, too. Can you give me a guess as to who is the Head?"

"I'm going to finish my dessert," Mary said. "My brain's going round and round in circles. I don't know what to think, and I don't want to answer your question."

Her comment stopped further discussion. We finished lunch in silence and then went for a walk. In the square, the traditional Maypole with its multi-colored ribbons stood ready for Midsummer's Day. Work had started on a platform in front of the Seythan House. Later, stalls would be set up around the green.

That night, after Rose had initiated a welcome cuddle—her word—I soon fell asleep. My dreams were full of happy penguins in an idyllic setting, up to the point in which a penguin appeared wearing a grinning mask. From then on, the dream went downhill into a nightmare of exploding digesters scattering debris over the rookery.

37.

THE *ST. JUST* RETURNED LATE ON THURSDAY THE EIGHTEENTH of December. A relief for Johnny, I suspected, because Midsummer's was only three days away. With Clara, I took the bus to the dock to check whether he had succeeded in getting all the replacement parts for Morley's digester. Clara was noncommittal about why she had joined me. Arthur and Sam Nancarrow sat in front of us, the normally chatty Arthur strangely silent, too.

The boat pulled in as the sun set. While I waited my turn to talk to Johnny—Susan had all of his attention—I noticed Sandy handing packages to Sam and Arthur.

"Personal items for the ladies," Sandy said with a self-conscious grin.

"I'm sure Martha and Jenny will appreciate them," Arthur said. Turning to me, he added, *sotto voce*, "Not easy for Sandy going in women's store, him not being married."

I had the transient thought, *why is he explaining this to me*, but Susan let go of Johnny for a moment and I grabbed my chance to speak to him. "Did you get everything?"

"It was easier than I'd feared and cheaper, too, with refurbished parts," Johnny said. "I got some spares in case we have more problems."

I wondered, with Midsummer's Day being so close, whether he would want to work on the digester. "Will you have time—"

"To start work at Morley's?" he said abruptly. "Of course. Susan and I can get this stuff there tonight. See you first thing in the morning."

Chance for a 'cuddle' with Susan. *Smart man.* "Right. What about the seed? Did they get everything?"

"It was waiting on the dock. Helped us make a quick a quick turn-around. Everything, I think." He spoke to someone behind me. "That right?"

"Yes," Young Artley replied. "Frankie and I are going to start handing seed out as soon as rest of you've cleared the dock."

I glanced around and noticed a group of farmers looking impatiently at the boat. "Message received," I said. "I'll get out of the way."

Clara returned from talking to Frankie and took my arm. "Seen what I wanted to see," she said quietly. We returned to the bus. Arthur, Sam and Sandy were already on board at the back. We sat in silence for nearly an hour, waiting for seeds to be handed out, before Elizabeth and Fred Gay boarded. As they moved down the aisle, she smiled at me and mouthed, "Thank you." Other farmers from the Veryan area clambered aboard over the next half hour and then the bus took us home.

Rose met me at the door. "I held dinner," she said. "The vegetables will be ready in fifteen minutes. How did it go?"

"Fine. Johnny got everything we needed and had money left over for spares. I'm going early tomorrow morning to help install with the new installation."

"I've got clinic in Veryan, then I'll be checking on a couple of older patients," Rose said. "Not sure how long that will take. Can you start dinner? We need to be done by six-fifty. They're showing the film, *Saturday Night Fever*, in village hall at seven."

After an early breakfast, Rose went to her surgery across the square and I cycled to Morley's farm. Morley had rigged up a temporary cover, and the stench of rotting manure was gone. It would not be until the *St Just* went to Cape Town in January that the new cover would arrive...if we were lucky. I hoped Dad would be able to get one made on such short notice. That reminded me that my parents would be on that boat.

Johnny and Morley were busy installing the replacement generator, water heater, and scrubber on the wooden base Morley had built.

"What do you want me to do?" I asked.

"Work on plastic pipe from sewer," Johnny said. He gestured at a point on a section of the wall that had been repaired. "Take it to there."

With that job finished, I switched to helping Johnny reconnect the power line. Following that job, I worked with Morley on the small sections of pipe that connected the various components while Johnny started on the controls.

Nicholas and his crew came after lunch and continued to rebuild the wall and roof.

By quitting time, we were within a day or so of resurrecting the place. I cycled home to find a note on the kitchen table with instructions on preparing dinner, using a recipe Rose had inherited from Mary.

The mutton stew was in the oven and close to ready by six-thirty. I waited impatiently for Rose to come home before cooking the potatoes and carrots to go with it, thinking that we'd never make it to movie in time. The moment I was about to put the water on to boil, I heard a sharp rap on the front door.

No one was outside when I looked out. "What was that?" I exclaimed and was about to close the door when I noticed a folded piece of paper on the doorstep. Taking it inside, I turned the light on in the kitchen, opened the note, and read, "We have Rose. If you want to see her again, come to Jago farm. ALONE! We'll be watching." A scrawled, leering mask was the signature.

My heartbeat increased and I felt a knot start in my stomach. I grabbed my parka and was on the point of rushing off when I reconsidered what to do. "Think," I said to myself. "It's a trap. Even if they have Rose, no masker is going to risk hurting a future Penseythan, and certainly not one who is a doctor and well-respected. Why Jago's farm? It's not far away. But so are other farms. What's special about that site?"

I paced in the living room and soon came to the conclusion that the special thing was the digester. I reckoned they were going to blow it up and try to get me at the same time. Should I go alone? Clearly, no. Who to talk to? No brainer: Clara.

After getting my binoculars, I turned the light off in the kitchen and with great care, opened the back door and crawled out. To my dismay, no lights were on in Clara's house. I had a moment of indecision before I crouched down and headed toward the Quick farm, praying that Frankie would be there. I stopped periodically and listened for sounds of someone following me but heard nothing and detected no movement.

Frankie's wife, Elspeth, came to the door when I knocked. "Is Frankie in?" I asked, holding my breath.

"No. Clara came and got him an hour ago. I don't know why."

My chest tightened. "Do you know where they went?"

"Sorry, m'dear, no." She paused. "Maybe Clara's back home by now."

She didn't sound as if that were likely. The last thing I wanted to do was go home and do nothing. "If they come back, please tell them I went to Jago's."

"I will."

"Thanks." I started back for Veryan, stopping well short of the houses. *What to do?* Because of the warning, I couldn't go into the village to get advice from Martha. It was a good bet that Sandy would be on the lookout for me. Staying low, I took a circuitous route around the village hall and chapel and up the hill toward the auk rookery. By now, the sun had started to set.

I stopped near the crest of the hill and dropped to the ground where I could see the Jago farm just over a mile away. With my binoculars, I scanned the farm buildings and the fields nearby, hoping to see something move. Nothing stirred and even the pigs were sleeping. For a moment, I thought I'd detected something, but it was only a trick of the fading light. I brooded about whether I should go down and investigate. My indecision lasted a good twenty minutes before I couldn't stand it anymore, and decided to visit George Anthony. He'd helped me before. Surely, he of all older people I knew couldn't be a masker.

My mother, the librarian, had made me an avid reader. She had schooled me in how novelists hooked a reader. "Whatever you do, don't go in the cellar, Janet!" You knew poor Janet was doomed, and you had to find out what ghastly fate awaited her. My mother had also introduced me to the English writer, John

Fowles. Her favorite hovel of his was The French Lieutenant's Woman. In my favorite, The Magus, Nicholas D'Urfe is tricked in the so-called "godgame," designed by the Magus and a rich group of friends to teach Nicholas a lesson. During my time on Roseland, I had often felt like Nicholas as my Magus, Clara Quick, had played games on me. But my life included the added complexity of being the punching bag for the Head Masker. I knew that now was the time for the game to play out. "Come on, Janet," I said. "Time to find out what's in the cellar."

38.

I TOOK THE PATH ABOVE THE CLIFFS AND THEN PICKED MY WAY carefully through the woods down to George's house. By now, the moon provided intermittent illumination to add to the light from a front room. I knocked and he appeared.

"Andy, what are you doing here?" His face had a strange look to it. "Come on in." He led me to the kitchen and turned on the light. "Let me make a cuppa."

"I'm not sure I have the time," I said. "I received a note that said the Maskers had taken Rose and I needed to go to Jago's farm." I gave it to him.

George read the note carefully then moved the kettle onto a hot part of his Aga range. "Don't sound right. Nobody's going to hurt Rose...not Rose." He motioned for me to take a chair.

I sat down. "That's what I thought, but I can't risk it."

"I see what you mean." He took one of two mugs on the table and placed it in front of me. At that point the kettle started to whistle. George swilled hot water around in a teapot and added tea and water.

I waited impatiently as George stood by the stove teapot in hand. He appeared to be gazing out the window. *What is he thinking about?* "George, I really can't stay long."

He turned, showing a strange expression...concern, lost in

thought…I couldn't tell. "Sorry, Andy, I was thinking about Rose." He came to the table and poured the tea. "Help yourself to milk and sugar," he said.

The tea was too hot to gulp and I sipped some before adding more milk. "Will you come with me? I think it's a trap. If something happens, you could let them know in the village." I had been going to say, tell Jacob, but now I'd got to wondering if he was a masker.

George hesitated. "Certainly. We'll leave as soon as you've finished your tea."

I took a big gulp and set the mug down. "I'm ready."

George appeared startled by my action before walking down the hall to get his coat. He turned the kitchen light out and we left through the back door, following a path to the nearest Jago field. We came to a stile and George climbed first, then seemed to fall sideways. I heard a grunt as if he'd had the breath knocked out of him and quickly followed. Hands reached up and grabbed me as I straddled the stile and I was manhandled over it. In the moonlight, I could make out two masked men holding George. Two others held me. They'd been hiding behind the hedge on each side of the stile. *Damn them.*

"Get George home," a man's voice said from the shadows. He stepped forward, revealing the wolfish mask I'd seen when they'd kidnapped me at the bonfire. "And take Ferguson to the barn," he said.

"Don't hurt George," I said.

The Head of the Makers—I assumed—gave a short, barking laugh. "Course not."

I hoped he meant it. They tied my hands behind my back.

Any ability to have a further discussion was prevented when they gagged me. The rag tasted salty and a faint smell of fish percolated up to my nose. Could that mean Sandy, crewman on the *St. Just*, was one of these maskers?

They manhandled me across the fields to the side of the two barns that was away from the Jago's farmhouse. A flicker of light in the grass ahead caught my eye as we approached a small door at the back of the barn that abutted the digester. I knew immediately what was there: wires going away from the barn. They'd rigged up the second stick of dynamite! *Oh shit!* They were going to blow up the digester and me. When one of the maskers let go of me to open the door, I twisted and kicked at the other masker.

He yelped in pain and swung at me. I ducked, and kicked up at the man by the door's crotch, connecting solidly. He doubled up in pain. I felt a sharp blow to the back of my head and hands grabbing me. Though dazed, I succeeded in kicking back at the man behind me. He gasped and let go.

The Head Masker came at me from the front. I launched myself forward, butting him under the chin. He fell against the barn. My momentum carried me forward into the wires. I kicked and they easily pulled away from the digester. *God, let them stay disconnected*, I prayed.

That was my last action. Blows rained down on me and I lost consciousness.

When I came to, my head throbbed, and the stench of pig manure caused my eyes to water. By feeling with my fingertips, I realized that the maskers had tied me to supports for some of the pipes from the digester. I had the obvious thought that my situation didn't look good. A faint scuffling noise from up in the rafters made me wonder if someone else was in the barn—Rose? I tried to call out, but the gag allowed only a grunting sound. But then I heard the fluttering of wings: only a bird. My hopes sank.

A creaking from the door being opened told me that someone had come in. Blinking away the tears, I glimpsed a figure holding a flashlight.

He came to a stop in front of me and illuminated his vulpine mask. "I warned you more than once to leave the island, and you ignored my advice. Through trickery, Clara got you and Rose married. Rose was promised to John Trevenna. I cannot change that he will wed Susan Thomas. You must die."

I had many questions and one came to the fore. "Where...?" My attempt to speak through the gag failed again.

The masker leaned forward and pulled the gag down

I flexed my mouth for a moment and licked my bruised lips. "Where's Rose?'

"Safe."

George had been right. They wouldn't hurt Rose. *Try to keep him here*. "Why destroy the digesters? How does that help the island?"

The eyes behind the mask stared at me. "Morley Thomas and Jacob Jago insulted us. I'm teaching them a lesson. Digesters can be rebuilt."

"Why do you have it in for me?"

A brief laugh was followed by, "You're a foreigner. You have no business being here disrupting our way of life. You killed Jane Trevenna." He reached forward and replaced the gag. "Enough of this. I have to reconnect the wires." He strode away.

My heart thumping, I tried briefly to free myself from the

bindings. I gave up when the pain in my wrists became unbearable. To have got so far and have everything screwed up. Tears of frustration welled up.

My agonizing was short-lived; I heard a thump from a far corner. *What now?* A faint scuffling sound followed, and a shadowy figure came up to me. "Don't move," Frankie whispered in my ear. "I'm cutting you free."

I held still until the cords fell away.

"Quickly." He propelled me to the corner he'd come from.

"Down. Cover your head."

I dropped to the floor. After I lay flat beside him, I removed the gag. "Thanks. Where's Rose?" I whispered.

"At Trewince. James told her Miriam wasn't well. She's safe."

Thank God. "Is Clara here?"

"With others."

They weren't alone. I took a deep breath, which was knocked out of me when the wall of the barn blew in following a sharp bang. Pieces of what I guessed to be barn wall and digester piping controls rained down on us. An eerie silence was followed seconds later by the crackling of flames.

Frankie prodded me. "We'd better get out."

Light from the blazing walls showed that the main door had blown out. We ran through it into the yard.

"You all right?" Roddy's voice called out.

"Yes," Frankie said. "Anybody hurt?"

"Watch out." Roddy rushed past us, a hose spewing water held in his hands. He directed water at the flames.

"Who set off dynamite?" I said.

"Head Masker, I reckon," Frankie said.

"Know who it is?"

"Mum knows." Frankie gestured at a contorted lump lying in the grass.

I followed him to the far side of what had been a digester. A garish smile—all that was left of a mask—reflected the flames. Closer to the pit, a body, its arms torn-up and bloody, lay rag-doll like on the grass. A flicker of red in the grass drew my gaze to where a ring remained on a bit of a finger. A sudden flaring of the fire illuminated what remained of a face—Arthur Nancarrow's.

"Deal with him later," Frankie said. "Get water." He gestured to where Jacob stood by a tap, his look distraught.

We ran over and began the business of ferrying buckets of water to douse the flames. Soon, we were joined by Johnny Trevenna, Young Artley, and Nicholas Thomas. In what seemed like an eternity, finally, we had the fire put out. The wall by the digester was gone, taking with it the generator, scrubber, piping, and controls. By some miracle, most of the roof had survived. Jacob's temporary cover had burned up, and the stench from charred and rotting pig manure had driven us to stand up-wind from the barn.

I had many questions for Frankie but needed to catch my breath first. I was on the point of asking how Arthur had succeeded in triggering the explosion when I felt a tap on my shoulder. I turned to see George Anthony. The minute I saw his crestfallen look, I knew what was troubling him. The light turned on in the kitchen had been the sign I'd arrived at his house. The delay for tea to allow the ambush to be set up. The light turned off a signal we were leaving. George motioned for me to step away from the group.

"I had no choice," he said. "I took oath. And after all you did for Ernie. I have no...." He wiped away a tear.

It must have been the high I felt from having survived an encounter with death, coupled with pity for this dejected old man, but I couldn't condemn him. "It's fine. Something best left to be between you and me. But tell me, why did you help me when I arrived on the island?"

"It was all part of Arthur's plan," he said bitterly. "But I did want to help you...because of Ernie."

"But what happened in Portloe? Maskers throwing my stuff in the sea?"

"Nancarrow boys did it on their own."

I sort of understood, but still didn't really get why Arthur had it in for me. He'd given some reasons in the barn. Surely there had to be more to it than that I was a foreigner and had caused Jane Trevenna's death. My God, she'd tried to kill me. It was self-defense. That left me taking Rose from Johnny. Might as well ask. "Why did Arthur want me dead?"

"Don't know 'xactly." George glanced to where Arthur's crumpled body lay: a shadow in the moonlight. Somehow, the dynamite had gone off when he reconnected the wires. "Best ask Clara...or Mary.... I'd better go." He stood awkwardly, indicating he didn't know how to leave gracefully.

I put my arms around his now stooped frame. "It's all right," I said. "Look after yourself."

He squeezed me. "Thank you," he said and walked away, his head held high.

"What was that about?" Johnny asked.

"George was worried I'd been hurt," I replied.

Johnny's face showed surprise. "That was it?"

"Yes." He raised an eyebrow but remained silent. My turn to ask a question. "Did somebody operate the detonator?"

"Nicholas reckoned they'd used the magneto blasting generator at Morley's," Johnny replied. "The bits of a clock were planted to confuse us. After that disaster, Martha gave the plunger to Nicholas for safekeeping. Frankie saw that they'd been forced to rig up a battery, voltage amplifier, capacitors, and a switch. When those maskers left to get you, Frankie disconnected the dynamite and I shorted out the switch. Whoever reconnected the wires signed their death warrant. It was Clara's idea. She decided Arthur had done enough damage to the island."

"Clever." I paused. "How did they get the generator and capacitors?"

"Frankie kept an eye on Sandy in Cape Town and saw him buy them."

Mention of Frankie reminded me of something he'd said in the barn. "I heard that James took Rose to Trewince. Will she be okay?"

Johnny smiled. "Yes. James Thomas is in enough trouble, and Miriam wouldn't let him harm Rose."

"So it was James who blew up Morley's barn?"

"Clara thinks so. James blamed Morley for their father's decision to leave Morley the farm." Johnny scanned the area. "Come on, everyone's leaving. I hope James has taken Rose home by now. People will be waiting for them. It's a long hike back to Trewince."

We joined the other islanders on the way back to Veryan. I had many questions for Clara, not least why she hadn't warned me. But she and Frankie were nowhere in sight. Questions could wait for tomorrow. I needed to get back to Rose. Johnny had better be right.

39.

It was a relief to see the Lagonda parked outside Nan-carrow's when Johnny and I reached the Veryan.

"I don't see James," Johnny said. "What the hell?" He point-ed at the center of the green where an unidentifiable figure was slumped in the stocks. His gesture distracting me briefly from checking if a light was on at home.

The faint flicker of candlelight reassured me that all was well. "You go see who it is," I said. "I need to find Rose." I ran to our house.

Rose came out before I got there and rushed into my arms, holding me tight. "Where have you been?" she gasped. Her words then flew out in a panicky stream. "I got here late. Your note said you'd gone to see *Saturday Night Fever*. I ate some of the stew. I wondered why you hadn't had any. When you didn't come back, I went to the hall as the film finished. Martha said you hadn't been there, so I came home." She pulled back to look at me. "Who's that in the stocks? And why is the Lagonda still here?"

"Either James Thomas or another masker."

"Why James?"

"We think he was the one who blew up Morley's digester. I reckon he also spirited you away this afternoon to make me think you'd been kidnapped. I nearly got killed."

Rose's face showed complete bewilderment. "How?"

"When Arthur blew up himself and the Jago digester, Frankie and I were in the barn."

"I don't understand."

"What explanation did James give to take you to Trewince?"

"Said Miriam had felt dizzy, fainted, and fallen over." Rose's expression changed. "Oh, I see what you're getting at. I checked Miriam out. Couldn't find anything. Told her to drink plenty of liquids and rest."

"So that didn't take very long. So, why weren't *you* back in time for supper?"

"Lagonda had some problem. James had the bonnet up and was working on it. I tried to call Nancarrow's to get a message to you. Phone was dead. My God. You're right. He kept me from coming home." Rose trembled and hung onto me for a second before regaining her composure. "But, what was that about Arthur?"

"He was Head of the Maskers. Arthur was determined to get me off the island, and if that didn't work, finish me off." I recalled a comment someone had made that I'd wanted to discuss with Clara. "That wasn't all though. Some issue connected to you and...I don't get this...maybe Mary."

"I think I know." Rose sighed. "Mum didn't talk about it much, but Arthur expected to be King when she was Queen. Instead, my dad got it and Arthur had to content himself with being one of the six. I think he took the opportunity to ask Mum to marry him. When she said no, he got aggressive. Mum fought him off. He never got over it."

"That explains a lot," I said. "He was getting revenge on Mary through ruining life for you and me."

"Yes, and he failed." Rose kissed me passionately. "Come on inside. I bet you're hungry. Then, if you feel strong enough, I can show you how it's a good thing he did fail."

"I think I could handle that."

***

Saturday, I slept in late, getting up just in time for the final band practice. I arrived last in the hall, and was met with a barrage of questions about the previous night. In my answers, I was cautious, not knowing how much it was useful to divulge.

Finally, Jacob took me aside. "What about my digester?" he said.

"The good news is that Johnny brought spares for the electrical system in Cape Town, and I heard yesterday that the cover Dad got is on the *St. Just*. They gave priority to distributing the seed."

Jacob smiled a rare smile. "Thank you." His rough hands clasped mine.

"If you're all ready," Charlie called out. "We'll practice here first. Esther Quick has taken, um… Arthur's place on violin. She needs to get to know our ways. Er…."

Esther turned out to be a quick read and we soon left for the entrance to the village. From there, we marched and played on the same route we'd follow for the main dance, which would take place later on this big day. We played only The Floral Dance.

That evening, Mary and the Captain joined us for an early supper before we all went to the chapel for a service, being held on a Saturday because Midsummer's Day fell on Sunday.

Martha, wearing black, sat in the front row with Elizabeth and Fred Gay, and Sam and Jenny Nancarrow. Martha had resigned as Penseythan, and Rose, who had replaced Arthur, and the committee had elected Elizabeth Gay as the new Penseythan. They had deferred sentencing Sandy, who'd been taken out of the stocks and now occupied a cell with James Thomas in the Seythan House.

Psalm number twenty-two, "Making Sense of Suffering," struck a chord with the congregation. Despite the vigorously played organ music, the singing of the hymn, "Burdens are Lifted at Calvary," was subdued. Equally, Isaac's normal hellfire and brimstone delivery lacked a certain bite. His message came from biblical stories in Judges that dealt with a God-sent evil spirit, treachery, violence, and even mentioned a house being burned down. As always, his sermon related to what had happened on the island, but it remained unclear to me whether he blamed God for Arthur's actions. The congregation sounded relieved in a rousing rendition of the final hymn, "Amazing Grace."

"I'm glad that's over," Mary said as we returned home. "Now I can look forward to Midsummer's."

Rose and I said good night to her and the Captain, and turned in for an early night. Sleep came quickly and, with no nightmares, I slept soundly.

40.

AFTER BREAKFAST, ROSE AND I JOINED THE THRONG IN THE square. Rose had on my favorite dress of hers, the white one with the blue ribbon tied under her bust. Her hair was up and tied with a second blue ribbon. She wore no makeup. That would come later. As on previous occasions, most of the island women were dressed in sleeveless, floral-patterned frocks, their men in white shirts and white or khaki pants.

Come nine o'clock, the stalls in the square were busy, selling food and crafts. An old wooden swing and merry-go-round for the children were in the field on the north side of the village hall. Next to it were tethered ponies and horses, and a sign announcing rides for sixpence—the price unchanged from three years earlier.

Rose and I tried our hand at the carnival games—ring toss, a shooting gallery, and darts—which were interspersed among the stalls. She beat me at all except the shooting, where my time hunting with my dad paid off.

Just before lunch, I put on my uniform and joined the band. After playing the national anthem, we played requests, with the children asking repeatedly for the march from Star Wars. The sun was shining and it was a relief when we took a break in the coolness of the pub. I ordered a pint of best bitter and a pub lunch—bread, cheese, and pickles— from Mary.

She leaned across and patted my cheek. "Thank God, we're nearly back to normal," she said with a smile.

When two o'clock came, I joined the band, some of them walking a little unsteadily as we headed down the road to the small round houses. The children came with us, accompanied by their mothers and some of the older girls. The girls looked cute in their party dresses and had flowers in their hair. The boys, neatly dressed, were self-conscious, as always. We lined up facing the square and Charlie signaled the beginning of the first Floral Dance.

As we marched, I pictured the couples behind me, each boy and girl stepping forward, side by side, then the girl twirling, with the steps repeated as they followed the band. In my head I heard, "Rum, tum, ti, rum, tum, tum."

We made our way between the islanders, who were two deep on each side of the road. As we passed, they would join in at the back. We circled the square once and went to the middle and continued to play. I could see, through gaps between the stalls, a hundred islanders dancing and singing.

For the remainder of the afternoon, Rose and I toured the stalls and chatted with friends until it was time for her to get ready for the evening. Taking Charlie's advice from previous years—"Best eat now, Andy," he'd advised. "Next time'll be after the main dance."—I joined him and other band members in the pub for a half pint and a pasty.

As was customary, around six, the parents took the young children from the square into the field for rides. Soon afterward, the very youngest were taken home.

"Time to go," Charlie said. "Get rid of beer now, lads."

We filed into the pub's toilet. From the pub, we strolled the short distance back to the two round houses. There, married couples and a few unmarried women with their escorts were waiting for us. In the first dance, the islanders had been wearing conventional clothes. This time, many of them had on their Guy Fawkes costumes and masks. Some of those without masks wore garish makeup.

Charlie lined us up facing the two small round houses. "Anthem," he said.

The first bars of the Floral Dance were the signal for the door of one round house to open. Seven men emerged, clad in white shirts, pants, and black shoes. Six of them wore flower-bedecked, floppy, white hats. They all wore masks. From his height, build, the way he walked, and a mask he'd worn in the play, I recognized Harold.

Johnny was the last to emerge. He was attired in a smart, white suit and white top hat with flowers around the rim. Each man carried a garland of flowers. They fidgeted as they lined up in front of the second round house. Johnny knocked on the door. At the seventh knock, the door opened and seven young women came out, the last being Susan. Of the remaining women, three were matrons of honor, and three were candidates to be the next Queen. They were all wearing low-cut white dresses, purple sashes, white pumps, and had flowers intricately woven in their hair. One by one, each went to her partner, who placed the floral garland around her neck.

Susan was the last, looking beautiful and smiling lovingly at Johnny when he placed the flowers around her neck. Johnny led her and the other six couples into the middle of the road. The rest of the dancers lined up behind them.

Charlie led us to the front of the procession and, walking backwards, signaled for us to start playing. This time the dance was in marked contrast to that with the children. The sides of the road were empty as we marched into Veryan. All of the islanders who had remained in the square joined in the dance. We circled the square three times and led the dancers up to the Round House and back to the square. When we stopped in the middle of the square, the dancers formed a circle around us. Charlie raised the tempo of the music. After one circuit, the dancers continued their cavorting, except for the chosen men and women. Many years earlier, when the Professor had told me the islanders practiced pagan rites, I hadn't really believed him. This fertility dance proved, yet again, he had been right.

Rose, her face now garishly made up, appeared and signaled to Charlie for me to join her. Charlie grinned and nodded. I placed my trumpet on the ground and Rose and I whirled around the square. Some of the locals cheered us on.

The music stopped and Rose and I joined the crowd waiting expectantly in front of the stage. It was then that I noticed the lone figure of Martha Nancarrow, wearing black, standing in the shadows of the store's verandah. When she noticed me, she looked away. Poor woman, I thought. I wonder how much she knew about Arthurs's secret role.

Elizabeth Gay, wearing an elegant blue gown befitting a Penseythan, climbed onto the stage. Her husband, Fred, in a black frock coat joined her. She spoke for a number of minutes to the seven couples, reminding them of the island's history and their role in continuing its customs. When she finished, the six matrons and candidate queens accompanied the seven men to the Maypole. They danced around it, intricately intertwining and unraveling the ribbons. It was obvious that Johnny had not had the time to practice much because, to the amusement of the crowd, he occasionally got his ribbon tangled.

While this was going on, Elizabeth took Susan by the hand and, when Fred opened the door to the Round House, she led Susan inside. About ten minutes later, Elizabeth emerged, stood by the door and pointed at the Maypole. Fred escorted the first of the young men to the Round House. Elizabeth spoke to him and he went in.

I rejoined the band and we played, "Anchors Aweigh." The crowd resumed dancing, spending more time between the Round House and the band so that they would not miss anything. My view was blocked, but I knew from the cheers that erupted when the first young man emerged. We stopped playing. He returned to the Maypole, looking rumpled. The other chosen men, with the exception of Johnny, surrounded him immediately, clearly asking him what it was like.

The second man up—appropriate words—was Harold, looking nervous when Fred escorted him to the door. And so it carried on until only Johnny remained. He saw me and gave a thumbs up. I reciprocated the gesture and he disappeared from sight. The music and the dancing stopped and we went to the edge of the square to watch him enter the Round House. In a traditional gesture, he tossed his white hat into the crowd to a great cheer.

Charlie signaled that we had to play. He used the words I'd heard at other times. "National anthem, lads, 'elp Johnny be upstanding. Least we can do."

"Don't reckon young Susan will give him any trouble with that," Clara said from behind me.

"I need to speak to you later," I said firmly. "Buy you a drink when this is over." I rejoined the band. We played a variety of dances, ending with a slow waltz.

When we had finished, I found Clara waiting with Rose. I didn't waste any time. "Why didn't you warn me what the Maskers planned?" I said to Clara.

Clara stopped and faced me. "Do you think the Head Masker would have stopped trying to eliminate you if I'd kept you away?"

"I guess not."

"If you hadn't been in the barn, would he have been in such a hurry to reconnect the wires we disconnected?"

"I suppose not." It seemed that Clara had used me to distract the normally cautious Head of the Maskers. "You're saying the Head of the Maskers acted rashly because he was impatient to get rid of me?"

"Yes, m'dear."

"And what if it had gone wrong?"

A smile flickered across Clara's face. "That's a chance we had to take."

I heard Rose gasp. "Clara, you should have told me."

"And have you give the game away to James Thomas…? Be grateful it all worked out for the best." She turned and headed for the pub. "Now, about that drink."

I watched her retreating back. "Do I have any choice?"

Rose kissed me, smearing her makeup. "Not really," she said. "That's Clara for you. Be grateful you're around for what I have planned for you tonight." She skipped away, dancing the steps for the Floral Dance.

"Rum tum ti, tum, tum, tum," I sang as I danced after her.

PENSEYTHANS

Florence Billing
1920-1924, 1925-1929, 1930-1934

Agnes Nichols
1935-1939, 1940-1944, 1945-1947

Prudence Nancarrow
1948-1949, 1950-1954, 1955-1959

Jane Cocking
1960-1964, 1965-1969, 1970-1974

Jane Trevenna
1975-1977

Martha Nancarrow
1978-1980

ABOUT THE AUTHOR

John Sheffield spent an enjoyable part of his childhood living in a fishing village in the Roseland Peninsula. Roseland is a scenic part of Cornwall in the west of England, with round houses to keep the devil out of the quaint village of Veryan. As a teenager he danced with his girlfriend, Judy, following the band in the annual Floral Dance on Midsummer's Day. He has used his experiences to set the background for Andy Ferguson's adventures on the remote island of Roseland in the southern Atlantic.

CPSIA information can be obtained
at www.ICGtesting.com
Printed in the USA
FSOW01n1355100117
29476FS